WYRFORRA

MCKENNA MILLER

Published in the United States of America First Printing: 2017

E- Book

ISBN -13: 978-1-943407-26-6

Print

ISBN -13: 978-1-943407-27-9

Trifecta Publishing House

1120 East 6th Street

Port Angeles, Washington

98362

TRIFECTA PUBLISHING HOUSE

VINTAGE HILL PRESS

Contact Information: Info@TrifectaPublishingHouse.com

Editor: Eilis Flynn

Cover Art by Designed by Rae Monet

Formatted by Monica Corwin

There are three people to whom I'd like to dedicate this book:

To my best friend, Jayna- people come and people go, but you're always there for me. Couldn't have done it without you, my true partner in crime.

To Mike, for putting up with me all this time, and never once doubting me even when I doubted myself. You're my everything.

And to Shirley. To this day, your light guides and inspires me. I miss you.

1 DAIRE

"DAIRE?"

I wanted to answer, but a punch to the gut knocked the wind out of me. I tried desperately to wheeze a response, but my attacker was too fast. Before I could get my breath back, he threw all his weight into my shoulder, knocking me sideways. I stumbled, falling into the low, crumbling banister of the old hotel. It didn't immediately register that I had actually gone *over* the wall, so I was a little confused when I was suddenly faced with nothing but open air between me and the ground...a good ten stories below.

Perhaps it was just shock, but right then, time seemed to freeze a moment. In midair, as I began to fall, I reasoned that, hey, maybe this wasn't so bad. I always figured I'd probably die in this war. With a small inward sigh, I thought, *No time like the present.* I mean, it's not like I could do anything but accept what had happened, and hope I wouldn't feel it when I hit the ground.

"Daire!"

Robin's voice. Just like that, my trance broke, time started again, and I was suddenly terrified. Not of pain, or of death, or even of losing the war. I was scared for her, and more than anything, I was scared that I would fail her again.

I had promised myself that I would make things up to her, make up for everything I had done, but here I was. Dying. *Great job, Daire. That's not going to help anything.* I looked to her, and tried to say with my eyes what I should have said weeks ago: *I'm sorry. You were right, all along.*

In the second before I lost sight of Robin, I cursed the broken world that, time and time again, tore me away from her. The politics, the fight for survival, the war... It was so hard to believe that we—humans, that is—had fallen so far in just ten years. I remember how, in the beginning, we had such hope. When it all started, we never imagined it would come to this.

We never thought that humanity could lose.

†

It began ten years ago, with the invasion.

I lived in a small, gray, ranch-style house in Denver. It was the last in a long series of moves, but after a few months I had finally started to settle in. My father was home, cooking breakfast in a clean but ill-fitting apron as he whistled some tune I didn't recognize. It was a special treat to have him home, as he was a high-ranking Navy SEAL who was almost always away on some assignment or another. Both my parents were military, so more often than not I was stuck with a babysitter or dropped at a neighbor's house for long periods of time. They were always nice, of course, but I constantly looked forward to having an actual parent home.

It was Saturday morning, and I sat cross-legged in the living room, watching SpongeBob in my Batman pajamas. The smell of bacon and slightly burned omelets drifted in from the kitchen. I pulled myself away from the TV and scrambled up into a chair at the kitchen counter. I immediately saw why Dad was burning breakfast —as usual, he was paying more attention to the kitchen TV than to the cooking. It was routine for him to watch the news every morning, but I always tried to ignore the anchor's shrill voices and bad news.

"We're entering day three of the massive power outages plaguing major cities," they droned. "New York City, San Francisco, Los Angeles, Houston, Seattle, Chicago, and most of Washington, DC, are still experiencing total blackouts. Everything from commerce to communication has been affected, and in many cases, completely halted. All attempts to start the backup generators has been met with inexplicable failure, and authorities are beginning to suspect foul play—"

Dad clicked the television off with a grimace. It was no news to him that things around the whole country had been getting...strange. My dad had a huge telephone-like radio that he kept on him at all times, and the past few weeks, he had been using it more and more. It was loud enough that I heard its crackles and beeps from across the house, and the noises often woke me up in the middle of the night. Some nights, when it was quiet enough, I could almost make out the words coming through—I knew I wasn't supposed to hear them, but I was desperate to know what was so important that they had to bother my dad at 3 a.m., so I listened as carefully as I could. But then I would catch phrases..."Lost another one"..."Communications have gone dead"...and I wished I hadn't listened at all.

But even as things got worse and worse, my father did his best to distance me from any fear or harm. I remember that on that morning, he forced himself to keep whistling a happy tune as he tried unsuc-cessfully to flip an omelet. He laughed when he saw me, staring at him with my wide eyes and messy hair, waiting less than patiently for breakfast.

"Well, kid," he said, his voice carefully constructed to sound care-free. "I hope you like scrambled eggs, because—"

Surprise silenced him as we were suddenly plunged into dark-ness. A momentary panic seized me even though it really wasn't all that dark, being midmorning. My mind started to race, wondering if we had been brought violently into the middle of whatever awful thing was happening, but my father's voice comforted me almost immediately.

"It's all right, Daire. It's just a power outage. Probably a blown fuse or something."

I was young, but not stupid. We both knew it wasn't a blown fuse. Though I'll admit that having something to blame besides the "great unknown threat" made me feel better. For a moment, I tried to convince myself that maybe it was just a fuse. Hey, maybe it was *all* fuses. Chicago, New York, LA...maybe everyone just needed to check the fuse box. As impossible as I knew that was, it put my mind at ease, if just for a moment.

"We'll just open the blinds and—"

He was interrupted again as a harsh static noise caught our attention. It was the radio resting on the counter, and my father grabbed it and pressed some button, causing the static to go dead. He held it up to his ear.

"Clark," he said.

A murmuring voice came through the radio, but I willed myself not to listen to the words, turning the voice into a word jumble in my mind. My father went very still as he listened. After a long moment, he reached to turn the stove off. Still listening to the radio, he moved quickly from the kitchen and through the house. I forced myself not to follow him as he disappeared from view. When he came back, he was carrying a black backpack I had never seen before and a heavy green jacket. Fear began to gnaw at me as I waited for him to explain what was happening. He knelt to look me in the eye, and I saw worry crease his forehead.

"Listen, Daire." His voice was calm but urgent, and I listened with all the intensity a child could muster. "Something is happening. I don't know what exactly, but it's not good. I need to go and help keep the country safe."

His words settled on me, and I struggled not to bend under their weight. I nodded, looking serious but brave like my father always did in scary situations. I understood. My dad was a hero, and he had to protect everyone. Not just me.

"I'm sending you to an old training base in Montana," he continued. "My former commanding officer is running it. Cap will keep you safe there."

I nodded again, trying and failing not to show my fear. He threw the jacket around my shoulders, though it was much too big and settled around me like a cape. I pulled it around me anyway, taking comfort in the faded fabric. He stood and led me to the front door, walking with his arm over my shoulders. We walked out into the driveway in time to see a black sedan pull up to the house. The engine idled but no one got out, and the suit-clad driver only stared through his sunglasses out the windshield. My dad ushered me into the back of the car, placing the backpack by my feet.

"I've got to go to DC, kiddo. I'm gonna meet up with your mom there and then, hopefully, we'll come check up on you. In the meantime, I want you to listen to Cap and do whatever he says. Can you do that for me, buddy?"

"Yes," I said, swallowing back tears.

My dad stepped back and closed the car door. He leaned in through the open window and ruffled my hair with a calloused hand.

"I love you, kiddo. Stay safe."

"I love you too, Dad."

The car began to pull out of the driveway. My father stood, watching with a forced smile and a face creased by concern. He was a brave man, but I could tell he was worried for me. He was worried for all of us. I watched him, standing alone in the driveway, as the black sedan started down the street. Then the car turned a corner and he vanished from sight.

I slumped down in my seat, feeling all my mustered bravery slip away. My lip quivered and I buried my face in my jacket as tears began to fall. It wasn't the first time I had been forced to leave my parents. But this time...I was scared. More scared than I had ever been.

"Hey, kid..." I looked up to see the man with the sunglasses in the rearview mirror. "You okay? You wanna stop and get a Happy Meal or something?"

I shook my head, unable to find words.

"Let me know if you need food or anything," he said. "It's gonna be a long drive."

Rows and rows of houses passed by out the window. Not one of them had any lights on. A few times, I saw families packing their cars with food and supplies, piling children and pets into the loads of whatever they could fit into the vehicles. I wondered where they were going. Then I wondered if they knew where they were going. Were they headed to their grandma's cabin in the woods until every- thing blew over? Or maybe they thought that getting out of the country was for the best? Perhaps they were just going on vacation. Or maybe...maybe they were running, with no clear destination in mind besides *not here. Anywhere but here.*

Then, all the houses disappeared as we pulled away from the suburbs, turning onto a big but mostly empty highway. I watched the street signs, feeling tears dry on my cheeks. I felt as though I was sitting as the world spun around me, moving outside the car with no effect on the people inside. I waited, in my Batman pajamas and my father's jacket wrapped around me like a blanket, to see what fate would decide for me.

I was eleven years old.

†

"Hey kid, we're here."

I was awoken by the voice, and I peeled my eyes open to see the man—no longer wearing his sunglasses—looking at me with tired eyes. I rubbed the sleep from my own eyes and struggled to take in my surroundings. It was dark, and from what I could tell the car was pulled up alongside a large building with no lights on. There was a loading dock off to one side, guarded by two large men with army fatigues and crossed arms. There was no one else around.

The driver got out of the car and I followed suit, slinging the backpack around my shoulders. I stuck close to the man as he moved toward the loading dock, pausing to show the guards some badge he pulled from inside his jacket. Then, with a backward glance to make sure I was still following him, he headed inside the building.

I recognized instantly that it was a hotel as we walked down corridors lined with ugly floral wallpaper and gray doors. The hallways were dimly lit at best, and the whole building seemed to be empty. There were no sounds coming from any of the rooms and when we entered the lobby, we found it abandoned. But the man didn't seem to notice as he moved quickly to a room off the lobby, guarded by more men and two large double doors. He flashed the badge again, and as one of the guards opened the door, my driver gently ushered me inside.

It was almost too crowded to move, as there were at least a hundred people standing in a circle around the outskirts of the room. Unable to see through all the people, I weaved my way through the crowd, struggling to get passed the tightly packed bodies. When I finally got close enough to see, I stopped, staring at a pool of light in the middle of the room. It was a conference room of sorts, with all the lights focused on the center. Three people stood there, holding the silent audience's attention. The first was a young woman with dark skin and a shaved head, high cheekbones, and a soft but commanding expression. Beside her was a much older man, and the only one of the three not wearing fatigues. He had white hair and a short beard and was standing with the help of a cane. He looked peaceful and happy but tired, and I wished someone would have gotten him a chair. Finally, there was a tall black man who had the posture of a drill sergeant and the fierce eyes of a commander. His clothes were clean but faded and his hair was all but gone. This man stood tall and fixed the room with a stare before he cleared his throat and began to speak.

"As you all know, we are here to address a new threat. This is strictly confidential information that I am only sharing with you because our situation is so dire. For the past few weeks, there have been invaders sneaking onto our land. We were unable to repel them on their initial landing and now, they have begun their attack."

The crowd broke its silence with confused and anxious whispers. I pulled my jacket tighter around myself. The man raised his arms, calling for attention, and the room quieted.

"They came by boat. We know this because we found them—the ships, that is. Thousands of them. They were disguised as things that wouldn't catch our attention. Cruise liners, fishing boats, even garbage barges. They all looked just like American boats...but it was them. These ships dropped anchor a few miles off the shores of San Francisco, Sacramento, Baltimore, New York City, Cancun, Vancouver, and hundreds of other places. We've started to find these ships, but they've all been completely abandoned. Some of them appear to have crashed, but we couldn't find any bodies or debris. The shipwrecks were picked clean, all information erased. We don't know how many people were on the boats, or what weapons they might have been carrying. So, in short, we learned nothing." He paused.

"Yesterday, we lost all contact with Australia. Today, we lost Europe. We've heard nothing, and there's been no indication that they are receiving our messages. International communications are going dead.

"To make things worse, communication lines from our own people are breaking. The President has disappeared. Whoever this enemy is, they are doing their best to separate and confuse us. But we have launched a counteroffensive, and we are all hoping that it will succeed."

The man paused, dropping his head. When he continued, looking up again, his eyes were somber.

"But there is the possibility that they will fail. That is why we are here. All of you have been chosen to help establish this place, which will serve as a secret military and civilian-rescue base in case these invaders manage to take control. This place is unknown and unmapped, and until the country is once again secure, it will be our home."

The man took a step back as the woman next to him began to speak, addressing the room with the same authority and a slight accent.

"We've gathered some information on their strategies. Army bases were their first targets—that's why we're meeting here. As we speak, the invaders are sweeping through towns and cities, rounding up as many people as they can...and killing thousands. It seems that their goal is to take our country, and our continent, for themselves. We've heard reports that the same thing is happening in Europe, Asia, and Australia, but as you know, since then communications have gone dead. I want to tell you about these invaders," she said. "But unfortunately, we know very little. These people...they are not like us. We do not know where they came from, why they are doing this, or even... what they are."

The crowd of people could not hold their silence at this. Exclamations of confusion and disbelief filled the room, and the woman had to wait for the people to quiet down.

"We do not know what they are," she repeated, raising her voice over the crowd before it fell back to silence. "But we have heard reports that they are faster and stronger than most people. Perhaps smarter, too. They have impossible reflexes, and somehow...bullets have little effect on them. They can see almost perfectly in the dark, and they heal much faster than should be possible. They look very similar to us, but you can distinguish them by their eyes. They don't follow the same iris color pattern as us; they can be yellow, red, white, or basically any other color. And when their pupils contract in a bright light, instead of turning into smaller circles like ours, theirs turn into slits. That is why our codename for them is 'Cat.'"

"There is a lot of speculation about these things." The man spoke again, retaking everyone's attention. "Some people think that they're the result of genetic modification. Some say they're just regular people on some crazy drug. All we really know for sure is that they're hostile, and they need to be stopped. This is real, and it's happening here, right now. You all know exactly what this means."

The man stepped forward again, slightly dragging his left leg. His eyes traced the room, so every person felt their gaze.

"We are under attack." The man paused, and the room echoed his words, repeating what no one wanted to hear. "*We are under attack.* And if we're going to survive, we need to work together. But if we can do that, if we can rally everything we have left, we can fight back, hit them hard, and *take our country back,*" he finished, his voice resonating with assurance.

The people filling the room nodded solemnly. Sensing that the meeting was over, they began to file out, murmuring among themselves in low tones. I stood still, unsure of what to do. I tried my hardest to look brave as the adults moved around me. The room seemed huge, so big that the ceiling didn't have lights, but tiny stars that hovered at the top and shone upon the center. The people in that light seemed like gods. Even as they spoke to each other in relaxed tones, their air of authority seemed to fill the gigantic room. As I watched from outside the circle of light, the old man smiled and the skin around his eyes crinkled, deepening long-set laugh lines. It took me a moment to realize that his smile was directed at me, and I almost jumped when my eyes met his.

The younger black man followed the old man's gaze, and after a quick good-bye he started toward me, leaving the other two to talk to each other. As the man approached me, I noticed he too had a slight limp. He knelt in front of me and scrutinized my face, and for a moment I was scared that he was looking right through me, as though I wasn't there at all. But then his intense features softened into a smile that looked rare but natural, and he held his hand out to me.

"So you're the little Clark," he said as I shook his hand with a firm grip the way my father had taught me.

"Yes, sir." He seemed important enough that I should give him some title.

"You look just like your dad. It's nice to meet you, Daire.

Everyone around here calls me Cap, so I guess you can too. I'm gonna look after you and keep you safe until your dad joins us, okay?"

"Okay. Will he come here soon?"

"I don't know, kid."

"Oh..." At my crestfallen response, the man sighed and stood, gesturing for me to follow as he headed for the door.

"In the meantime, I can tell you all the embarrassing stories from your dad's time at boot camp. Did he ever tell you how much trouble he got into?"

I shook my head, staring at Cap in awe as I stumbled alongside him. Even with a limp, the man walked fast. But he adjusted his pace so I could keep up and glanced at me to make sure I was following.

"One time, he got in so much trouble he was told to go outside and mop the ground dry during a thunderstorm." Cap chuckled, half caught in the memory. I followed along with wide eyes, having finally forgotten my fear. "He deserved it, of course. Clark pulled the best damn prank I've ever seen on the drill instructor. I tried to cover for him—or maybe I pulled the prank and he covered for me. I don't remember. But what we did was..."

2 CAP

MY FATIGUES WERE WORN and faded, and I pulled the jacket tighter around me. The sun was setting; the city was getting cold. Wind whipped around me from my post on top of the abandoned factory, but I ignored it and focused on the small alley below me. The long shadows and my failing eyesight forced me to concentrate on the scene to make out any details. For a while, all was quiet.

A small figure turned into the alley. Though a hood covered her face, completely obscuring her features, her small, thin stature made it obvious she was a woman even from a distance. She walked with quick, sure steps, hunched over in her thick hooded sweatshirt and black pants. Old combat boots clicked against the sidewalk. I thought it odd for a moment that she didn't seem to look anywhere but the ground, as though keeping her head low. She should have been looking around, checking over her shoulder. After all, she appeared to be unarmed, and she was alone in a dangerous part of town.

Another figure slipped into the alley. He was much larger than the woman, with a broad chest and shoulders. He was muscular and a good foot taller than her. Dark hair hung in his eyes, and a long coat added to his menacing look.

He moved silently, easily catching up to the woman with long, quick strides. She didn't turn around as he drew close. Just a few feet away, he withdrew a knife from his coat.

From my place above, I watched. I didn't move or make a sound, so as not to draw attention to myself. I was careful not to do anything that would affect what was unfolding before me.

The man moved closer still, and slowly withdrew his hand from his pocket. I saw fingers wrapped in black gloves gripping a large knife. Dying sunlight flashed off the weapon in his hand, and he lunged forward, closing the distance and thrusting the knife into thin air as the woman spun away from the path of the blade.

She faced her attacker, dropping into a low battle stance. She rested on the balls of her feet with her legs set wide, one positioned farther forward for stability. Her back was curved forward, like a waiting snake, and her knees were bent to keep her low. The woman's arms were raised in front of her chest and slightly to the side, ready to guard or strike. Her eyes were hidden in shadow, but I could see her lips curled in a grin.

The man swung the knife toward her, but she ducked it easily. With impossibly fast reflexes, she caught the man's arm with one hand and his shoulder with the other. Before he could shake her off, she spun into him and flipped him over her back. He landed hard on the ground.

In less than a second, she was on him. With one boot-clad foot she pinned the hand with the knife, pushing it into the dirt. She kept one hand locked on his throat while the other was pulled back, clenched into a fist and ready to deliver a devastating blow.

I sighed, and moved to the fire escape to make my way down to the alley. The man coughed and winced in pain. He didn't struggle, but seemed resigned to his fate.

"Jesus, Robin," he choked. "If you don't start taking it easier on me, I'm going to have to find a chiropractor."

"Hey, it's not my fault you always give away your position,

Daire." She grinned. "Next time, make sure no light reflects off your weapon. Any Cat would've seen it."

I reached the bottom of the steps and called out, "If you're done kicking my star student's ass, could you help him up?"

"Sure, Cap," said the woman, extending a hand and helping Daire to his feet. I made my way over to them as Daire rubbed his back in pain and Robin smirked in triumph.

"So tell me, what did you do wrong that allowed Robin to get the upper hand?" I asked.

"Picked the wrong training partner," Daire mumbled. After an elbow to the ribs from Robin, he continued in a stronger voice. "I, um...didn't take the sunset into account. I wasn't properly aware of my setting."

"Correct. So what will you do differently next time?"

"Um...be more aware of my surroundings?"

"Good. Robin, you did well as usual. Now head back to the Fort."

I did an about-face and marched back toward home, ignoring the sharp pain in my leg, a reminder from my time in Iraq. As we walked, Robin pulled a white half-mask from the pocket of her jacket. Its features were fine but worn, and it seemed to mimic a bird's face with small carved feathers sweeping up around her cheekbones. Two particular feathers were thick and hooded, casting shadows over Robin's eyes and making them almost impossible to see. While I marched as a military professional, the children bickered behind me.

"I know you need to keep your identity a secret," said Daire in a teasing whine. "Being an ambassador and all, but there are other ways than a weird bird mask. Besides, it's safe enough so you don't have to wear it here. There's just me and Cap."

"You know it's not that simple. If there were Cat spies around here, they'd recognize me. And then you'd lose your double agent. They barely trust me as it is, since I'm a human. Damn things won't even let me use the coffee machine." She laughed. "Besides, I like this mask. It's pretty, and my name is also a bird, so it's fitting. Plus it makes me feel like a superhero."

"Yeah, but do you have to wear it at the Fort? There's only humans there, and new refugees are gonna think you're weird."

"We've gone over this, Daire. The new refugees are exactly why I have to wear it. Any of them could be spies and then my cover would be blown. Trust me, I don't like it either. I'm pretty sure that most of the children there think this is my real face." Robin sighed, running a hand along the mask. "Plus it's uncomfortable. And sticky."

"Well, it is pretty," said Daire. "The other day, Fox said it reminded him of some old opera mask or something. Personally, I think it makes you look like someone at one of those mask parties."

"A masquerade?"

"Yeah, that. And that's pretty cool. I've always wanted to go to a costume party. Hey, Cap, why doesn't our military/refugee camp throw many masquerades?"

I didn't even glance back at Daire and Robin, just shook my head as they giggled to themselves. We had been fighting, running, and struggling to survive for ten years, and those two had managed to hold onto a sense of humor. They were young and stupid, but somehow they were able to laugh through the whole goddamn apocalypse.

3 ROBIN

"HOL-DA- IN-" read the sign perched on top of the building, the "i,"
"y," and "n" having fallen off long ago. The grass by the door was
wildly overgrown and the trees skirting the parking lot had gotten so
big that their roots cracked through the pavement. The lot led to a
small curved road in front of the doors, where a decade ago families
could pull their cars up and have bellhops take their luggage. Above
that was a large canopy built into the building, but time and weather
had caused it to sag in the middle, so it seemed ready to collapse at
any moment. The parking lot was scattered with abandoned cars,
some flipped over and others left with their doors gaping. The sun,
now just above the horizon, cast harsh early-morning light on the
metal, which would hopefully reflect and blind any unfriendly eyes
that might be watching. Nevertheless, I scanned the rooftops dili-
gently, shielding my face with one hand.

"Clear," I said.

Cap, Daire, and I rose from the shadow of the truck we were
hiding behind and headed quickly for the building. Cap rapped a
short, precise beat on the door, which opened cautiously upon
receiving the password. We stepped inside without hesitation.

"Morning, Port," Cap addressed the man who closed the door behind us.

"Morning, sir." The young soldier inside nodded at us. Curly brown hair hung low over his wide eyes as he greeted us with a shy smile. I returned the boy's smile and a light flush spread across his cheeks. Cap had asked me to spy on this one because he might have potential, and from what I had seen, I agreed. Port was only 18, but he threw himself fully into every task. If he continued in the direction he was going, he might end up leading the Fort someday.

The hotel lobby was, aside from Port, deserted. The ugly wallpaper had long since faded, leaving pale squares of color showing behind the permanently askew pictures. Thousands of boots had left the carpet torn, and in some places, bloodstained. The corners of the lobby were littered with fake plants and discarded luggage, all haphazardly shoved out of the way of foot traffic. Off to the side of the room was an elevator shaft with the doors open. There seemed to be no actual elevator in the shaft, but hundreds of wires tied together, running from far below the lobby to the highest rooms in the hotel. The wires reached down to the generators in the basement, bringing power to the rooms above and spreading it across the building. The rooms served as living quarters for our small army, a handful of hard-working army vets and refugees, as well as children, families, and even a few animals trained to warn us of intruders.

The view from the far lobby window showed what had previously been the hotel's second building. It had collapsed years ago, leaving only high outer walls. It was impossible to see from the outside, but the debris had been cleared out and the walls fortified. Alcoves for lookouts had been added, and though the destroyed building appeared unusable, it made an excellent courtyard for training.

But everything from the lobby to the courtyard to the training rooms made up only half of the Fort.

We made our way to the other side of the lobby and through a heavy metal door. From there, it was down six flights of stairs until we were several stories underground. We reached a door, and after tapping out another pass code, we entered into a flurry of activity.

It was originally an extensive parking garage, but the network of makeshift walls configured from boards and blankets left no room for cars. The garage extended ten floors underground, and every inch of space had some purpose. There were strategy rooms with tabletop displays, armories, storage areas, kitchens, and even a more or less functioning doctor's office. This section of the Fort was almost its own little city, a self-sufficient pocket of humanity. It was a sight to behold.

A man leaned on one concrete wall by the door, under signs that read "Parking Area H" and "No Smoking." His arms were crossed over a tattered black tank top, and his olive drab cargo pants were in dire need of a wash. Tendrils of smoke swirled up from his cigarette, faintly obscuring knowing brown eyes and sandy, short-cropped hair. He looked to be about eighteen, but the freckles dotting tanned white skin made him look almost child-like. His demeanor, however—like the way his shoulders seemed to droop with exhaustion and how his eyes were ringed with dark circles—made him seem much, much older. An iron hatchet hung in its sheath by his side, and he rested with an easygoing, lopsided smirk.

"Hey!" Daire called out, approaching him. "Can't you read?"

"What can I say?" The man's slight Southern drawl added to his air of relaxation. He stirred, stood straight and crushed the cigarette under his foot. "I'm a rebel."

Daire grinned. "Aren't we all? Fox, guess what? I beat Robin at the training exercise today. I finally managed to get the upper hand, using stealth and Cat-like reflexes. Pun intended."

I turned to Daire with a raised eyebrow, but his excited smile made me hesitant to ruin his fun. He winked at me, and for a second his eyes seemed to shine in the florescent lights. He nudged me playfully with his elbow, and I couldn't help but smile. Fox didn't say anything at first, but regarded us carefully with knowing eyes.

"Yeah...I'm gonna call bullshit on that," he said. "You haven't beaten her yet, and something tells me you're not gonna for a long time."

"Dammit. Why don't you ever believe me? Is it really so hard to think that I could win a fight against her?" Daire frowned with exaggerated features and I chuckled.

With an easy smile, Fox sauntered over and draped an arm around my shoulder. "Sure is. 'Cause there ain't a human alive could take down our Robin. Hopefully ain't a Cat, either. If that mask doesn't scare 'em off first."

"Hey, Fox?" He was so tall that I had to look up to meet his eyes. "Have you been keeping an eye on Port like I asked?"

"Oh, I've been keepin' an eye on him, all right. And speaking of eyes, he sure is easy on them." He whistled, and Daire and I giggled in response. "But more important, he's smart and dedicated. I can see why Cap's groomin' him to lead."

"Cap wants Port to replace him?" said Daire, with confusion rather than anger. "But he's only been here a few years. Fox, you and I grew up here, and Robin's been here for about five years now. Why doesn't Cap want any of us to take over?"

"None of us are exactly the leading type." I said. "Fox could, but he seems more like an advisor. Not really one much for the spotlight."

"You're right there. I'm too quiet for anyone to listen to me, except Cap. Daire wouldn't want the responsibility of leading, and Miss Ambassador here is too busy with her day job. And besides, you two are too busy making doe eyes at each other to lead anything," Fox teased.

I felt a blush crawl across my face, but Daire only laughed. "Maybe Port is the right guy for the job. He seems like a nice-enough kid."

"Oh hey, don't y'all forget, Doc's givin' physicals today. I'm headin' over to get mine now," said Fox.

I drew in a sharp breath in surprise. All my muscles tightened as panic shot through me. Fox, sensing the change, looked at me questioningly. But true to his character, he said nothing.

"I almost forgot. I have a meeting tomorrow that I haven't prepared for." I kept my voice steady, allowing only a fraction of my fear into my words. "I need to get back to my apartment."

"A meeting?" asked Fox. "With the Cats?"

"Yeah. I'm supposed to go to them and report back what I've seen. Basically I tell them 'I think there are a few humans in the woods north of the city or wherever but I haven't found them yet.' And then they say 'Keep looking, and tell us where they are when you find them.' And then they threaten me and say that if I continue to spy for them, they'll continue to not kill me."

"And they believe you?" asked Daire.

"I'm pretty convincing," I said. "And sometimes, I lead them to little 'human camps' that I set up, spreading old supplies around so it looks like I'm leading them in the right direction. I have my tricks, and they haven't caught on yet."

"I'll escort you home so you can prepare, Miss Ambassador," said Daire. "Just make sure that during your meeting, you tell those Cats that we're going to kick their asses."

"Or better yet, tell them we're weak and most certainly *not* going to kick their asses." Fox disentangled himself and started toward the infirmary at the back of the Fort. "That way, the look on their faces when we do will be *priceless*."

Daire turned to me, his moss-green eyes kind and trusting. I hated lying to those eyes.

"Ready to go?" he asked me.

My apartment was only about a mile from the Fort, but getting there meant checking every corner and rooftop for Cat spies. On occasion, I had gotten stuck hiding in a ditch or behind a trash can while an enemy patrol marched by, but there were usually no Cats around this part of the city. With the coast clear, Daire and I arrived at my mostly abandoned building in about twenty minutes. Then it was up seven flights of stairs and around two corners until we reached the only door with five deadbolts. I had a code for the locks—

the day of the month determined which ones I locked. Daire always asked me how I memorized all the numbers.

Seventeenth, I thought, *that's number one, four, and five.* I opened the appropriate locks and stepped in hurriedly.

"Thanks for walking me home," I said, closing the door. "See you tomorrow."

"Hold up." Daire stopped the door and pushed it open again. I tried to swallow my fear as he regarded me closely. Just as always, his dark brows hung low over eyes that were somehow both gentle and fierce. *Don't ask,* I begged silently.

"Why don't you want to get your physical?"

Damn. "My meeting—"

"You're a terrible liar, Robin." His tone was lighthearted, but I could tell he was hurt that I wasn't telling him the truth. I sighed, defeated.

"Actually, I'm a fantastic liar. You just know me too well."

He smiled, open, reassuring. "So what's up?"

"Truth is, I really, really need some sleep." And it was the truth. Not the whole truth, of course, but as much as I could afford to tell him.

"Nightmares again?"

"Yeah."

Empathy shone in his eyes, and a genuine desire to make things better. "That sucks. I've heard chamomile tea can help you sleep. I'll see if we have any at the Fort for you to take home tomorrow. In the meantime, I'll clear you with Dr. Hanson. You just get some rest."

"Okay, Daire." I smiled gratefully. "Thank you."

In that moment, I was glad he couldn't see my eyes. The force of holding back a secret I so desperately wanted to tell nearly brought me to tears.

"See you tomorrow, then. And sleep tight."

He set off down the hall, back toward home. When he was well beyond earshot, I whispered a final "Thank you" and shut the door.

4 DR. HANSON

"SO YOU EXPECT me to believe that Robin can't make her physical because of a meeting?" I asked the young man before me. "Roll your sleeve up."

"Yes, ma'am," Daire replied, sitting on my examination table, which was really just a rectangular dinner table with an almost clean sheet on it. He obediently rolled his sleeve up past the elbow, and I placed the cuff to test his blood pressure.

"Don't call me that," I said gruffly, squeezing the instrument and watching the dials. "What's the real reason?"

"Well, it might have something to do with this area not being entirely...well, secure." He poked at my "door"—a tattered blanket hanging in front of the entrance. "Someone could easily see her in here, and her identity might be compromised to some Cat spy. And then we lose our double agent and connection to the Cats. Or she could be telling the truth, and she has a meeting in the morning," he added innocently. I paused to scowl at him before taking note of the numbers on the dial. 145/89. Not too bad.

I considered this. "Yes, I can see why this wouldn't be the safest room to show her face, since it doesn't have any real walls. Still...

there's more to it than that. This wouldn't have anything to do with what you asked me for, would it?"

"No, ma'a—um, Dr. Hanson. Not at all." He flashed a wide, disarming smile, but I wasn't fooled. "Speaking of, did you find any?"

"The team I sent out brought a box back this morning. Consider yourself lucky they found any at all. Every grocery store has been stripped of...well, everything. Even unnecessary things. But there just happened to be a box left." I walked back over to my desk and grabbed my old stethoscope. I reached into my medical bag/old suitcase and brought out a small cardboard box, which I tossed over to Daire. "What do you need chamomile tea for anyway?"

He caught it easily. "I'm having trouble sleeping, and I read that some types of tea can help with that. Ah, that's cold," he exclaimed as I placed the stethoscope against his skin above his heart.

"Daire, I know you don't have trouble sleeping. Fox is always coming to me and asking for earplugs. Apparently, he lives in the room next to you and can hear your snoring through the wall. I know this tea isn't for you. But I think I know who it is for," I said.

"I don't know what you're talking about," he replied, staring pointedly at the ceiling. I removed the stethoscope, hanging it around my neck.

"Tell me, does that girl know about half the things you do for her?"

Daire looked at me in surprise, and I could see a faint embarrassed flush spread across his face. It was gone in a moment, though, replaced with an endearing half-smile.

"Nope," he said. "And with your help, Doc, she never will."

I shook my head in resignation. "My lips are sealed. You're healthy, by the way. Now get back to work."

I paused for a second after the door swished closed behind Daire. I always try to be completely objective with my patients. That's kind of a necessity when there are hundreds of people with battle wounds, infections, and all sorts of other ailments coming through my office constantly, especially when so many end up in the tiny cemetery out back. It's good practice not to get attached. But that kid...I couldn't help but like him. He was unique, that's for sure. Always thought of others before himself, as if that was the natural thing to do. And he never thought twice about risking his life for a friend, or even a stranger. Fox sure thought highly of him too, and *that* guy was smart. All the leaders of the Fort secretly went to him for advice—even Cap, that grizzled old veteran. And Robin...well, she was something else entirely. The toughest and most loved person in the Fort, she was like the final piece to our puzzle. Those three set an example for the others, on and off the battlefield. And more important, they gave us hope. We were lucky to have them, the whole lot. But that didn't mean they could go skipping physicals.

I shook my head, clearing my thoughts, and moved to lean out of the doorway. "Next patient!"

5 ALMYRR

I STOOD to the back of the strangely round room, near the tall rein-forced windows and their flowing curtains. I had been standing still for hours, but I didn't sway or show any signs of weakness. I knew better than to draw any attention to myself. I stood at the ready, silent and unmoving as stone. I was very good at fading into the back-ground. That was part of what made me so deadly. But for the moment, my task was not to kill, but to protect, and I would not let my charge come to harm. I could not fail him.

The ruling king of the world sat with his feet propped up on a desk in the center of the round room.

His cape, made nearly six feet long to reach from his shoulders to the floor, hung unceremoniously over the back of his chair. His clothes were expensive but not flashy, with a black suit and simple white undershirt. His hair was white, but not with age—it had always been a stark white color. His face fell into a natural expression that spoke of a calm with rage boiling just below the surface, with a soft smile that was just a little bit too wide. He always seemed friendly but quietly dangerous, and he looked quite like what the humans would call a "politician."

But every Wyrforra—or as those disgusting humans call us, *Cat*—knows, the terrifying thing about the King is his eyes. It is highly believed that they change color, but no one has ever been brave enough to ask. They say when he's happy, his eyes are a light shade of maroon, an attractive color that adds to his unfailing charm. But when he's angry, they turn a bright, stark shade of red. With those he could strike fear into a nation, maybe even a planet. As much as his armies and countless soldiers, those eyes were a weapon.

For the moment, they were focused on a strange little cube in his hands. He was fiddling with it, moving the colored boxes around with deft fingers. His brow was slightly wrinkled in confusion, but he seemed more entertained than frustrated.

At the sound of footsteps approaching the door, I reached silently for the dirk at my side, keeping it hidden under my coat but ready to slash out at a millisecond's notice.

"Sir, your captai—" called a voice from outside the door.

"No, no," interrupted the King, the first time he'd spoken in hours. "Knock at the door, like humans do. I'm still trying to understand the concept."

There was a pause, then a hesitant tapping.

"Come in," he said.

A porter poked his head through the doorway. "Your captain of espionage is here, sir."

"Excellent. Send her in."

"Right away, sir."

The door closed, and I heard the King mumble, "Knocking...why? I don't understand. Isn't it just easier to call through?"

The door opened again and a soldier in strikingly clean battle clothes entered. Her hair was dark red, like blood on pale skin, and she wore it in an unusual fashion—tied back into one long tress with a series of bands, and the sides of her head were shaved. She wore simple silver chest armor, one sheet of plate mail, secured with one shoulder strap. Under that she wore sleeveless black underclothes that covered her from neck to toe, except her arms. Belts crossed her waist and thighs, and her arm and leg armor was made of simple metal guards buckled on with straps on the sides. Crossed short swords were strapped to her back, both cleaned so much that they shone. She stepped forward and dropped to a knee, bowing her head low. "Sir," she said.

"Odyra," he replied, rewarding her loyalty with a wide smile. "Stand up, you needn't stay like that. I'm glad you're here, in—what is this place called again? The Pale House?"

"White House, sir."

"Right, right. So, any news from the East?"

"Not yet, sir. The European and Asian invasion forces are still establishing communication. Most of their messenger ships bear good news, however. Colonies are being established with little difficulty."

"That's good. But why haven't communication lines been settled yet?"

"The rebel forces on other continents are strong, sir. They keep sabotaging the radio towers and phone lines. But we *will* crush the insurgents, sir."

"Yes, we will." He paused for a moment, playing with the cube. "Is there any new information on the rebellion here?"

"We now know that we overestimated their numbers. We believe there are only a few thousand, stationed somewhere in the center of the country."

"We haven't figured out the region— er, state they're in yet?"

Odyra shifted uncomfortably, but stood firm and spoke clearly. Her pink eyes were neutral and stoic, the only expression she allowed others to see. "No, sir."

"Shame. Any more news?"

"No, sir."

"Very well. You're dismissed. Wait—take this." The King handed the multicolored box to Odyra, who took it uncertainly. "Bring it to the humans we've imprisoned and find out its purpose."

"...Yes, sir." She turned quickly and marched out the door,

cradling the odd object as though it was a precious but fragile treasure.

He paused for a moment, silent and pensive.

"She didn't bow as she left. I must have surprised her with the cube," he said, his voice thoughtful. I stayed silent. After a moment, he spoke again.

"Do you think I should have her killed, Almyrr?"

I considered this a moment. "Good messengers are hard to come by, sir," I answered.

"That's true. And she's never failed me. I suppose she can live." The King leaned back in his chair and shut his eyes, crossing his arms behind his head. "Thank you for your council, Almyrr. You know I always rely on your advice."

"Of course, King Erenvyr."

6 DAIRE

I STOOD watch on top of the outer wall of the courtyard. There was a small platform built into the wall, with an overhang for when it rained. It made for a cozy little alcove that overlooked the wooded area to the west of the Fort. And above the trees, thousands of stars shone bright with nothing to block them out. After all, there was no light pollution for miles around. The Fort kept all aboveground lights permanently off so as not to give us away, so the nearest well-lit area was the small Cat base on the other side of town. The invasion was the worst thing to happen in recent history, but at least we could see the stars.

When the night was this peaceful, it was hard to concentrate on scanning the ground for enemies. The wind rustled through the trees and the courtyard was empty. The air was cold but my old green jacket was warm. It was so comfortable, I couldn't help but slip into a daydream.

Perfect, I thought, observing the scene laid out before me. Yes, it was all ready. The plates were laid out nicely, all the silverware was in the right place, and the vase of flowers in the center of the table tied everything in so well. Everything was just perfect.

"Robin!" I called, trying to keep my voice neutral. "Dinner's ready!"

"Daire, you made dinner again?" She sounded annoyed, but there was a smile in her voice. "It was my turn."

"I know, I know, but I just wanted to make sure you're eating healthy. You understand." I carefully took the chicken out of the oven, placing it on the table. It smelled delicious. "Besides, you shouldn't be doing any work now. You should be resting."

"Well, if you insist. That smells amazing! The table looks wonderful, too. And are those calla lilies? Aw, you set out my favorite kind of flowers!" She reached over and pulled me toward her, close enough to plant a kiss on my cheek. She looked as beautiful as always, with her intense purple eyes, arching brows, and a slight smile that seemed to invite a challenge. "You're the best!"

I couldn't help but smile. "Make sure you leave room for dessert. There's a pumpkin pie waiting for you. Your favorite."

"Oh my God, Daire. You are perfect." Robin's eyes sparkled at me from across the table. I smiled in response, feeling warmth in my cheeks.

"Well, take a bite," I urged. "Tell me how it is."

She obliged without hesitation. "Mmm...it's amazing! What's your secret?"

I thought for a minute. "Oregano."

"Oregano...well, I'll have to remember that for when I'm cooking for you. This is phenomenal. Hey, how about after I clean the dishes, we watch a movie? I'm thinking maybe one of those old kung-fu flicks. Those are great!"

"Sounds like a plan." I was still smiling, mostly because Robin was, too. "Except for the part about you doing the dishes. Let me handle that."

"What? No way. You made dinner."

"I know, but I don't mind. Really." I reached over and held her hand, savoring the moment. "You just relax. If not for you, then for the baby."

"Daire."

"It's okay, really."

"Daire!"

"Please, honey?"

"Hey, Triple Dog Daire, are you planetside?"

I was awoken from my pleasant daydream by Fox's distinctive Southern drawl and his footsteps coming up the stairs. I shook my head clear of the fantasy as the cold night air woke me back up. I grinned with embarrassment, but I doubted Fox would think too poorly of me for drifting off.

"Roger, roger, do you copy?" he said, reaching the top of the stairs leading to my outpost.

"Yeah, I'm here, Fox." I rubbed my eyes, trying to knock the sleepiness out. "You can stop shouting."

"You were pretty deep in that daydream, kid. I almost sent a recon team in after ya. Say, what were you dreaming 'bout, anyway?"

"Ah, the usual. Killing Cats, kicking ass, taking names. You know, tough, manly things."

"Yeah, sure." Fox gave me that knowing smirk. That bastard knew me better than anyone. "Well, your shift is over, so feel free to head home. Oh...and say hi to Robin for me."

"Yeah, yeah." I stretched and started to head back inside. "Hey, do you know what oregano is? I've read about it in books and things, and I think my dad used to cook with it, but I'm not really sure what it is."

"Sounds like a plant. Vegetable, maybe?" Fox shrugged.

"I don't know. Just sounds fancy, I guess." I sighed. "Wish we had time for the fancy stuff."

"We will someday, after this damn war is over. Don't worry. Someday we'll get regular life back and you can be the happy suburban home owner you always wanted to be," Fox said, lighting a cigarette. "You and Robin can have 2.5 kids and a minivan, just like in all those old magazines. And the only cats around will be those little furry bastards."

"I hope you're right." I laughed. "I like *those* kinds of cats."

"More of a dog person myself. Anyway, I've got watch now so

you can go get some dinner. They're serving steak tonight, with a side of caviar and fine wine." Fox chuckled. "It's actually beans and hotdogs, like from a can."

"I'd better go get some before they get cold, on the off chance that there's some left. I'll see you later, Fox."

Fox nodded a good-bye, and with that, I turned my back on the stars and my dreams and retreated inside the Fort.

7 FOX

THE THING about guard duty is, when you're standing out under the moon with no trouble in sight, the conditions are perfect to let the mind wander. That's why I couldn't blame Daire for daydreaming like that. Lord knows he always pulled more weight than the rest of us. He and Robin, anyway. And when I was standing out under the stars myself, more often than not I'd end up lost in thought. I'd start thinking about my friends and family...and the two people who were somehow both.

Not many people understood why we made such a great team, all three of us. Then again, not many people knew the full story. Daire and I had joined the Resistance around the same time, about ten years ago. He saved my life the day we met, and we've been friends since. And the second Robin joined the team, I knew that those two would a perfect match.

I remember the night we met her. She sought us out, which was no easy task, as the Resistance tends to keep quiet. Cap, Daire, and I were training on a rooftop in the middle of the city when she approached us. She was wearing that hood and mask thing she always had, explained that she was an ambassador and had to keep her identity a secret. She said she wanted to join, wanted to help us fight the Cats.

None of us trusted her at first, even after she showed us her eyes and proved she was human. We never trusted strangers. But there was something so sincere about her that I said we should give her a chance. Cap took one look at her and disagreed, saying that she could join us as a refugee but not a fighter, seeing as how she had no experience in combat. Really, I think he was concerned for her safety.

She was 16 years old and tiny, and truthfully she didn't look like she could lift a baseball bat. But Robin made history as one of the few people to stand up to Cap and demanded a chance to prove herself. She challenged Daire to a fistfight.

Now, Daire had about 150 pounds on this girl, all in muscle, and he was almost a foot taller. He was always too proud to turn down a challenge, so he stepped up with doubt in his eyes, probably thinking he couldn't beat down on someone so small. I remember that fight perfectly, and how Robin took the first swing and immediately gave Daire a black eye. That was an eye-opener. Sort of.

They were evenly matched for a bit, but the fight got one-sided real fast. Daire had strength and reach, but Robin was quick and creative. Daire would throw a punch and Robin simply wouldn't be there, having predicted where he would aim and moving just enough to let the blow pass her. She would step in close and land a punch of her own and then step back before he could react. She would go after weak spots he didn't expect and then use his momentum to her advantage. She finally hooked her leg behind his knees and pulled him off balance, throwing him to the ground. In the end, she gave him the best ass kicking I've ever seen.

Daire was the best fighter on our side, and I'd never seen him get it handed to him before. I figured his pride would be hurt, and I honestly had no idea how he'd react. But when Robin helped him up off the ground, I saw genuine respect in his eyes. Something between them connected in that moment. I saw it in the way that their smiles seemed to mirror each other, and how on the way back to the Fort, they had both fallen slightly behind to talk.

"Could you teach me how to fight like that?" Daire had asked.

"Actually, I really like the way you fight," she responded. "Maybe we can train together."

They've been the perfect team ever since, complementing each other in every way. When they fight together, it's like watching a thunderstorm—lighting and rain coming together to create something *more*. They make up for each other's weaknesses and encourage each other's strengths. And I was quick to catch on to their connection, and tease Daire about it relentlessly.

"So what do you think of Robin? Should I start planning your wedding?" I asked him once. It was a couple months after she had joined, so about five years since he and I had met.

Daire was silent for a while, looking thoughtful. "I think I really like her, Fox," he said.

I thought a while. Daire was my best friend, maybe my only friend, and adding another person to the mix could be risky. But I wanted Daire to be happy, and I liked her. As I was getting to know Robin, I found that she wasn't just great in battle, she was kind and caring and she liked to laugh. She was perfect for him, and I knew he could make her happy.

"Do you love her?" I asked.

"Hell, I don't know. Maybe I will someday, but I don't think now's the time." He sighed, running a hand through his hair. "Maybe I'll...love her after the war."

"I don't think you can put things like that on hold, friend. But good luck." I patted him on the back and offered a reassuring smile. He only sighed again.

As time passed, he did his best to be disinterested. He had plenty of chances with other girls but always politely declined. He'd say he was a soldier, and he wasn't at the Fort to date. I asked him about that once, why he never accepted, and he just looked at me and said with that smile, "No time, Fox. We're fighting a war." Bless him.

Now, to the untrained eye, it might seem like I had more interest in their non-relationship than Robin did. After all, she never showed any interest in dating anyone. She was always concentrating on the next battle plan, preparing strategies, training, devising undercover counterstrikes—always so busy. But if you watched closely, you could see her change when she was with Daire. It was subtle, but not much gets by me. Her shoulders set back a little, her tone gets less serious, and she smiles a little bit more. It was like she was always in the heat of battle, but when Daire was around, she was comfortable enough to drop her guard. The few times I've seen her whole face, there was an unmistakable look in her eyes when she was with him. There has never been any doubt in my mind that they'll end up together, someday.

Standing my post on that cool night, thinking of my two great friends and feeling the breeze on my face, I couldn't help but smile a little.

I was torn from my thoughts as movement below the wall caught my attention. I peered over, spying two people scuttling around the base in a hurry. I squinted in the darkness, trying to determine what species they were. Then one of the creatures stopped and turned his face sharply upward, lifting his nose into the air. *He's scenting,* I realized. *So they're Cats.* I silently unclipped the sheath on my hatchet and slid my crossbow from my back, holding it ready. I glanced down the other side of the wall, and noticed that my movement had caught the attention of some of the soldiers in the courtyard.

"Trouble," I called down to them before setting off quickly in the direction the Cats had gone. " 'Bout time something happened around here."

8 HADRYLL

THE FALLEN BUILDING hardly called for scrutinizing. The...*hotel*, I think it was called, looked to have been destroyed years ago, and I caught no movement from the cracked walls. It was quiet, too. Almost silent. There was no reason for this part of my new patrol route to be suspicious.

Except for one thing—it absolutely reeked of humans.

"Lycel," I called, drawing the attention of the other half of my patrol team. He looked over his shoulder to me, his eyes calm and his pupils round to catch as much light as possible in the darkness. He walked over, one hand on the crowbar at his side, scanning the woods for danger.

"Do you smell that?" I asked, keeping my voice low.

"Yeah." He wrinkled his nose in disgust. "Humans. Should we check it out?"

"Better not," I decided. "Let's report it first and get the whole squad to investigate."

"Good plan. Let's hurry. I don't want this stench to stick to me."

I nodded, and turned to lead us back to our squad. It was a long trip, and we broke into a run, skirting the old hotel.

The faint sound of shouting from behind us made me glance back.

"Lycel!" I called. "Did you hear tha—"

He pitched forward without warning, thrown to the ground by some intense force. A thick arrow protruded from the middle of his back. I stopped, turning back toward my comrade.

"Lycel?"

A second too late I realized I should have kept running. Another arrow flew from behind me and struck me in the back of my leg, sending me to the ground. I was laid out on the old road as the arrow pierced me through and stuck into the dirt.

"Hadryll," I heard. The voice was weak and panicked, but alive. "Can you move?"

I thrashed about but was unable to get up, as my leg had collapsed under my weight. I felt fear rise in my throat, and I reached over to grip the arrow, tried desperately to pull it out. My hands shook as blood from the wound coated them, making the arrow too slick to hold on to. The arrowhead was much thicker than any I had ever seen and three-sided, like a huge bayonet.

"There's no use for y'all to struggle now."

Lycel and I both went silent at the sound of this strange new voice. Slow, heavy footsteps approached, and I raised my head as much as I could to see what was happening.

A human walked toward us, casually swinging an axe in one hand.

"Those bolts are barbed," he continued, seeming almost disinterested. "They're designed to tear as much muscle as possible and they're almost impossible to remove. Y'all won't be getting up without help."

The human reached Lycel, who was writhing around in an adrenaline-fueled attempt to free himself. The human just gazed down, with an almost sad look.

" 'Fraid one of y'all won't be gettin' up at all."

My blood ran cold, and I had to fight down a wave of hysteria. *It had only been a normal patrol. Boring, actually. Nothing like this should have happened.*

"Hadryll!" Lycel's voice was strained with fear. Pinned facedown, he screamed at me to tell him what he couldn't see. "Hadryll, what's happening? What's going on?"

As much as I wanted to comfort him, my throat was too dry to offer any reassurance. I could only watch as the human held the axe in both hands and angled his face skyward.

"Lord, if you're still watching over us wretched people," said the human, "please send this stray soul to Cat heaven."

He raised the weapon so the sharpened metal pointed to the stars.

"Hadryll!"

The metal cleaved Lycel's head with such force that his skull split in half, echoing a resounding *crack.* The axe had wedged itself right between his eyes, cutting his forehead in a straight line down the middle. My legs were splattered with warm chunks of gray matter and bloody skull fragments, some still loaded with hairy bits of scalp. Gore covered the human, who didn't even flinch as blood dripped past his eye.

"Amen," he said, then shifted his eyes to me.

I held my fear in, fought to remain resolute. I said nothing as the human trudged toward me, holding the weapon in both hands.

When he finally reached me, I hissed, "There are thousands of us. Kill me, it won't matter."

"*Kill* you?" The blood that had splattered across his face shone in the moonlight as he smirked at me. "Sorry, Cat. You ain't that lucky."

I remember him raising the weapon again, sky high. I remember him turning it, so the blunt end of the metal faced me. Then I remember it falling toward me, falling—it seemed so slow.

After that, there was only darkness.

9 DR. HANSON

"CAP! THERE YOU ARE," I called after we finally located his balding head bent over a strategy table.

"What do you need, docto—" He turned, then fell silent as his jaw dropped at the sight of us. Fox and I were struggling to carry a body's worth of dead weight, with one of the Cat's arms around each of our shoulders.

"Well," I sighed. "Somehow I found myself helping Fox carry an unconscious Cat around the Fort in the middle of the night. And that was after I patched up a hole clean through the creature's leg."

"...Why?"

I shook my head. "Ask the redneck."

Cap eyed the Cat suspiciously. "Fox, you'd better start explaining. And good God, boy. You look like you've been working in a slaughterhouse."

"Don't worry, sir, it's Cat blood." Fox grinned good-naturedly. "There was a two-man patrol, and I took one of them out. He's outside, and I feel like we should send someone to bury him. But I figured we might have a use for this one."

"A use?" It was my turn to be suspicious. "What use?"

"Wasn't construction on the basement finished last week, Cap'n?"

I saw comprehension dawn in Cap's expression, and he nodded slowly. Apparently I was the only one still in the dark.

"What basement?" I demanded.

"The one under the courtyard. Used to be a boiler room and a storage room," Cap explained. "We've just finished converting it into a makeshift prison."

"And who better to test it out than a half-dead Cat?" Fox grinned.

"Yes, it's perfect!" Cap showed one of his rare smiles, and clapped Fox heartily on the shoulder.

Fox shifted the weight of the Cat on his shoulder. "I was thinkin' maybe after he woke up, we could ask him where the rest of his squad was, and probably a couple other questions."

I stopped myself from asking if they really thought the Cat would just tell them. *Of course* they didn't, and that was the scary part.

"Yes, good idea," said Cap. "Find someone else to guard the door and get Port. Maybe he can get something out of him."

I felt my face turn white. "Port? He's just a kid! He can't be more than sixteen! You can't expect him to..." I trailed off, unwilling to finish the unpleasant thought.

"He's seventeen. So?"

"You'd have a teenager *torture* someone?" I demanded, staring hard at Cap and Fox.

"What? No! We do not torture people here. Not even Cats."

Cap looked startled. "Don't worry, Doc. I only want Port to talk to him. He's a smart kid and he picks up on things that other people don't, so he's got the best chance of getting some information."

I sighed with relief. "In that case, let's get this guy to the basement before my back gives out."

10 PORT

I STOOD—OR sat—guard in a room that a few weeks ago had only held boilers. For some reason most of the machinery had been locked in large rooms with cement walls and glass partitions, each with a door. For us, the setup was surprisingly ideal.

I, along with my fellow soldiers, had taken part in the transformation of the basement. We had cleared out all the glass and used the metal frames for the partitions as a base for the walls. After that, we set about constructing the bars. Luckily, there was a lot of spare pipe around—it had been a storage area, after all. Once, when we were shorthanded, Robin and Daire even came to help us weld. It was an honor to be working with them, especially since they were usually raiding for supplies or going out on patrol, generally doing much more dangerous things than construction.

Robin, I remember, even spoke to me that day. I couldn't see her eyes because of the hood and mask, but she was smiling kindly at me.

"Wow, you're great with a welding torch. Keep up the good work, Port," she said.

I must have blushed bright red, and I grinned like an idiot the rest of the day. I couldn't believe that Robin—half of the Resistance's hero team—knew my name.

When construction was finished, we had twelve cells, barred floor to ceiling and as secure as could be. The doors were barred too, and fitted with the biggest locks we could find. All in all, our little prison served as a metaphor for the whole Human Resistance: it was crude and thrown together, but tough as nails and got the job done. And I was damn proud of it.

I was also pretty excited to see it tested out. A Cat lay passed out on the ground of the first cell, and I waited patiently for him to wake up. His armor had been taken, so he was left with a dark T-shirt and clean cargo pants. A thick bandage was wrapped around one leg, just below the knee. His hair was short but seemed too thick and unruly, so it stuck out in some places. Even as his face was relaxed in uncon-sciousness, his eyebrows were severely arched, giving him a frantic look.

As I was scrutinizing the Cat, he stirred and slowly sat up with a groan.

He looked around, rubbing a spot on his head. Cats are quick, and he took in the situation immediately. His eyes grew wider as he looked at the bars. Panic worked its way into his features and he grabbed one of the bars and pulled, but of course it didn't budge. He gripped the bar with white-knuckled intensity as his breathing started to become fast and shallow. At first, I thought he was reacting to being captured, but the way he whipped his head around trying to find a way out convinced me that something was off. There was defi-nitely something wrong with this Cat.

"Hey." I walked over and knelt in front of his cell, meeting his crazed eyes. I kept my voice low and calming. "Are you all right? You don't look so good."

He didn't answer me for a moment, as he seemed caught between a hatred for humans and his intense desire to leave the cell. After a few seconds, his fear won out.

"I am...extremely claustrophobic." The inflection in his voice rose and fell as though he had no control over it. There was no hiding the panic in his words.

"I understand. I'm actually claustrophobic too," I said. "I can see why you're, well, freaking out. But we can't just let you go."

"I know, but isn't there something you can do?" The Cat couldn't make eye contact with me. He kept shifting his gaze from one wall to the next, as though they would move closer if he weren't looking at them. "Like tie me up outdoors or something? Or just a bigger room? I won't try to escape, I swear."

"I don't know…"

"Please!" he shouted, then brought his voice down to almost a whisper. "Please. Anything. I can't stay here. If I'm in a place like this too long, I'll…" He trailed off as he shook his head furiously, as though trying to chase away a thought.

"You'll lose your mind?" I finished. It wasn't hard to believe. He'd only been in the cell a few minutes and he'd half lost it already.

"Yes. You understand. You know what it's like! Isn't there something you can do?" His voice began to shake along with his hands.

"…I think there might be a bigger room we can put you in." His eyes lit up with hope, but I raised a hand in caution and his face fell. "But my commanding officer won't let me move you unless there's something in it for him."

"But I don't have anything!" the Cat nearly screamed.

"You have information," I said, clearly and carefully. "I'm sure he'd let me move you if you told us how many Cats are in your squad and where it's stationed."

"I… I can't tell you that." The Cat's eyes darted wildly as he battled his fears. He bit his lip, hard enough to draw blood, but he didn't seem to notice. He was trying to decide, and it was tearing him apart. "They'll kill me if I tell you."

"They can't get you here. And the other room is very safe, and much bigger. You'll have no problem with your claustrophobia there," I said.

"...No. I'm not a traitor! I won't tell you anything." The Cat's eyes narrowed as he glared at me, conquering his fears. Temporarily.

"Fine," I said, rising to my feet and turning from him, moving back toward my seat. "I'll give you a week before you can't remember your own name."

"Wait!" he called, more panicked than ever. I looked at him over my shoulder, and his proud expression was now pleading.

"Look, I'm sorry. But I can't do anything without a bargaining chip." I shrugged, and took another step away, waiting for him to call me back. He didn't disappoint.

"All right! I'll tell you." I hid a smile and went back to kneel in front of his cell. His whole body was shaking like a leaf now, and I did my best to look worried for him. He kept his voice low with shame and he wouldn't meet my eye as he spoke. "There are twenty more of us fifteen miles north of here, camping out in the woods. Is that the information you need?"

"It is, yes. That's very helpful. Here, I'll let you out of there before you shake yourself to death," I said, grabbing the keys from my belt. I saw hope return to his eyes as I brought the key to the lock, and he almost smiled as I touched it to the metal...and then I paused with the door still locked, and he looked to me in confusion.

"Say, do you want to know how I became claustrophobic?" I asked, letting my concerned facade fall away. The Cat's mouth fell open, but he said nothing.

"It happened a few years ago, right before I came here," I said, watching how his eyes moved from my face to the keys and back as I talked. "I was still real young then, and my family and I were trying to find a safe place. We had heard rumors about a Resistance base in this city, so my mother, father, big sister, and I traveled all the way from Washington to find it. And somehow we all managed to get here alive and together. I remember how happy we were when we entered the city.

"But before we could find this place, we were ambushed by a Cat patrol. We had no weapons and we were heavily outnumbered—we didn't stand a chance. My parents were killed immediately. They didn't have time to even try and protect us. I remember...my sister was just old enough that they weren't sure if it would be 'all right' to kill her, since the Cats claimed they never hurt children.

"But ultimately, they figured she was almost an adult, so they slaughtered her too. She was fifteen, by the way. And as they stood over her body, they argued about what to do with me. They didn't have the means to take prisoners, see, but they didn't want to just let a human go. So they decided to throw me in the back of one of their supply trucks and take me along until they found a place they could dump me. But the door to the truck didn't lock right, so there was no way to secure my capture. So what they did was take one of their supply crates and shove me inside, before nailing the lid shut.

"*Three days* I was inside that damned box. There was no room to move, so I was stuck in the same curled-up position for *three days*. Luckily for me, the Resistance stole the truck from the Cats in order to get whatever supplies they had. Imagine how surprised they were to find me."

All color had drained from the Cat's face. With a slow smile, I put the key to his cell back in my pocket.

"I went pretty crazy after three days," I told him. "I wonder how long it will take you."

I think he started to cry as I made my way back to my seat by the door, but I didn't turn back to look. To be honest, I almost felt sorry for the Cat, but what did he expect? A luxury suite? Besides, even if I tried to find other accommodations for him—which none of my superior officers would even *think* to allow—there was nowhere else in the Fort that was secure enough to hold a dangerous enemy. He would have to be under constant guard anywhere else, and we certainly couldn't spare the manpower for that. No, there was no other place. I didn't love the idea, but he'd have to remain here.

There's little room for mercy in wartime. The Cats taught me that.

11 DAIRE

FOX, Cap, and I were waiting outside the door when Port emerged from the basement. As he swung open the thick steel door and stepped through, the distinct sounds of sobbing followed him. With a shy smile, he shut the door, blocking out the noise.

He turned to Cap. "There's a squad of twenty Cats camping in the woods about fifteen miles north of the city, sir."

"That's what we wanted to know. But what exactly did you do to the Cat?" said Cap, watching Port.

"I didn't lay a hand on him. He had a particular...weakness that I was able to exploit," Port said. Suddenly the kid seemed a lot scarier.

Cap shook his head with a sigh. "The important thing is, we got our info. Do you think there's any possibility he could have been lying?"

"No, sir. He didn't seem to have his wits about him, certainly not enough to lie," mused Port.

Cap rubbed his chin, considering. "In that case, let's run with this. I'm thinking a careful ambush."

"Cap'n," Fox said, his tone all business. "If I may make a suggestion? It won't be long now 'fore the Cats in the woods to notice their patrol's gone missin'. I'd suggest we take the fight to them first."

"That's a good point. All right, Fox, you're lead. Pick your squad, but keep it small. Stealth is the way to go for this one. Daire, I want you to stay behind with me and organize a counteroffensive in case we're too late."

Fox aimed his next question at me. "Think I should get Robin?"

I thought about saying yes, but then remembered the exhaustion in her voice when I left her apartment. She wouldn't be much use in her current state. Best to let her get some sleep.

"No, I don't think we should wait for her. Take Arianna instead. She's been itching to do some fighting," I answered.

"Good idea. I'll take her, and the twins too. I'm sure I can wrangle up the rest of a team in no time flat."

"Great," said Cap. "Then you can leave almost immediately. And I want you to take Port as well. It's thanks to him we can do this mission at all."

Port's face lit up, and he turned from Cap to Fox with an excited smile. Fox returned with a warm lopsided grin, and the two shared eye contact for a moment.

"Yessir," said Fox. "Port, go to the strategy room and get a map of the area, and see if you can start planning a route. I'll get the others, grab some gear, and meet you there."

Port nodded and dashed off toward the strategy room. I almost laughed at his enthusiasm, but it was encouraging to see. He was eager to get things done, and I was sure the Fort's governing body would be happy with that when it came time to find new leaders. But for now, I hoped he would focus on not dying during the preemptive strike.

Cap marched off down a hall, beckoning me to follow. I hurried to catch up, but called behind me as I ran.

"Be careful, Fox!"

He waved his hand in response, as I was already too far away to hear him.

12 ROBIN

MY APARTMENT WAS ALWAYS TOO dark. I had candles placed on the scarce furniture, but I rarely bothered to light them. There was no electricity here, or running water. Most of the surfaces, from the bare kitchen counters to the ancient sofa, were covered in a thin layer of dust. The only area that saw regular use was my bedroom, and the oversized mattress where I would collapse after a long day. It wasn't that I didn't cook or clean or relax—I did all of those things, at the Fort. That was basically where I lived, where I spent almost all of my time. My apartment was just where I usually slept...and hid. I hated it, but it was the only place I had privacy.

Even so, I always dread getting home. Or rather, getting back to my dusty apartment, which was in no way a home. After Daire or Fox escorts me here—more for their peace of mind than my safety—I have to face my empty apartment.

That's the worst part. My friend leaves, I close the door and lock three of the five deadbolts, and I'm left alone with my own worst enemy.

There's only one mirror in my apartment and I try to avoid it as much as I can. Every night, I go about my routine: checking the windows, making sure all my stashed weapons are in place, making sure everything is secure. Once I'm convinced, I recheck my locks once more and get ready for bed.

For the first time that day, I pull off my hood and remove the mask, hanging it from another hook by the front door. When I can avoid it no longer, I go into the bathroom. I pour some bottled water in my hands, splash it onto my face, dry off, and finally lift my head to meet my reflection.

The bright moon throws its light through my blinds to illuminate my face. I see...high cheekbones, purple almond-shaped eyes, and thin lips. I run a hand through my pitch-black hair, which is short in the back but hangs around my face in the front—an easily maintained cut. My heart always sinks when the moonlight hits my eyes...

...And I watch as my pupils narrow into slits.

In that moment, all the lies and self-deceit in my life come into view. The reality—that no matter where my heart is, I'm still one of *them*—forces itself upon me. The uncertainty of my situation weighs on me, and I think about how everything I've worked for can be stripped away so easily. The only thing holding my future in place is a mask.

And what if I lose that mask?

I shiver at the thought, wrapping my arms around myself. Humans... I love them, but they don't handle the unknown very well. And my kind is *very* unknown. When humans are surprised—and when they feel they've been deceived—they grow scared and angry, and they lash out. If the worst happened, I could tell them I'm actually one of their enemy, but I've been fighting for humans since the beginning. But they'd never listen. They'd probably never even give me a chance to speak.

Because, at the heart of the matter, I'm *not* one of them. And no matter how much I wish I was, I can never be one of them. I'm different, and frightening, and in their eyes...dangerous. No matter what

I've done or said, it is my species, and my species alone, that would determine how they see me.

That is the thought that haunts me, night after night. When sleep escapes me, or haunts me with nightmares, it's all I can think, all I can feel. That horrible truth...

I can't change what I am. And I can't hide it forever.

13 ODYRA WARRINGGATE

I HURRIED down the dark hallway. The curtains were drawn shut, but there was enough light to see the eyes of the human presidents staring down at me from their portraits on the walls. I ignored them. The leaders of a fallen civilization meant nothing to me. All that mattered was the small cube in my hands and the message I had for the King. He was waiting for an answer and there was no time to waste.

Another figure strode toward me from the end of the otherwise deserted hall. His long black hair was tied back, and he wore a low-cut white shirt under a long, stained coat. As we approached each other, I recognized something familiar in the way he moved. His head was bent down slightly, steps quick and silent, one hand loosely hanging by his belt. He had the kind of walk that accompanied the fresh bloodstains on his coat and boots. There was no mistaking him as he drew near. The walk of a murderer for hire was easy to spot.

"Almyrr." I kept my greeting cold and professional.

"Odyra," he answered. He stopped, and though I wanted nothing more than to keep walking, politeness forced me to a halt.

I noted the fresh blood dripping from his traveling cloak onto the formerly pristine carpet. "Coming from something important, I see."

"Indeed. Do you have an answer for His Majesty?" *Typical.* Almyrr considered everything that involved King Erenvyr to be his business.

"Yes, I do. I am on my way to tell him."

"What is it?"

I hesitated, reluctant to tell him anything. But I knew I couldn't avoid a direct question.

"A human informed that it is some sort of prize puzzle," I explained. "When the right combination is set, the box opens to reveal a surprise."

"I see. How droll." *Pretentious bastard.* "Humans are such petty creatures. Well, you'd best be on your way."

I nodded, then moved to pass. I only made it a step before I saw Almyrr whirl into action from the corner of my vision. Before I could react, his hand snaked out and grabbed my hair, pulling back hard. He jerked my head back, exposing my neck in a way that made me think he was about to cut my throat. My hand flashed to my knife, but I stopped myself from drawing.

He *might* kill me right now, I thought. But if I fight, he definitely will.

"The King was not happy about how you behaved at your last meeting," Almyrr murmured in my ear. I could feel his breath on my face, and I was disgusted. "So be sure you *mind* your *manners* this time, or the consequences will be severe. Am I clear, Odyra?"

"Yes, sir." I fought to keep my voice neutral, but I could not restrain all of my contempt.

With that, he released my hair and shoved me forward so hard I nearly fell. I turned to snarl a response, but he was already halfway down the hall, getting farther by the second. I let him go, watching him leave as I stood. I waited, my fists clenched, for him to be far out of earshot.

"Enjoy it now, Almyrr," I whispered. "Someday, I'll have your job. And with it, I swear, your life."

14 ROBIN

IT WAS 5:28 A.M., approximately 22 hours after Daire had walked me home, when someone started knocking on my door.

I had been awake for a while and was almost finished getting ready to head to the Fort, though my hoodie and mask still hung from their pegs in the entryway. I rushed for the door, snatching a knife from the counter on the way, and threw open the latch on the eyehole. I held the weapon close as I peered through, and was equal parts relieved and uneasy to see Daire, looking unharmed but upset.

Alarmed, I paused with my hand on the door, checking the lighting. The room was still dark, and the hallway would be too. With all the blinds closed, there was no way for any light to take me by surprise. In other words, it would be safe to be seen without my mask for the moment. I opened the door.

Daire's expression was desperate, and he wasted no time getting to the point.

"Fox has been hurt."

I paused only to grab my hoodie and mask before I ran with Daire toward the exit, sprinting to get to the Fort as fast as possible. Daire explained the situation on the way, while I concentrated on fastening my jacket and keeping up.

"Fox left to raid this Cat camp in the woods at about 10 last night. He just got back, and things don't look good."

Needless to say, we made it back to the Fort in record time.

†

I burst into Dr. Hanson's office with Daire right behind. Fox was sitting up—that was good—but he didn't appear to be in great shape. Cap, the doctor, and some other man I didn't know stood in a semi-circle around the table, but I was focused only on my friend.

Large cuts crisscrossed his chest, carving bloody Xs into his skin. In addition, blood flowed in rivulets down his leg from a deep gash on his thigh. I silently prayed that his wounds were nonfatal, though they were definitely not superficial.

"Fox, what happened?" I asked, not bothering to keep the worry out of my voice.

"Damn Cats heard us coming," he murmured. For some reason, he wouldn't meet my eyes.

"The Cats set up noise traps." The stranger in the back spoke with cold confidence. "These guys fell right into them."

All eyes turned to the man. He stared back from behind crossed arms, his dirty ski jacket crinkling at the elbows.

"Who are you?" asked Daire.

"I'm a hunter. Name's Truman. I was hiking through the woods, on my way to cause some trouble for the same group of Cats, when I met your squad and we decided to join forces."

"We killed five Cats total." Fox winced in pain as the doctor applied bandages to his chest. "Truman musta took out two of 'em all by himself. He's good."

Cap eyed the new man with suspicion. "If you're meaning to stay here, we won't turn you away. This is supposed to be a safe haven for humans, after all. But you can't fight with us again until you've been properly trained."

Truman stiffened, his hand resting on a machete attached to his belt. "I'm not handing over my weapons."

"You won't have to. We have very few internal conflicts. People can carry whatever they want here, unless it becomes a problem." Cap's words were calm, but the implied threat wasn't lost on the room.

"Well, we gained an ally and some Cats are dead," Daire said, optimistically. "Other than Fox's injuries, I'd say this was a victory."

To my growing fear, the room went silent. Fox hung his head, and even Dr. Hanson averted her gaze.

Cap's voice was quiet. "Fox getting hurt wasn't the worst part."

Daire's smile faded as we waited for someone to tell us what happened, but no one seemed willing to admit anything. My heart jumped to my throat, and I had to fight it down in order to speak.

"Fox?"

He stared at the floor, back bent in pain and exhaustion. When he finally spoke, his voice held both sorrow and guilt.

"We lost Arianna."

The weight of his words settled on everyone in the room. I heard Daire draw breath sharply, then let it out. I braced myself to take in the news, but I still had to stabilize myself against the table to keep from sinking to the ground. Arianna was one of our best. No one would have ever expected to lose her.

"She's dead, then?" Daire asked.

"Probably." Though Fox raised his head, it was the stranger who spoke. "We didn't see her die, exactly."

Daire looked hard at Truman. "Explain."

Fox's voice was weak, though it wasn't clear whether emotion or injury was draining him. "We left her behind. It's my fault. I gave the order."

"She was mortally wounded. She wouldn't have made it back, anyway. And she told you to leave." Truman's voice was harsh but honest. "She stayed behind to draw them off. It was her choice. And we wouldn't have made it back if she hadn't sacrificed herself."

"I let her." Fox cradled his head in his hands. "I let her go off on her own. I should never have done that. I should've made her come back with us."

"Then we *all* would have died." There was no emotion in the hunter's voice, and I could barely restrain a glare.

Daire spoke up, his voice strong through the pain. "There's no purpose in blame. What's important now is to figure out where to go from here. We all know that's what Arianna would have us do."

Cap straightened, retaking his role of the fearless leader. "That's right. Robin, Truman, you come with me. Truman, I need you to explain what these 'noise traps' are and how we can bypass them next time. Daire, you stay and help Dr. Hanson."

"What can I do, Cap'n?" Fox moved to get off the table, but Daire stopped him, placing a hand on his shoulder.

"What you can do is heal. We need you in top condition as soon as possible." Daire's voice was kind, but his unspoken thought rang loud through each of us. *We can't lose two people today.*

Fox nodded slowly, and lay back on the table.

"Robin?" he croaked. "Can you, uh...tell the others for me?"

"Of course, Fox. Don't worry about anything, okay? We'll take care of it."

"Okay." He squeezed his eyes shut, but it wasn't enough to keep a tear from rolling down his cheek.

15 ARIANNA

I STOOD, unsteady on my feet, at the top of a small hill. Dark, rolling clouds peered above the tree line, bringing an early dusk to the forest.

Look at that, I thought. *Storm's coming.*

Pain seized my side and I collapsed, falling backward against a tree. I sank into a sitting position, clutching the spot just below my ribs where some Cat had got me with an axe.

Not that I'll live to see it. Such a shame too—I love storms. Back home, the sound of the rain on the tin roof would calm me like nothing else. I didn't mind the thunder, or the flash of the lightning, as long as there was rain. It seemed like the world was a better place when it rained.

Not that it matters now. I had a sewing kit, but I knew that I'd pass out from pain halfway through trying to close the wound, and bleed out even faster. *An axe. I can't believe it. A freaking axe.*

The wind brushed through the trees, whipping the leaves into a blind frenzy. The storm was on its way, and in a hurry. I needed to find shelter—but the blood seeping through my armor reminded me that if I tried to move without help, I wouldn't make it more than a step. Two at the most.

" 'Ask for me tomorrow, and you shall find me a grave man.' " I laughed to myself. Everyone always said I had a dark sense of humor. Maybe that's why I found my current situation so funny. "And 'a cat to scratch a man to death.' But I bet Shakespeare didn't count on this kind of Cat," I said aloud. I chuckled at my own joke, which was more of an effort than I was expecting. Exhausted, I rested my head against the rough bark and closed my eyes, resolved to accept my fate.

"Ah, fate," I sighed. "Thou art a heartless bitch."

It was while I was congratulating myself on my gallows humor that I heard a *thump* a few feet away. I jumped, turning to meet the stare of a soldier in chipped red armor, bracing himself against a tree. Lightning lit up the sky for an instant, and I held the stranger's gaze long enough to watch his pupils shrink into slits.

I *wanted* to hiss "Cat." I *wanted* to throw something sharp. At the very least, I wanted to look menacing. But all I could do was watch in wide-eyed terror as my enemy stood straight and drew a small triangular knife.

Well, looks like the storm won't be the one to kill me after all, I thought. *At least now I'll know—know exactly what they went through.*

With pain clouding his yellow eyes, my soon-to-be killer stepped toward me...and fell to one knee with a grimace. I glimpsed the start of a large gash on his shoulder, which must have extended pretty far down his back to slow him down this much. Then I understood—the blood on his armor was his own. He couldn't move without help either, and without a place to rest, he wouldn't last much longer than me. Since we didn't have the strength to kill each other, the storm would take us both.

Around me, I had a dangerous adversary, an impending potential hurricane, and a profusely bleeding, probably mortal wound. Three ways to die. But was there one to live?

The forest we were trapped in was thick, rugged, and hilly, so the odds of finding workable shelter nearby weren't bad. The problem would be getting there. I couldn't make it alone, and neither could the Cat—but perhaps, if we worked together...

It took me a while to find my voice. I had never spoken to one of them before, except for derogatory terms and shouting from across the battlefield, of course.

"Your wound is mostly on your right side, isn't it?" I shouted against the rising wind. He looked up at me in surprise, but said nothing.

"You fell after stepping on your right leg. So you can move your left side all right—right?" I tried again.

After a moment, he slowly nodded.

"I'm hurt on my left side," I continued. "Can't move very well, and I have to keep pressure on the wound. But if we lean on each other, maybe we can walk."

He shot me a confused glance and remained motionless. I bit back the urge to ask him, "*Cat got your tongue?*"

"We need to find shelter or the storm will kill us both," I shouted.

He considered this for a while, apparently oblivious that we were on a time limit.

"Why should I trust you?" he finally asked.

I braced myself against a tree and, keeping one hand firmly clenched on my side, got to my feet.

"Look," I said. "I'm unarmed. I'm hurt, and I'm probably gonna die soon. If I tried to fight you, I'd end up doing more damage to myself than to you. I'm literally no threat. But if I'm going to be killed, I'd rather die someplace warm and dry. So trust me or not, I don't care. It's up to you whether or not you're willing to work with me to try and survive."

Standing was sapping my strength, and I could feel my last hopes fading as he continued to kneel silently. After a few long minutes, he struggled to his feet, letting the knife fall from his hand.

"There's a cave about a half mile to the north. That's where I was headed. Think you can make it?" he said.

"I can try."

He nodded, set his shoulders back, took one step and fell to his knees again.

Going against every instinct I had, I moved toward the Cat. I put his arm around my shoulder and stood, bringing him up with me. I was leaning on him as much as he was on me, but we managed to support each other just enough to walk in an almost-straight line. Weary and unbelievably uncomfortable, we set off for the north, one painful step at a time.

"Try not to get your filthy human blood on me," he muttered.

"Quit whining, or I'll step on your paw," I retorted.

The rest of the journey went by in silence.

16 TYLOS, WYRFORRA SOLDIER FIRST CLASS

WE FELL APART at the entrance to the cave, with the human falling against one side and myself retreating to the other. It took my eyes a second to adjust to the darkness, but the frequent lightning of the strengthening storm helped me locate the bundle of dry wood in the corner. With the last of my strength, I dragged myself over to the pile, bringing the wood to the center of the small enclosure. I was looking around for some flint when the human spoke up.

"I got this one, Cat," she said, withdrawing a book of matches from her pack. With a shaking hand, she tried to strike a match but it broke against the box. She swore under her breath and reached for another, which she was able to light and touch to the kindling to start the fire. Soon the cave was warm, well lit, and comfortable enough for me to have time to consider what the hell I'd gotten myself into. I was a top-class soldier, on my way to being an officer, and here I was, half dead and in the company of a human.

"Well, I'm beat. That was a pretty nasty little scuffle there, wasn't it? You look pretty worn yourself. Maybe you'd feel better if you took..." The human winked , pointed at me, and with an over exaggerated smile, said, "a *cat* nap?"

A *snarky* human.

"It's a pun, get it? Anyway, I've got to admit, this is a nice little setup you got here. On a hill, so we don't have to worry about floods, and not too dank or damp. Nice little foxhole," said the human. Her face was drained of color, and I got the impression she was talking to take her mind off the pain.

"It's a military campout for lost soldiers. Hence the firewood." I shifted my back against the wall, leaning on the shoulder that wasn't bleeding. It was indeed a good cave, though it only extended back fifty feet or so and was barely tall enough to stand in. It was probably only ten feet across at its widest, which meant being uncomfortably close to the injured enemy combatant I had somehow managed to end up stuck with.

"So. Do you have a name, or am I gonna have to keep calling you 'Cat'?" She was smirking half-heartedly, like she was trying to be friendly with her worst enemy. Then again, I suppose she was.

I sighed. "Lysander. Tylos Lysander. Soldier first class."

"No shit? Lysander? Like *A Midsummer Night's Dream* Lysander?"

That threw me off. "Exactly. You've read Shakespeare then?"

"Every play and sonnet. I'm a literature buff. Call it a hobby."

"Well...you're well-read for an ignorant human."

"And you're proud for a half-drowned Cat. I'm Arianna. I'd get up to shake your hand, but I'm afraid all my guts would pour out."

"Charming."

"So sue me. Now if you'll excuse me, I've got to get this properly wrapped up. Hope you don't mind a little gore."

I turned from the grisly scene as she bandaged the wound. But from what I saw out of the corner of my eye, her fate was pretty obvious. Without proper medical treatment, she was done for. It was only a matter of time.

17 ARIANNA

IT TOOK me a long time to bandage the wound. By the time I was done, I could barely hold my head up to watch the Cat across the fire, and I eventually settled against the wall of the cave. I lost consciousness pretty quickly. And when I did, I dreamt of my sister. She smiled and said, "Do you want to go for a ride, Arri?" Just as she had said so many times before. And just as always, I agreed in a heartbeat.

In this particular memory, she was eighteen and I was nine, so it was two years before the invasion. I was so small, she had to lift me onto the seat of her pride and joy—a bright red 1992 Suzuki DR650 dual-sport. She loved that motorbike, and so did I. I always felt safe when I rode with her. Really, it was the only time I was safe.

That day, she had asked me to go with her as soon as she saw my parents begin to argue. We were just pulling out of the driveway when the screaming started. But soon the unhappiness was drowned out by the roar of the motorcycle and my sister's voice.

"Hang on, Arri! We're gonna go fast!"

In my young mind, the bike was magical because it allowed us to escape. We spent countless afternoons riding down back roads, often parking by a hill with a view. Those peaceful days were my favorites.

We would stare into the sunset, dreaming of the day when we could escape for good. At that age, I wondered why she didn't leave. She was fully capable of driving away and never coming back. Though she never said it, it was evident that she wanted to take off more than anything. But she stayed. I didn't realize until much later that she stayed for me.

I was eleven years old when the Cats attacked. When I dreamt of that night, I remembered wondering why my parents were shouting at three in the morning. Then, slowly...I recall the smoke and the heat, the fear. Finally a voice breaks through the panic—

"Arri, we have to go!"

And then I'm on the bike, speeding away faster than I've ever gone. I cling to my sister in terror, and finally gather the courage to look back toward home. The flames seem to touch the clouds.

"Don't look away, Arri," she shouts. "Keep looking at the fire."

I stared until the burning was lost to the distance. Only then did I understand why she wanted me to watch that light. She was protecting me from the terrible darkness, the uncertainty that lay ahead.

We were on the road for three years. We wandered for a long time with no clear destination, until we overheard talk of a sanctuary in Montana. It was a long and dangerous journey but she protected me, kept me fed, and somehow brought us to the Montana border. We were on our way through the state, checking every city we came across for the supposedly safe human settlement.

But before we found it, *they* found us.

Two Cats cornered us in the woods skirting town. We had stopped to rest when they snuck up on us. Two soldiers, big and lean, stared down at us with bloodlust in their eyes. They wore faded fatigues, and they were both so tall that I had to crane my neck to see their faces. Their eyes seemed so *wrong* to me, and I couldn't understand why they were strange colors. I glanced at the knives on their belts while my sister took a protective stance in front of me and locked eyes with one of the monsters.

"You girls look like you've been on the road a long time. Why don't you come with us? We'll take you somewhere safe," the Cat said, beckoning.

"Thank you for the offer. We'll be glad to go with you," my sister said, but squeezed my shoulder—our signal for me to remain silent and not move. I obeyed as she stepped up to the Cats.

"And how about you, little one? Come now, we won't hurt you."

But I refused to budge, shifting slightly toward the trees as if about to run. The Cat moved toward me, and my sister struck, grabbing the knife off the other Cat's belt and stabbing him in the chest. By the time he screamed for help, she had sunk the blade hilt-deep into him four times.

The first Cat spun around with a surprised curse and launched himself at her. I stood, frozen, as he drew his own knife and sank it in her back. Her face contorted with pain, but she didn't make a sound. Her body folded in on itself as she collapsed silently. Blood spread across her back like unfolding butterfly wings.

The Cat gathered his wounded companion's arm around his shoulder, moving with careful urgency. They began to leave, but the healthy one stopped to fix me with a deciding stare. My brain screamed to run, but the signal wouldn't reach my legs. I couldn't move. He was going to kill me.

But then the other one grunted and grabbed his bleeding chest. His failing condition prompted the other to give me a final look before hurrying into the woods. It wasn't until long after their disorganized footsteps faded into the distance that I found the courage to move.

I spent the rest of that day and night burying my sister. The grave was shallow, but it was as deep as my tiny hands could manage. I mourned while I dug, and long after. I was forced to stop digging from time to time as sobs heaved through my body, shaking me to my core.

Around midnight, I found and placed a flower on her grave: A daisy with a missing petal. I stayed there until the moon faded into the horizon. As dawn broke, so did my vigil. As I climbed onto the motorcycle, I reminded myself that I could no longer afford to cry, as I needed to see clearly.

I was lucky enough to be tall as a teenager, and the years on the road had made me strong, and my sister had taught me how to ride. Even then, I was barely able to control the bike at first, but I pressed on anyway. I rode into the city, and wandered even more. I had almost given up when I was approached by a strange girl wearing a bird mask, who brought me to a place called the Fort. They took me in as a hungry, traumatized child and raised me to be a fighter. And then, through a few crazy turn of events, I wound up trapped in a cave with a Cat.

The feeling of being watched woke me. It was hard to get a restful night's sleep with a painful injury and dangerous creature nearby. If I wasn't going to be able to sleep, I figured I should do something to pass the long night.

"Hey Cat," I said without opening my eyes. "Do you have a family?"

"Of course."

"Siblings?"

"No, just a mother and father. They didn't want any children so they only had me."

"Why'd they have you if they didn't want kids?" I sat up, fully engaging myself in the conversation. The Cat was not likewise engaged, but rather giving most of his attention to the dying cinders in the fire.

"To contribute to the military efforts."

I didn't really know how to respond to that. "...Are you close with your parents?"

"No. They sent me to boarding school at a young age and then military academy. I haven't spoken to them in years."

"Why not?"

"Because." He sighed. "For my people, strong family ties are very unusual. Bonds are generally only formed with close companions. My squadron is my family."

"You mean the squadron that abandoned you when you were injured."

He grimaced and narrowed his eyes at me.

"Sorry. I'm only curious. I thought Cats formed clans or something."

"Many of us choose a primarily solitary life. Introversion is common."

"So do you guys mate for life, or is it a breeding season–type thing?"

To that, he scowled at me and said nothing.

18 TYLOS

"SO, CAT," said the human with a wide yawn. She hadn't been asleep long before pain woke her again. "Do you have motorcycles where you're from?"

I shot her a suspicious glare, searching for some ulterior motive in her words. Finding none, I shook my head.

"I've got one back home. It's real nice. Big engine. Red." She shifted, wincing and lightly pressing her wound.

"It's a machine?" I asked, curious about the humans' world. It wouldn't hurt to learn all I could from this Arianna before she died.

"Yeah, it's a two-wheeled transport vehicle, to put it in technical terms."

The human leaned against the wall again, and her eyelids drooped. After a second, she shook herself, fighting off drowsiness. It seemed she had worsened, and feared that if she fell asleep, she'd never wake up. From the look of the fresh blood seeping through her coat, she was right to be worried.

"You operate the throttle like this, and the brakes with this hand, and the clutch..." She mimed the actions, trying to hold back a grimace.

"We have vehicles that work just like that back home," I told her. "I'm quite good with them, actually."

"Yeah? Well, look at that. We have something in common."

"Wonderful."

"Hey, sarcasm is *my* thing."

Her voice was fierce, but weak. We lapsed into silence, letting the sound of the rain fill the cave. She stared out into the storm, her chest rising and falling with obvious, arduous effort. Very suddenly, I thought of her as an injured bird, with its tiny heart beating furiously to survive. A songbird, fragile but lionhearted, trapped in a cage with a big, hungry cat.

I felt a pang of...*empathy?* A largely unfamiliar experience, I could only guess at where the feeling came from and if I had even experienced it before. And then I realized: my promotion. When my captain was carried off the battlefield all those years ago... He was in tatters, torn to bloody pieces.

"Lysander. Take command." And then, when he thought I couldn't hear, he muttered, "I don't want to die."

That was the first time it had occurred to me that I might die in this war. Just like the human in front of me. It was...sobering. And the empathy tugged at me more than I could have possibly guessed.

"So...human—er, Arianna," I said. She turned those weary gray eyes to me. "Tell me more about this motorcycle thing."

Somewhere in the depths of those eyes, something lit up. She smiled, so faintly.

"Well, it was a gift from my sister. A really beautiful bike. Let me tell you how to drive it."

No, not a songbird, I realized as she spoke. *An eagle.*

†

By the time the human finished explaining the inner workings and functionality of her "bike," it felt like hours had passed. She was still fighting sleep.

I kept my eyes on the distance, or what I could see through the storm. I had escaped a few dangers, but I was well aware that if my regiment caught me in the presence of a human, I would be killed. Or removed from service, which was probably worse. But the wind and the rain made an effective barrier, and I was fairly confident that no squad would be out in this. And it wasn't like they were looking for me. When they made their retreat, they were certain I was dead, or very close. I told them to leave me behind, and they followed orders. While this was painful, it meant one very important thing—it was safe to sleep.

I started to tell this to Arianna, but when I looked across the fire I saw that her eyes were already closed as she lay against the back wall. For an instant I thought she had died, but the steady rise and fall of her chest and the color that had returned to her face convinced me otherwise. For some strange reason, I was relieved. *It's natural,* I quickly deduced. *No one wants to share a cave with a dead person.*

With my only companion unconscious, I resolved to keep watch for a few hours, and fell asleep immediately.

The sound of thunder woke me. Unwilling to get up, I lay motionless and slowly opened my eyes. Though my vision was unclear, I made out a figure approaching, holding something large. Details sharpened, and I realized that Arianna was coming toward me, with something that looked like a large rock in her hands.

Adrenaline shot through me as I realized what was happening. *That filthy human was planning to kill me in my sleep!* I tensed my muscles and waited for her to get close. In an instant, I kicked out at her leg, snatched the knife from my boot, and by the time she hit the ground I had her pinned with my blade at her throat.

She looked surprised, to say the least. She didn't make a noise, but her eyes were wide with fear and confusion. I waited, unmoving, for her to say something.

"Whoa now." She gulped. Her voice shook, but she managed to sound almost nonchalant. "If you didn't want breakfast, you could've just said so."

"...Breakfast?" That was when I took a closer look at what she was carrying, and was surprised to see that it wasn't a rock—it was her pack, food rations tumbling out.

"Oh," I said. I could feel my face heating up.

"Um, Tylos? I know you have the whole nine lives thing going on, but I've only got one. So if you could kindly, well, not kill me, that'd be great. And Jesus, how many of those knives do you have?"

"Sorry, I thought you were—doing something else." I took a food ration as I put my knife away, opening the brown box to find the usual dehydrated gruel.

"Oh, you thought I was attacking you?" She sat up, shooting me a bemused look and rubbing the spot on her neck where I almost cut her. She stood up and went to move back to her side of the fire. "At the moment, I couldn't lift a rock above my head if I—"

She cut off, grimacing in pain as she staggered against a wall. She sat down hard with a thump, a hand firmly pressed on the bandage at her side. "...tried."

Shame cut through me. "I reopened your wound."

"Yeah," she said. "Hey, that almost sounded apologetic. Careful now, or I might start to think you have emotions."

I scowled. "You fell asleep very quickly last night. Even in my state, I could've easily killed you with your guard down."

"Yeah, you probably could've killed me with my guard up, too. So I figured, I might as well trust you. This wound is probably going to kill me anyway, so really there's no harm. I mean, what's the worst you could do?" She smirked. "Kill me a little quicker?"

I saw fresh blood starting to seep through the bandage, and I turned my attention to my food ration, trying not to look affected. Silence descended for a moment as we each chewed through a stale cracker. I gritted my teeth, but it wasn't the food that made me so...uncomfortable.

"Do you have a sewing kit in there?" I said, motioning to her pack.

"I do indeed. Why, did you get a hole in your blouse, princess?" She laughed, but I could see she was in pain. "I've also got a compass, bottled water, rags, bottle of whiskey—don't tell my commanding officer—more food rations, and some other random crap. Real bag of mysteries here."

"I see. Pass me the whiskey and the water bottle, would you?"

"Fine, but you owe me." She gently tossed them over the fire and I caught them easily. She rummaged through her pack for fresh bandages as I drained the water bottle in a few gulps.

"Hey, how's your back anyway?" she asked. "It looked pretty bad last night."

"Much better." I drained the whiskey from the glass bottle into the plastic one.

Arianna gave me an odd look. "Why on earth did you do that?"

"You'll see. Could you take a look at my back? I want your opinion on how far it's healed."

"Fine, but you owe me even more now that I have to get up."

We both got to our feet, though it was obvious that it was a struggle for the human. They are such fragile creatures.

"What's that?" I said, pointing to the empty cave wall behind her.

She turned, saying "I swear to God, if you say 'Made you look—' "

In one motion, I broke the bottle against her head, knocking her out instantly. I caught her just before she hit the ground and laid her out carefully.

"Sorry about that," I muttered, before turning to her pack to look for the sewing kit.

19 TRUMAN

I WATCHED these people carefully from the corner of the room. They were just kids, besides the old vet and the doctor, but they seemed to have a lot of authority. They were important somehow, and they knew it.

That could be a problem.

It was young hotheads like these that got me demoted in the army —the *real* army—almost forty years ago. Stupid kids thought I was "inhumane" with the enemy, when really they were the ones who didn't understand how war works. It's not a tea party, I told them. Things get *unpleasant*.

But the head brass demoted me anyway, right out of active combat and into records and archives. And even then I could've done something great, changed the tide of a few battles at least, if they hadn't put children in charge of running the forces. When I found "resources" from way back, some really useful stuff, it was some eighteen-year-old punk who told me we couldn't use them. I tried to explain to him that when you're losing a war, you do *whatever it takes* to win—and now we had the tools: ingredients for mustard gas, napalm, explosives, and so much more. Enough to make a difference.

But the kid said no, and when I insisted—well, a demotion turned into a dishonorable discharge real fast. At least I was able to sneak out a few parting gifts.

After *this* war broke out, I thought that maybe it'd be my chance to do what I was made to do—lead. I'm naturally charismatic and intelligent, a born leader, though Mom always said I should've been a con man. No, I was destined to lead, but all these damn kids in charge never gave me the chance.

I almost had my opportunity at the first settlement I'd been living in for a few years, but they kicked me out. So did the next one, and the next, and soon there wasn't any place left—at least that I knew of. I couldn't afford to be thrown out on my ass again. There was nowhere left to go.

But this place...this Fort...it could work. I liked the system, or what I'd seen of it. I could live here, and if I played my cards right, I could *lead* here. All I'd have to do was work up through the chain somehow, and I knew from experience that the quickest way to do that was to get a following. But how?

I surveyed the room. The old man, Cap, was no doubt secure in his position. I could tell that by the authority in everything he said and did. The kids, on the other hand, seemed too inexperienced to have a real foothold in the power structure. I probably had more than double their experience, but they had the trust of the people living here. Unless...

I studied the girl with the mask. They had explained to me why she had to hide her identity—some BS about "ambassadors." But still, she wore that mask and hood all the time, so it was reasonable to suspect that not many people, if any, ever saw her face. She was a mystery even among her intimates. An unknown. And whether they realized it or not, most people fear the unknown.

And fear is easy to use.

20 FOX

MY BACK WAS STARTING to hurt from sitting hunched over on the examination table. I stretched, moving my arms and shoulders to relieve some of the tension. Pain shot through my body at the movement and I couldn't restrain a wince. Truman, who was in the corner, didn't even look my way. Robin was standing next to the table and watching me like a hawk—albeit a concerned, caring hawk—and her worry visibly increased when she saw me grimace. She had one hand on the edge of the table, and I suspected it was to keep herself from pacing. It seemed she was trying not to speak, but finally the words came out in a rushed jumble.

"Are you sure you're okay to walk? It's only been a few hours. Did you get any sleep? If you can't sleep, Daire brought me some tea that I can give you. Trust me, it helps a lot. Or I can get some pills from Dr. Hanson. And there's always tequila—that'll knock you out quick. I'll go get all three and you can decide—"

I grabbed her sleeve before she was able to dash out. "I'm all right, really. Slept like a baby. Thanks, though."

Idleness is not in Robin's nature, and the helplessness of the situation was driving her mad. She kept looking around the infirmary for something to do, and I wished she would just sit with me and relax. I hoped Truman would speak up and tell her to calm down, but he just stood and stared off into space. He had seemed like a decent-enough fellow at first, but I was liking him less and less. He hadn't spoken in a long while and the silence was starting to get uncomfortable.

Finally, Daire entered the room carrying a wooden crutch, which he brought over and handed to me. I nodded my thanks.

"Cap's waiting for us in the strategy room. We're supposed to go over plans for a counteroffensive on the Cats," said Daire. "Can you move, Fox?"

" 'Course I can move," I grumbled. "Why does everyone keep asking me that? I'm a little scratched up is all. I ain't dead yet."

I made to hop off the table, which turned out to be more difficult than I anticipated. Daire and Robin helped me to my feet—Truman made no move to assist anyone—and I was able to keep myself upright with the crutch. With a brisk "Let's go," I headed out toward the hall at an aggressive hobble.

Robin took the lead, and Truman caught up and kept pace, apparently unwilling to be behind anyone. Daire kept back with me, ready to help in case I fell.

Unwilling to be a burden, I turned the conversation toward the impending battle. "What do y'all think we should do?"

"Easy." Truman's voice carried unfounded authority. "We've already killed a few and wounded some others, so they'll need rest. And since they got some of ours, they'll be expecting that we'll take time to recuperate. We should attack at once and take the bastards by surprise when they're at their weakest. We leave tonight."

"I don't think that's a good idea," said Robin. "There were dark clouds headed that way last night. I'll bet there's a huge storm right over the Cats' camp. We should wait a few days, let the weather wear them down and get our own strength back."

"But that'll give the Cats time to rally their forces."

"Not at all. If they sent for reinforcements, it would take them weeks to get through the forest and they won't travel in a downpour. They'll be easier to finish off if we wait."

"Or they'll attack us first." Truman was beginning to sound annoyed.

"Twenty Cats launching a head-on assault against the Fort? They couldn't be that stupid."

"They could sneak in and destroy us from the inside!"

"The Fort is guarded by the best sentries we have. No Cat could sneak in."

"Unless someone let them in." Truman stopped walking suddenly. "Someone like you."

Daire, Robin, and I stopped dead in our tracks. Robin didn't turn but kept her back to Truman. Her voice changed instantly, turning from professional to calmly threatening.

"Excuse me?" she asked, but it wasn't a question.

"You heard me. I haven't seen your eyes, so how do I know you're not a Cat?"

"You don't. You'll just have to trust me."

"Not likely. I don't trust anyone who won't show their face."

"So, let me get this straight." Robin's entire demeanor had changed in an instant. Her voice was low and venomous, her muscles had tensed up, and though she kept her composure, she was obviously fuming. "You can't trust me because you can't see my face, but I'm supposed to take it on faith that you're not a Cat spy. I've just met you. For all I know, you're working for them to blow my cover."

"For all I know, you're not human. And I'm not trusting you until I know for sure."

"I guess you won't be trusting me then. I'm an ambassador to the Cats and a double agent—my identity is top secret. I'm not letting a stranger see my face."

"We're going to have a problem then." Slowly and deliberately, Truman drew a machete from its sheath at his side. "Because I'm not leaving here until you take off that mask."

Robin didn't move except to look over her shoulder at Truman. A small and devious smile showed from beneath the shadow of her hood. "Is that so?"

"'Ain't you going to do something?" I whispered to Daire.

"Nope." He seemed content to be a passive observer to the imminent confrontation. "She can handle herself."

Without further warning, Truman lunged forward, reaching with his free hand toward Robin's hood. She remained motionless until his fingertips brushed the fabric, then sprang into action. What happened next was so fast it looked like a dark blur, but I knew Robin's fighting style well enough to understand what was going on.

A second before the impact, she spun and grabbed the machete handle, twisting it out of his hand. At the same time, she used the momentum of her turn to throw her weight against his legs, just below his center of balance. His knees buckled, and as he began to fall Robin rammed her knee hard into his stomach. The impact threw him a few feet down the hall, where he landed hard on his back. He lay there, stunned, as Robin tossed the machete in the air and caught it in a carefree fashion. Then she launched the weapon at Truman. It stuck into the dirt an inch from his head.

"We wait a few days," she said, before continuing down the hall, stepping over Truman without glancing down.

Daire turned to me as we began to follow her. "Told you."

21 ARIANNA

WHEN I CAME TO, I felt only groggy confusion as I tried to figure out why I was on the ground. Then I remembered the sound of breaking glass and the sudden pain, and my confusion turned to fury.

"What the *hell?*" I sat up and turned the full force of my anger to the Cat sitting across the cave. "You broke a bottle over my head? Why would you do that?"

With only a glance at me, Tylos continued to sit quietly and tended the fire.

A new abrupt pain pulsed through my side, and I frantically tore at the bandages to find the damage. "*Ow!* And what happened to my wound? What did you do to me?"

Panic rose in me as my mind raced, wondering what the Cat could have done while I was unconscious. My hands shook as I peeled away the bandages, and I found the bloody wound to be... surprisingly clean. The gash in my side had been closed, sewn up with neat, even lines. The bleeding had stopped, and the overall wound had started to heal.

"You—you stitched me up." I was shocked, to say the least. The last thing I had expected from this Cat was help.

"Yes, I did," he said casually. "Don't move around too much, though. I'm not a doctor and I don't know how well those will hold."

"You stitched me up," I repeated, still unsure of how to handle the information.

"Sorry about the bottle, by the way. I knew using a sewing needle would be difficult, so I figured knocking you out would be less painful. Oh, here." He tossed me the water bottle, now filled with whiskey. "You probably need this. I imagine those stitches will hurt for a while."

"Why'd you do it?" I asked.

Tylos shrugged. "You gave me food. I had to pay you back somehow."

Still shocked, I took a swig of the whiskey. Then another. I was at a loss, and trying to comprehend my situation. I had honestly expected the Cat to kill me the first chance he got. They were supposed to be cruel, heartless creatures that had no regard for human life. And yet he had quite possibly saved mine. It made no sense that I was still alive, let alone on the mend.

"Besides," he continued, "it was my fault that your wound reopened. I fix my mistakes."

"Apparently." I smiled, bemused. "I suppose I should say thank you, Tylos."

Now it was his turn to be caught off guard. He returned my smile for a half-second, before he seemed to realize what he was doing and looked away, embarrassed. "You're welcome."

The cave became quiet as the sounds of the campfire failed to cover the awkward silence between Tylos and me.

"How's your back?" I asked, mostly just to say *something.*

"Oh, right. I actually meant for you to take a look at that."

"Sure." He took his shirt off and turned his back to me, and I winced at the sight. Long gashes stretched across his back, in some places crossing from his shoulder to his waist. "Jeez, what happened to you? Did you lose a fight with a chainsaw?"

"Not quite. I believe they were...what you call samurai swords? I got cornered and ambushed from behind before my regimen was forced to retreat. Does it look bad?"

"Actually, no. You—" I stopped myself from saying *Cats* at the last second. "You guys heal fast."

"Yeah, we do." He redressed, and I caught a glimpse of a tattoo on his chest before he pulled his shirt over it. "I'd say I'm good enough to fight."

Fear resurfaced in my gut. He might have been good enough to fight, but I was far from battle ready. If he decided that I might be a threat and attacked, there wouldn't be much I could do. I took another swig of whiskey.

Tylos crossed to the mouth of the cave. "Looks like the storm won't let up for another day at least."

"So we're still stuck. Great." I turned to rummage through my pack. "At least we've got some booze, and... Hey, you want to play cards?"

He turned to me, momentarily dropping his default skeptical expression. "Cards?"

I held up a deck of playing cards. "You know, cards. Blackjack, poker, crazy 8s, go fish. Any of this ring a bell?"

"I've never played...cards."

"Have a seat." I motioned to the ground in front of me. "We've got time to kill and I'm bored. So let's play."

22 DAIRE

"I'M nervous about Robin leaving tomorrow. I think it might be too soon to attack," I confided in Fox, as we moved slowly down the hall. I had walked Robin home after the strategy meeting, and Truman had disappeared, probably to tend to his wounded pride. I was helping Fox get back to the infirmary—not that he needed the help. With one crutch, he was moving along almost as fast as I was.

"She'll be fine. The storm will have cleared up mostly by then, and she'll have a dozen of our best. Don't worry about her."

"Yeah, you're right. I just—" I stopped. Fox began to speak, but I raised a hand, telling him to wait.

Voices. It wasn't uncommon for people to gather and chat, but the pitch of the voices I could hear sounded...angry. I couldn't make out what they were saying, so I inched down the hallway until I came right next to a doorway, and then one voice became clear.

"That hood and mask keep her eyes in shadow. Have any of us ever seen them clearly? We have this *thing* living among us, and we haven't even seen her face! How can we be sure she's even one of us?"

I knew that voice, and I knew exactly what the bastard was talking about. *Truman.*

I heard a low murmur from the room. I had to wonder just who Truman was talking to. Even if a few people agreed with him, he couldn't be that influential...right?

One voice rang out from the crowd. "He's right!"

"Yeah!" another person answered. My heart began to beat faster. *How many people agreed?*

"Some of the higher-ups claim to know she's human, but how can we be sure? Would they know? Maybe she tricked them, too. Maybe she's fooled all of us! None of us are safe until we know for sure."

This was met with murmurs of fearful agreement. Bile rose in my throat.

"If she doesn't have anything to hide, she should show us her face. If Robin is human, make her prove it!"

That was all I was going to take. I barged into the room. There he was, standing in the middle of the room like some great speaker. To my disappointment, almost twenty of my fellow soldiers were there with him. I could feel their eyes on me for a second before most of them looked away in shame. I kept my stare on Truman as he turned to face me. He didn't seem contrite or ashamed as the others did, but met my glare defiantly.

"Welcome, Daire," said Truman with a triumphant smile. "Do you have anything to say about your pet Cat?"

"She's human, you *son of a bitch!*" I lunged forward, but a hand on my arm stopped me. Fox tried to tug me back while balancing on his crutch.

"This ain't the way to solve this, man," he said. "He's lookin' for a fight. Don't give him one. It'll just make more people side with him."

"You don't even believe she's not human," I snarled at Truman, fighting to keep my fists at my sides. "You just want to cause trouble."

"I only trust what I can see," he responded with a smirk. "And it looks like she's hiding something."

I scowled and turned to confront the audience. "How many of your lives has she saved?" I demanded. "How many times has she risked her own life to keep us all safe? How can you *still* not trust her?"

No one spoke for a long minute. But then an uncertain voice rose from the crowd, though the man speaking would not meet my eyes.

"She works with the Cats," he said. "You say that she's on our side, but...she never shows her face."

"She could be a double agent for *them*," said a woman in an anxious tone.

I could only shake my head in disbelief. I felt a hand on my shoulder and turned to see Truman. I didn't believe his friendly gesture for a second, and I wasn't surprised when he stepped in closer to me and said, "She could be lying to you, Daire. Don't trust her."

"You don't know what you're doing," I whispered through gritted teeth. "This place is held together by trust. These people are scared enough of the Cats without you making them think there's some inside threat. You're putting everyone at risk."

"Maybe. Or maybe I'm saving everyone from a threat you won't acknowledge because you're too wrapped up in your little love story to see it. You care more about her than the safety of this place. If you're not careful, you won't see how dangerous she is until she puts a knife in your back."

"This is a warning." Truman stepped away from me and raised his voice for the room to hear. "Your emotions are clouding your judgment, Daire. You need to face the truth before it kills us all."

The room broke out in murmurs again, and I realized they were agreeing with him. Truman had filled these people with fear and doubt, to the point where I wouldn't be able to fix it. They weren't going to listen to me anymore. It took a lot of self-control, but instead of giving Truman the beating he deserved, I turned around and left the room, marching down the hall and leaving Fox on his crutch to keep up. My mind ran ahead of me, dreading what was going to happen next. Truman was chipping away at the stability of the Fort. If he kept making people afraid... Whether he meant to or not, he could bring down everything.

And if Robin heard the lies he was spreading about her, she would be crushed to know that people believed him.

23 TYLOS

ASIDE FROM THE crackling of the fire and the roar of the wind outside, the cave was dead silent. I didn't dare make a noise for fear that my opponent would judge me by it. I also attempted to keep my expression as neutral as possible, and, failing that, I did my best to hide behind my cards. I had a terrible hand—I thought. An eight with sideways squares, a five with something that looked like a fat fleur-de-lis, a human female with a heart, and the letter A with something that looked like a clover.

Arianna had explained all the cards to me, but I hadn't really understood. She was most obviously winning, judging by her snide expression. She was silently watching me, with a look that made me think she could read my mind. Trying to read hers was pointless. She wore a blue shirt with a torn sleeve and a high collar that offered little protection against the wind. She had black pants and high boots, but nothing that could be mistaken for armor. Her light brown hair fell in waves down her back, and she seemed to have one eyebrow always slightly raised. She showed an expression of amusement, and her cheeks held a light glow that could have been the reflection of the fire, or a reaction to the now half-empty bottle of whiskey.

But even in her inebriated state, I could only see what she wanted me to. Her thoughts, her emotions, her inner workings...she kept those skillfully hidden.

I cleared my throat. "You know, when my people first started studying humans, we thought these things were for identification." I gestured to the cards. "Mostly because we always found them in snipers' helmets."

"That makes sense. But trivia won't get you out of taking your turn, Tylos." She was grinning, as though she knew that would confuse me more.

"Oh, fine. Do you have any...As?"

The human threw back her head and laughed. "They're called 'aces,' kitty. And no. Go fish."

I swore under my breath and reached for another card, only to find myself once again in a state of bewilderment.

"Tell me, why does this human appear to be attacking his own head with a sword?"

"Ah, that card's known as the suicide king. He's supposed to represent Charlemagne, a human king from way back. Really, I don't know why the card was designed like that. But I do know...you have an eight that you want to hand over to me."

I scowled and passed the card to a grinning Arianna. "How did you know I had that?"

"It's all in your eyes." She winked, and took another sip of whiskey.

I found this to be a very interesting answer. Most humans were afraid to look me in the eye, because of my pupils. I've been told that humans consider them unsettling or even frightening. Arianna, however, seemed to have no problem maintaining eye contact, a fact she used to her advantage in that infuriating card game. Though I would never admit it, her eyes were quite mesmerizing—for a human, of course. They were the color of storm clouds, a dark gray that always seemed to be reflecting moonlight. They were the kind of eyes that hid mysteries.

When Arianna turned to gaze outside, I realized that I must've been staring for longer than I thought. She didn't seem annoyed, or even distressed. She just stared out at the rain with a thoughtful look that made me want to stay silent, as though if I listened hard enough, I could hear her thoughts.

"Tylos," she said after a moment. "Why haven't you killed me yet?" Her tone was entirely casual, with no hint of fear or suspicion, only genuine curiosity.

"I'm too lazy to carry your body outside," I answered without missing a beat. "Do you have any queens?"

She tossed a card over to me. "You're hilarious. From the second I met you, I figured that you'd get rid of me as soon as you were strong enough. Threes?"

"Go fish. Honestly, I did plan on killing you as soon as I could. Fives?"

She handed me another card, then turned those eyes to me again. "So why didn't you? We both know you could have by now. And I'll bet you're armed to the teeth. I wouldn't be surprised if you pulled another one of those knives out of your ass."

I chuckled at that, but her question made me pause to think. *Why hadn't I gotten rid of her?* She was right, I could have. It would have taken almost no effort, and it would have kept me alive if my squad found me. I couldn't think of a single logical reason why I had spared her life. After all, we were enemies. Or we had been.

After a long hesitation, I decided to tell the truth, or as much as I understood of it.

"I didn't kill you...because I didn't want to." The words sounded strange, even to me, and I frowned, trying to think of a better way to say them.

But she only smiled. "Makes as much sense as any. Well, I'm glad you didn't want to kill me, ca—um, Tylos."

I felt my face heat up, and I turned away so she wouldn't see. "Don't push your luck. We still have another night in here. I may change my mind."

To my surprise, her response was a hearty laugh, so sincere I couldn't help but smile a bit myself. "It's your turn, stupid human."

"Indeed it is. But you see, my friend..." she set down the last two cards in her hand—a pair of aces. "I have already won."

"Damn." I absent-mindedly reached for one of the aces. I pretended to examine the card as I watched Arianna stand and move to the mouth of the cave, drink in hand. She raised the bottle to her lips again, drinking for a long minute. There was a serious air about her all of a sudden, and I slipped the card into my breast pocket as she began to speak.

"Why are we even fighting this war?" she asked, her voice barely audible above the relentless rain. After a moment of silence, she looked back to me, and asked, "Why are you in the war?"

"Well, my parents were in the military. It was expected I follow their footsteps."

"Did they...did you lose them?"

"Yes, they were killed in the initial attack."

"I'm sorry."

I shrugged. "I never really knew them well. My real family was my squad, but they were quick to leave me behind when things got tough. So I guess I don't really have a reason to fight." Arianna was silent, and her stormy eyes gazed at the fire, revealing nothing. "What about you?"

"That's a long story." I looked up expectantly at her.

After standing a moment, she took her place on the other side of the fire and sat, resting her chin on her knees. "I grew up on a farm by the sea. It was attacked one night while I was asleep. The house, the barn, the fields—everything was burned to the ground. The Cats killed my whole family. I didn't have anywhere else to go, so eventually I joined the Resistance. They see me as a bit of a role model, but I never really fit in there." She grinned, though her eyes still reflected sadness. "The old military people don't appreciate my sarcasm. But it was the only place I could go. Joining the fight...just seemed like the next logical step. So here I am."

I couldn't help but drop my eyes to the ground. I had to gather up courage before I was able to speak.

"We...took your whole family from you? You must hate us."

"I did, for a while. Then I realized...when it comes to humans, there are good people and bad people. I figured it was the same with your race. You can't all be the same. Besides, more killing won't bring my family back."

I was at a loss. As hard as I tried, I couldn't come up with a single response. She was right. And she was also far wiser than I would have ever guessed. Many of my people believed that all humans were the same, and that there was no variation in the inferior species. It was what we had all been taught. It was what even I had believed.

"Tylos?"

"Yeah?"

"I don't want to die in this war."

Arianna seemed to be close to tears, and I realized her confession must have been incredibly hard to make. She was baring her soul to me. I wanted to be encouraging, but all I could do was listen.

She took a deep breath. "I want to die on my front porch, in a rocking chair, watching the rain."

I felt strangely somber at the mention of her mortality. Confronted with this unusual sadness, all I could do was nod.

She fixed her gaze on me. "I don't want you to die in this war either."

I felt my breath catch in my chest.

"You're not like they said the Cats are like. You're not heartless or evil or cruel. You seem like a good person," she continued. I couldn't tell if it was the alcohol or exhaustion that was making her speak so honestly. "No more good people should have to die because of this... petty land squabble."

"You're right" was all I was able to say. "But neither side will agree to compromise."

"Yes. And because of that, odds are we'll both die in a battle neither of us wants to be part of. We might even be forced to kill each other. Honestly—I can't imagine anything worse than that."

I couldn't speak. But I had to do something—seeing the pain in Arianna's eyes was too much to bear. I had to be brave, for once.

I slowly rose to my feet and made my way around the fire. I sat next to her without a word, and put my arm around her, like she had for me when we first met, when she did the last thing I expected and helped to save my life. I held her silently, knowing she would speak when she had something to say.

"Do you think this war will kill us?" Her voice was barely a whisper.

"No, I don't. We've beaten the odds once and survived situations that would have killed most other people. But we're okay. You are, without a doubt, the strongest person I've ever met. Something tells me the two of us are going to be fine." She turned to look up at me in surprise, and I could see the hope growing in those unusual eyes.

I hadn't planned to say any of that, but it was the truth. Never before had I spoken right from the heart like that, and I was pretty afraid at how she'd react.

Arianna leaned into me, rested her head against my chest. Somehow I knew she was smiling.

"You're right," she said simply. "We're going to be okay."

There was a war outside that was tearing the world apart. But right there, wounded, trapped in that cave by a raging storm, and forced to share the space with a dangerous enemy, I felt calm. With her...there was peace.

24 ROBIN

THERE WAS something so refreshing about being in the forest again. The rain had eased considerably, leaving just enough to cause noise and eradicate smells. In other words, the weather was helping my squad be almost invisible. Even with their heightened senses, it would be very hard for the Cats to find us now, and they probably wouldn't even bother to look. During the march out here, it had been easy to let myself get lost in the survival mindset. I focused on keeping myself and my team safe and headed in the right direction.

But when we camped for the night, there was no longer anything to distract me from what was weighing on my mind. We had decided that Daire and Fox should remain at the Fort, which I understood, but when I led the team out and Daire had come to say good-bye... There was something very wrong. I noticed that he was upset, but he tried to hide it. And unfortunately, I didn't have time to press him about it.

"Good luck," he said. "Give 'em hell." He was smiling, but it was too tight, too forced. There was something bothering him. But I would have to wait until I got back to find out what.

The waxing moon seemed almost within reaching distance from

my spot high in a pine tree. I let myself gaze upon its brightness for a little while before looking back down at the campsite where my squad was sleeping peacefully. Everything was quiet. In a few hours, I'd trade places with one of them, leaving the final watch for someone else. We'd keep our group safe for the night. And in the morning... we'd attack.

A part of me was worried. We were a small group going up against as many as twenty enemies. And my squad...these were good people. They were my friends. I was terrified of leading them into what might be their last battle.

My own morality did not concern me. In fact, I rather hoped I'd die heroically in battle. Maybe not this battle, but someday, for sure. I planned on going out fighting. That was the best I could hope for, because if I did die in battle—well, no one would ever find out what I was. Not Cap, or Fox—and not Daire. They would never know what I had been hiding. I'd die a human.

Another part of me let all thoughts of fighting fall from my mind. I gazed at the stars, locating my favorites. *Those three are Orion's Belt...that's Venus over there...and the North Star, of course.* The night sky always held a fascination for me. It made me think of a giant, shifting canvas that some great painter had made his masterpiece. I suppose there's a romantic part of me, after all.

Somewhere, in the back of my mind, I wondered what Daire was doing and if he was feeling better. I almost wished he was with me. Then I remembered the fighting I had to do when the sun rose, and I was glad he wasn't.

25 PORT

"WE HAVE TO DO SOMETHING. Truman is causing dissent among the soldiers."

That was Cap's voice. His barely concealed frustration terrified me, and I was glad my back was to him so he couldn't see my fear. I lingered at the doorway, standing tall and holding an aluminum bat in a threatening manner. Three of the Resistance's leaders tasked me with keeping guard over their meeting, and I took my job seriously.

"Daire, you know as well as I do that the Fort needs people to trust each other. We can't have doubt over one of our senior members."

"But that's no reason to punish Robin! She's done nothing wrong. She has no reason to prove herself."

"Daire's right," said Fox. "She's saved our hides more times than I can count. Ain't right to do this to her."

"We have no choice." Cap sounded weary. "I don't want to do this either. But we need a show of proving Robin to be human. That will eliminate all doubt and restore faith in our cause. We need to eliminate all uncertainty now before things get out of hand."

Daire sighed. "I don't like it—but Cap's right. We don't have a choice. Besides, if Robin was here, we all know that she'd volunteer to prove herself."

"I dunno. This don't bode well with me. I still say it's a real bad idea."

"I know it is, Fox. And damn Truman for forcing this on us."

"We'll do it tomorrow, all three of us," said Cap. "And once we prove she's human, Truman will have nothing he can use against her."

"I've got a bad feelin' about this. But I guess it's gonna happen anyway," said Fox.

Daire sighed again. "I guess so. I just hope Robin will forgive us."

26 HADRYLL

HOW MANY DAYS...HOW long have I been here? It feels like I've been in this tiny, claustrophobic cell for months, even seasons. The tiny window near the ceiling doesn't let in enough light or air, and I feel like I'm slowly suffocating during this endless imprisonment. But it hasn't even been a week, has it? No, it can't have been... Every hour this damned cell gets smaller. If it had been weeks, I would have been crushed completely. So, days. But how many? How many days?

"Three."

What?

"Three."

Three days?

"Three."

Wait, who said that? Who's there? There...there's someone in here with me!

I sat bolt upright, screaming at whoever was in my cell. Only, I wasn't making any noise so I suppose the screaming was internal. No matter, as there didn't seem to be anyone else in my cell after all. I was alone. And apparently my slow descent into insanity wasn't as slow as I had thought it would be.

"Three."

I almost hit my head on the ceiling. I lurched to my feet, but the source of the sound eluded me. Was it even real? Or another hallucination? No, the way the voice echoed off the walls was just too haunting to be anything but real. My fading mind had unnerved and upended me, but never surprised me. There was something near... and my Wyrforra pride urged me to challenge it.

"Who's there? Show yourself, stranger!" I shouted in a voice cracking with thirst.

"Three. Three!"

The trill was coming from the high window. A minuscule black and white songbird was pecking along the ground, occasionally raising his tiny head to chirp. He seemed disturbed by my outburst, and hopped angrily toward the window bars. "Three," he said. "Tree!"

"Have you come to rescue me, little bird?" I sighed. He hopped back and forth a few times. I swear his beady eyes held sympathy.

"You'd best hurry. I fear I'm going insane."

"Three!" he shouted at me, before turning tail and flying off in an indignant flurry of loose feathers.

I muttered, "Stupid bird."

"Stupid Cat," it responded.

Wait...what? No, the bird didn't say that. The...the walls did...they were still echoing.

Someone was laughing.

It's me.

27 ARIANNA

I REMEMBER FALLING asleep feeling as though, for the first time in years, everything was going to be all right. That was why I found it so confusing when I woke up with a hand clamped tight over my mouth.

I started to struggle for all that I was worth until I realized the hand belonged to Tylos, who was giving me a desperate *Be quiet* look. The panic in his eyes terrified me, and I nodded, letting him know I'd understood. Tylos let me go and stood, moving silently.

To my confusion, he moved to the stack of burned firewood and rearranged it into a big pile in the back of the cave. He dashed over and grabbed my pack with one hand and then scooped me up in his arms, which was an unusual experience and it took all of my willpower not to resist. He took me to the firewood, dropped my pack, and set me down behind everything, motioning for me to stay low. There was real fear in his eyes and it paralyzed me.

"Lysander!" called a harsh voice from the mouth of the cave. "Is that you?"

From my place behind the firewood, I watched Tylos straighten up and force his expression to be neutral. "Here, sir."

"I can't believe you're alive, soldier!" There were more voices now. Tylos walked out to meet them, and I shifted to peer through a gap in the log pile. My breath rushed from my chest and I had to force myself not to gasp when I saw them. There was an entire squad, twenty Cats at the least. If they found me, I'd have no chance.

"With your injuries, we thought you were dead for sure," said another voice. "How'd you get away?"

"I managed to drag myself here. Then I just waited out the storm." Tylos's words were crisp and official, and no one dared question him. "I would like to have a medic look over my wounds. I'm worried they might be infected."

"Let's head out. Say, did you find anything in the cave?" I tensed, staying as still as possible, but I couldn't still my trembling hands. "We could use some extra supplies if you have them."

"No sir," said Tylos. "Just burnt firewood."

"Very well. It's good to have you back. Move out."

I heard footsteps as the squad headed back out into the forest. I peered back through the woodpile in time to see the Cats leaving, with Tylos in the back of the group. He looked back toward me, a worried expression on his face. After a moment, he turned and followed his squad.

Knowing it would be unwise to leave right away, I waited behind that woodpile for a long time. *Everything had gone well,* I thought. *I hadn't been killed, I didn't have to kill anyone, and I could go back to my own people now. Somehow, I survived being trapped with a dangerous enemy. I was incredibly lucky.*

But why did I feel like everything was wrong? If there was no way this could have gone better, why did I feel like...I had failed?

I sat in that cave, listening to the rain slowly dying down, until I understood what was making me feel so wrong.

When he had looked back at me, Tylos's yellow eyes reflected such a profound sadness that I wondered if he was going to be okay. I gathered myself and rose from behind the woodpile, though the movement shot pain through my side. As quietly as I could, I made my way to the mouth of the cave.

The Cats were gone. I knelt to the still-wet earth and took note of their footprints, which were—thankfully—headed away from the Fort. My path was clear.

I stood, gathered my pack, and headed off.

28 FOX

THE SUN HUNG almost halfway between its morning horizon and its midday zenith. From my perch on the wall, I looked out over the courtyard and watched the shadows change shape. I felt as though this new day didn't hold the promise it usually carried. Instead, it brought an ominous responsibility.

Daire approached my seat on the wall, interrupting unhappy thoughts. He wasn't set to take over my shift as lookout for a few hours, but I didn't protest when he sat next to me.

"Coffee?" He handed me a lukewarm Styrofoam cup. I accepted, swirling the powdered cream around to mix in the sugar.

"Little late for coffee, innit?" I said.

"Blasphemy. It's never too late for coffee."

I couldn't help but agree, and I sipped it gratefully. We held a pensive silence for a moment. A few people entered the courtyard below, carrying boxing gloves and punch mitts. Daire and I watched as they set up, punching and coaching each other. Even from high up, we could hear their laughter.

"You've been quiet. Are you upset about Arianna?" Daire asked. "You know—"

"Don't say that it wasn't my fault. Please," I interrupted. "I've heard that so many times, I...don't think I can hear it again without losing my mind."

I leaned back in my chair, running my hand through my hair and over my eyes. I patted my pockets, searching for a cigarette, but they were all empty.

"She's gone." I said it, without meaning to. "No matter whose fault it is...it doesn't change that she's...dead."

"It's a war, Fox. People have been dying for a decade because of it. There have been tens of thousands of casualties."

"Yes, and doesn't it feel like every one of them is counting on us to make it worth it? If we don't win, they'll have died for nothing. Our country, our parents, our friends. Every loss makes it more important for us to succeed, but every casualty makes it more certain that we'll fail." Daire looked at me in surprise, but I wasn't controlling my words anymore. It was simply raw emotion that I needed to get off my chest. "I just want..."

"You want everyone you care about to be safe and happy," Daire finished. There was no hint of criticism in his words.

"Yeah." I sighed. "Is that naive?"

"Yes. But you have to be a little naive to be human. Otherwise, people turn into numbers. Number of soldiers, number of casualties... And you can't fight as hard for numbers as you can for people. It's people who can drive you to win. At least, that's what my dad used to tell me."

"That was pretty damn poetic, Daire," I said, with a smile. We both knew that nothing he could say would make me feel better. But just showing that he cared helped me smile just a bit. In the courtyard down below, the boxers switched places. One clapped the other on the back. Both wore wide smiles. Daire watched them and said nothing.

"You're worried about Robin. About what's going to happen when she gets back," I said.

"Yeah." Daire sighed. "Is everything set up for that?"

"Mm-hm. Cap and I got everything ready a few hours ago. Are you sure 'bout going through with this?"

"No. But we have to. There's no doubt she'll pass, but she'll hold it against us that we had to prove it. And she should. It's invasive and wrong, especially after how much she's done for the Fort. We should trust her."

"We—you, Cap, and I—do trust her. She's saved our lives more times than I can remember, and she's been our best friend for years. You two are head over heels for each other, for Christ's sake." Daire shot me a scowl and I winked. "Come on, it's obvious. You aren't the problem here, Daire. It's Truman. He's the one putting her through this, and she'll understand that."

"God, I hate that guy."

"Me too. Wish I'd never found the bastard," I said, staring into my coffee. "He ain't all there. If I could do it all over again, I'd leave his ass in the woods and find a way to get Arianna home."

The boxers below were wrapping up their training, removing their gloves and heading back inside. Their voices carried up to us, but I couldn't make out their words. Their tones were light and tired, like children coming in from the playground.

Daire put a hand on my shoulder and squeezed. We stopped talking, and settled for drawing strength from each other's presence. We each had our own pain, but somehow, the burden seemed lighter. We drank our coffee and allowed ourselves to heal.

29 ALMYRR

THE KING WAS ANGRY.

His fingers were flying on the little cube, manically twisting and turning the colored boxes. He was leaning forward in his chair now, intent on solving the puzzle. He was growing more and more frenzied with the thing, and I was glad his back was to me. I didn't want to see those undoubtedly blood-red eyes.

"Damn it all!" he roared. "I've tried every combination I can think of! Why won't this work?"

A soft knock sounded at the door, and I was glad I was spared from answering the king.

"Enter," he said, and the captain of espionage strode into the room. She immediately knelt, bowing her head low in a gesture of subservience. Odyra had taken my warning to heart.

"Stand up." His eyes never left the cube. "What do you want?"

"It's about the Australian colonies, sire."

"Yes, and?"

"Their messenger ship was supposed to arrive a few weeks ago. There's no sign of it."

"What do their forces say about that?"

"Nothing, sire."

"Nothing? What do you mean nothing?"

"We haven't heard anything from them, sire." Her voice was quiet and unafraid. "The Australian colonies are silent."

"Damn it!" With a shout, he threw the multicolored cube at the wall. It collided and shattered, spreading small boxes across the carpet.

Wordlessly, the King rose from his chair. He moved around the desk, heading to the scattering of cubes from the broken puzzle. Odyra and I held our breath as Erenvyr inspected the wreckage. For a few long moments, he looked for the secret prize until the unavoidable truth presented itself. There was nothing but small broken pieces.

He straightened. "Almyrr, Odyra, excuse me. Send in the door guards."

We lost no time in leaving the room. Once outside, I nodded to the guards on either side of the door, motioning them inside. They obeyed with some hesitation, and the door closed behind them.

Then the screaming started. Odyra and I stared forward, away from the door, and tried to ignore the cries of rage and pain. There were disgusting, unmistakable tearing sounds. We heard the snap of bones. A plea for mercy was abruptly silenced. I began planning for new guards and a cleanup crew. Everything had to be done discreetly and the word spread that the current guards had been transferred. If I arranged everything myself, I could keep it quiet enough to avoid spreading fear and possibly starting a mutiny. I glanced over to Odyra, searching for weakness, but her expression was unchanged as she gazed impassively ahead. Perhaps her resolve was stronger than I imagined.

After a few minutes, the sounds of violence stopped. We waited, and the doors swung open, revealing the terrible scene.

The bodies were unrecognizable as people. I averted my eyes from the bloody masses of pulp and bones and observed the ruined room. There would be no way to remove the blood from the walls, and the carpet was thick with body fluids.

Erenvyr stood holding the open doors. His suit was saturated with the gore, but he didn't seem to mind, not even bothering to brush away the bits of brain matter from his breast pocket. His calm expression and soft maroon eyes stood in stark contrast to the splatter of blood across his cheek.

"Send another ship to Australia," he said, the picture of professionalism. "And I'll be needing new door guards."

30 TYLOS

THE FOREST FLOOR clung to our feet, slowing progress as we marched, heads down, eyes forward. No one spoke, for their own reasons. My comrades were most likely mourning their fallen brothers and sisters. I was praying that Arianna's stitches held. The walk seemed endless, but we were all too tired to run. I wasn't even sure we knew where we were going. It was so easy to imagine that we were lost, nineteen soldiers wandering aimlessly through unknown territory.

And then there were eighteen.

A hood-clad human with a mask blocked the path, standing over the body of our squad leader. She had appeared in a split second, as if she had fallen from the trees as divine intervention sent to rain destruction on us. For a second, I saw her cast in stained glass, standing fearless like a masked angel bent on retribution. Her black clothes and high boots were glittering with dew, and she held no weapons. The human was confident, unflinching in the face of so many enemies. No one had seen her strike, but one of our own lay at her feet. The hilt of our squad leader's k-bar knife protruded from one oozing eye socket.

A cry from behind marked the next victim, as the rear guard was struck with a barrage of thick pointed sticks coming from somewhere in the woods. He died before he hit the ground.

All at once, the humans stepped out of the woods around us. There must have been a thirty at least, all armed, all with that hateful glare. Many of us moved to defend ourselves, but few were quick enough. The seventeen of us remaining braced ourselves for the slaughter.

I was numb and unarmed. My squad was killed before me, people I had known for years and yet never really known, dying left and right. Not one of them asked for help from their friends. Not one allowed themselves to rely on each other. I wondered if that was the true cause of their downfall—*our* downfall.

I closed my eyes against the thick mist of blood and in my mind's eye I saw Arianna approach me as we were both wounded and dying. She offered me help, allied herself with her sworn enemy so that we would both have a chance. And here...among squad mates, not a single one of us thought of doing the same. The thought that we might team up and rely on each other never crossed our minds. We faced the humans one on one, and we died, one on one. I had seen this in battle so many times before, I had assumed that was the only way to fight. It was our culture. And if we could not learn from the humans, it would be how we would lose this war.

I felt no fear as I opened my eyes and walked through the blood bath. In all honesty, I had no idea why I felt so apathetic at my own impending death. It was as though my fate had been decided long ago, and there was no going back. My world had been altered irrevocably, and dying in battle almost seemed like a better option than facing the change. So I walked, until I stood face to face with the masked human.

She looked at me and I looked at her, and for a moment, an unspoken understanding passed between us. Perhaps she saw it in my eyes, or perhaps she only guessed, but I knew she acknowledged my wish. The human nodded, and reached down to pull the k-bar out of my squad leader's skull.

Shrieking a death cry, one of my comrades fell against me from behind, throwing me onto my knees. He ricocheted off me and fell forward, landing on his face. He made no move to rise. He made no move at all.

Stunned and still kneeling, I stared up at the hooded figure as though she was a heavenly warrior I had read about in an old human book—a Valkyrie. She raised the knife. Blood ran from its hilt, dripping thick red tears. I couldn't see the human's eyes, but I imagined they looked to me with grim acceptance. I idly registered that the sounds of battle behind me had ceased. The only sound was the human's sharp intake of breath as she prepared to slash the blade across my throat.

As the knife began its journey toward me, I let my mind wander, seeking happiness in my final moment. My thoughts came to rest on a human with a sharp tongue and storm-cloud eyes. I could almost hear her voice as the k-bar swept down to meet my throat.

"Wait!"

At first, I thought my desperate imagination had conjured her voice. It wasn't until I noticed that the knife had stopped, coming to rest with the edge not quite at my neck, that I understood that everyone else had heard it too.

"Arianna?" The hooded woman spoke, her voice ringing with fearful optimism. "You're alive?"

I froze, not daring to turn and look. I wasn't half as scared of the knife as I was of blowing Arianna's cover. I didn't know what humans did to people who associated with the enemy, but I doubted it was pleasant. And selling Arianna out would be a poor way to repay her for dragging my ass to a cave and saving my life.

"Robin, wait." Arianna sounded winded—and in pain. "Don't kill him."

I could almost feel the humans' questioning stares focus on her. They were confused, but she recovered quickly.

"This Cat is a high-ranking officer— he knows things. I overheard them talking after I retreated. He'd be more useful alive."

There was a terrifying silence, which was finally broken by the hooded human.

"She's right. We'll take him back. You two—get his hands." She spoke with authority, and I soon found myself manhandled as my hands were tied behind me and I was dragged to my feet. The humans, who seemed to have suffered no casualties, began to fall into line. Four men stood around me, as though guarding me from the humans instead of the other way around. We all began to walk.

"Arianna, thank God you're alive." The hooded human stood just ahead of me, leading and beckoning for someone to join her. "Are you hurt?"

"Just my pride. Oh, and this axe wound."

She came into view, moving to stand next to the woman. She had one hand clamped on the stitches at her side, but there was no fresh blood on her. Her face was bright but weary, and she met her friend with a tired smile. She would not look at me.

I hung my head, playing the part of the defeated prisoner. I did not allow myself to sneak glances at Arianna, but I listened with all my strength, hanging off of her every word.

I wondered what fate had in store for me as I walked for miles in her footsteps.

Hadryll

Hadryll. I wrote it again and again, scratching at dirt on the cell wall. *Hadryll. Hadryll.*

Remember it. Remember my name. I had to remember my name. *But was that why I was writing?* No, not really. *Then why? Why write?*

Because it made the walls close in just a little slower. Every name. Every word. Every spot of blood on the walls made them stop moving, stop suffocating me so much. *Wait, blood? Why was there blood?*

The walls are bleeding...? The walls—they're bleeding.

No, you fool! You're losing your mind! You've hurt your fingers with all the scratching. It's your blood, Hadryll. My blood.

It didn't matter. I had to keep writing. It distracted me from my confinement, and the screaming of the walls. *Hadryll. Hadryll.*

I focused hard on writing, but flashes of memory interrupted my concentration. I remembered...my illness, as a teenager. The rashes, the weakness to cold, falling unconscious for no reason. I remembered how my parents, the doctor, everyone was so sure I was going to die. And then...I did. I was pronounced dead. After the traditional one-night vigil, they took me to the...*crematorium,* that was the word. An idea we had gotten from the humans and altered slightly, changing the mechanics of the machine to fit into our climate. The practice of cremation fit so perfectly with our culture's views about the deceased, though I've been told the humans honor it in different ways than we do. We also don't hold services for the dead like they do. One night of mourning for close friends and relatives. And then they disposed of the body before it could freeze. I don't remember it happening, but I know they put me in a box with my name on it. *Hadryll.*

Wait. Hadryl? Was there one "l"? Or two? I can't remember. I can't remember my own name!

No! I can remember it, I just need to concentrate. But I can't think with all the screaming!

The room is silent. Just like the box was. The box that I woke up in all those years ago, after I died. I was so confused that I lay there for a moment, wondering why I was in this strange place. It wasn't until I heard the *click* of the burners turning on that I realized. And I started screaming.

It's the walls! They shriek as they close in on me. It's my death song the walls are singing. They're going to crush me!

I shook my head violently. The walls weren't closing, or making noise, or doing anything besides triggering my fear of confinement. This fear that followed me even after they had pulled me out of the furnace, just as the flames began tearing through the box, a millimeter away from my body. The rational part of me knew that, and resented my own claustrophobia. But the logical part of me was fading faster and faster. I was going mad.

I'm going mad. Keep writing. Hadryl. Hadryll? I'm mad. Madryl. Ha! Madryl!

I threw my head back to laugh, but the sound of a padlock clicking stopped me. The prison door opened.

31 TYLOS

THWACK!

The slap landed hard across my face. I felt blood welling up on my lip, but I shrugged off the pain, opting to stare at my captor. This seemed to upset him. The human grabbed me by the collar and dragged me toward him. With my hands tied behind my back, I could make no move to fight back.

"What was your squad doing here? What did they want?" he shouted, quite unnecessarily, in my face. The belowground room I was being held in was small, and my cell far smaller. I could have heard him clearly if he had whispered.

"I don't know," I answered for the fifth time. "My squad leader never told us anything he didn't think was immediately necessary. He never told—"

"Stop lying!"

He shoved me, knocking me over so I sprawled backward on the concrete floor. I landed hard on my unarmored shoulder. The human raised his arm, preparing for another attack.

The sound of a door closing startled him. A familiar voice echoed through the dungeon.

"Hey, I heard—what? What the hell are you doing?"

Arianna swept into the room, shouting at the man. She stepped through the open cell door and positioned herself between the human and me.

"Truman! What are you *doing*? Did Cap agree to this?"

With her back to me, I could only imagine her stormy eyes. Her body language was clear enough. Her shoulders were set back, causing her long coat to fall like rain around her legs. She carried a basket in one white-knuckled hand and held the other balled in a fist. She looked ready for a fight.

"I don't answer to Cap," said the human.

"You're going to answer to Cap's famous right hook when I tell him about this."

Truman ignored the threat, gesturing to Arianna's basket.

"Is that food?"

"You tried the sharp stick approach. I'm gonna try the carrot."

"You can't give him food until he tells me what I need to know."

"I can and I will."

"Don't."

"Stop me."

Truman raised his hand suddenly, palm facing in, ready to back-hand Arianna. Every muscle in my body tensed and I barely stopped myself from crying out. *No! She's injured!*

But Arianna never flinched. Despite being thinner, shorter, and wounded, she stood up to Truman's threat without blinking. She stared him down.

After a moment, he lowered his arm. With a scoff, he abruptly turned to leave, slamming the prison door as he went through.

"Asshole," Arianna muttered after him.

When she looked back to me, she was smiling. Carefully, she lowered herself into a cross-legged sitting position on the floor. I struggled into a sitting position myself, stopping to loop my arms under my legs to bring my tied hands in front of me.

"So, Tylos," she said brightly. "How have you been?"

I almost smiled. "Well, I have a dirty cot to sleep on, not much food, and a bucket to relieve myself," I answered. "It's just like being back in the barracks, only less crowded and slightly more comfortable. How's your wound?"

Her hand flickered to her side, as if guarding the fragile stitches holding her together.

"On the mend. The doctor was just amazed that I managed to 'stitch myself up.' Hurts like hell, though. But it's nothing that lots of alcohol won't solve." She reached into the basket and pulled out a thick slice of bread. "I'm going to be transparent. This is a bribe. I have some questions."

"Ask away." I took the bread and barely refrained from stuffing the whole thing in my mouth at once.

"Where are you from?" she asked.

"North. I'm afraid I can't tell you exactly where—not because I'm withholding information," I added, trying not to spew crumbs everywhere. "I actually don't know where I'm from in relation to where I am now. On the boats they wouldn't tell us where we were for fear of deserters. The officers thought that if we knew where we were, we wouldn't be afraid to take off."

"So you're from somewhere to the north?"

"Yes." I finished off the bread. "It's much colder there."

"All right, good enough. Next question." She handed me another piece of bread, which I accepted gratefully. "What are you? Like your people? Your name?"

"We're called Wyrforra."

"What does that mean?"

"It's what we are. It means...well, us."

"Hmm...so if you're from some mysterious place to the north, why do you all speak perfect English?"

"We used to have our own language, but it was guttural and rough. The story goes that a couple hundred years ago, a ship crashed on our land carrying missionaries. My people liked their books and their way of speaking, so we adopted their languages. Many of us also adopted their religion."

"Wait, languages? Plural?"

"English and Latin."

"But if you learned English from priests hundreds of years ago," she said, "why is your vocabulary so modern?"

"In the last fifty years or so, the Wyrforra has been...listening, especially to North America. We've been tapping into radio frequencies and intercepting any physical mail that passes by us. My generation was raised on the information they learned, teaching us how to speak like you in preparation for the invasion. That's how we've kept up with the rest of the world, and how I know so much about life here in Canada."

"You're in the United States."

"Oh."

Arianna laughed, and I couldn't help but smirk through my embarrassment. But my smile faded quickly as she rose to her feet.

"That's enough questions for one day." She moved out the cell door and locked it behind her. "I'll be back tomorrow. Try not to miss me too much, eh?"

"You forgot your basket."

"Shh," she whispered. "I most certainly did not forget any basket with lots of food in it. And you should hide that. You wouldn't want the next guard to find the basket I didn't leave behind. Catch ya later, Tylos."

And with that, she was gone once again.

32 ROBIN

"COME WITH ME, TO THE COURTYARD."

Daire was acting strangely. For one, he was leading me by the hand, which was out of character. Fox was the touchy-feely one, while Daire rarely made contact with anyone. But I let him pull me along. His hand was warm.

"Daire, what's going on?"

"You'll see. Don't worry."

He was being nice, too. I mean, he was a kind person but it was odd for him not to tease me or joke around. I was suspicious, of course. It was impossible not to be. But I trusted Daire. If he said it would be okay, it would be okay.

We entered the courtyard, which was surprisingly deserted, at least as far as I could tell. Even my light-sensitive eyes couldn't see its farthest corners. The darkness made it hard to navigate, but Daire and I stumbled to the center of the space. The night was silent.

"What are we doing here?" I asked.

"Look at the stars, Robin. They're so beautiful tonight."

"Yes... What's this about?" I asked again.

"Robin."

Daire was facing me now. I could only see the outline of his face, but I could feel his eyes resting softly on mine. My heart began to beat a little faster.

"Yes?" I tried to keep my voice even and neutral.

Slowly but suddenly, Daire's hands found mine in the dark. He held them gently, rubbing his thumbs in tiny circles on my wrists. Blood rushed to my face, and I was glad he couldn't see how red I was. I tried to think of something to say, but I couldn't seem to string the words together. I let the moment hang in silence.

"I want you to know that I care about you." His voice was soft, not quite a whisper. "Since the moment I met you, I knew you were going to be a very important part of my life. And you are. You're my best friend, but also so much more than that. I...I really care about you, Robin."

"Daire, we've talked about this. We're in the middle of a war, there's no time for—"

"Let me finish."

He dropped my hands and reached up to my face. Slowly, delicately, he pushed back my hood, letting it fall against my back. My heart skipped a beat. *What was he going to do?* I waited, breathless, as he reached to my mask and slipped it off, letting it fall to the ground.

"Robin... You mean more to me than the whole world," he said. "That's why...I hope you can forgive me for this."

Forgive? Fear coursed through me as I was flooded with uncertainty. For the first time, I had no idea what Daire was thinking. He stepped away from me, and I extended my arms toward him, as if asking for a reassuring touch. But he was beyond my reach. I was about to call out to him when his voice rang across the courtyard.

"Now, Fox."

An impossibly bright light appeared from the far corner of the yard. Its beam struck me in the face with more force than light should have. I raised my hand to protect my eyes from the pain. Why wasn't my hood helping me?

Wait. No.

I wasn't wearing my hood, or my mask. Daire had taken them from me. I was unprotected and completely exposed.

No. No!

Understanding dawned on me, and my stomach dropped to my knees. I thought about scrambling for my hood, but it was far too late. They set up the perfect trap.

No, no, no, no! God, this can't be happening!

And they had caught me. Anger rose amidst my despair. I trusted him, and he had betrayed me.

"Daire, *why?*" I cried. I had to understand. "Why would you do this?"

He moved toward me, a look of guilt on his face. He felt bad about setting me up. I saw that apologetic expression and my anger melted. He had never meant to hurt me. Of course he hadn't. He was my friend. But...*why wasn't he mad? Had he not seen yet?*

"That idiot Truman raised doubts about your humanity. He's already been gathering support, and we thought there might be a mutiny if we didn't act," said Daire. He was nearest me, but he still didn't seem to realize. "We had to promise we'd double check. You're safe though, it's just me, Fox, and Cap here. I'm sorry we had to do this, but things will go back to normal now that we've proven you're..."

He trailed off as his eyes finally met mine. His smile slowly faded. I'll never forget the way his happy expression fell...or the look of shock that replaced it. He had the look of someone whose whole world had suddenly been thrown into question. Betrayal...even fear crossed his face. He was afraid of me.

I dropped my hand, letting the light flood over me. He had seen my eyes. From the direction of the light, I heard a sharp intake of breath, and a heavy curse that must have come from Fox or Cap. But I kept my focus on Daire. I couldn't look away from the pain across his features.

"You're not human," he said. His voice held dying traces of denial and rising despair. The hurt in his voice killed me. He took another step backward, getting farther away from me, and his hands rose into a defensive pose as if he thought I was going to strike out at him.

"But I am on your side!" I pleaded. "I've always been!" I tried to let my eyes convey my honesty, trying to persuade him I was telling the truth.

"You're one of them." His voice seemed almost distant. He stared at me. I had never seen him look at anything like that before. It left a knot in my stomach. "All this time, you've been one of *them*... How could you have hidden it for this long? How could you have lied to us for *years?*"

"I couldn't tell you! I wanted to fight with you, for the humans, but if you had known what I was you would have killed me on sight." I stepped toward him and he recoiled, as though a snake had stuck at him.

"You lied to the Fort," he said. "You lied to *me!* I've saved your life countless times—"

"And I've saved *yours!* Why can't you see that no matter what else I am, I'm your friend!" It was the first time I had ever raised my voice to Daire. I heard footsteps approaching, and I guessed that Cap and Fox were sneaking toward us in case of a violent confrontation.

"You're not an ambassador. You're *their* double agent." Daire's voice was hoarse.

"No! I've never even talked to another Cat. I'm fighting them, just like you are!"

"How could I believe that? After everything else you've tricked me into thinking? How do I know that anything you've ever said or done is real?"

"You know who I am and how I feel. You know me, Daire." I couldn't bring myself to raise my voice above a whisper.

"Apparently, I don't."

That's when I saw it. He had reached a turning point. It was written on his face and etched into his hands, clenched into fists. The trust we had built for so many years was gone. The weight of every word and every emotion had shifted. Everything he had ever thought about me was now working against me, completely changing me in his eyes. I wasn't his friend anymore. In just a matter of minutes, I had become the thing he hated most.

"Daire, please. I'm on your side." I was almost begging now. I would give anything for him to understand. But he was wrapping his head around what I was...and that I had been lying since the moment I met him. The deceit was not lost on him. The fear and hurt in his eyes had smoldered into a cold burning anger. Those eyes, so kind just a few minutes ago, now spoke of fury and promised retribution. And now...*I* was afraid.

"You betrayed me." His voice was chilling. I had to force myself not to shudder.

"I fought for you, and for the Fort!" I answered, but I was starting to understand I had already lost. "You have to know that I would never cause the Resistance harm! You know I'm a loyal—"

I cut off as he stepped up to me, closer than he was when he had held my hands. He didn't touch me now, but loomed over me, his face inches from mine. He stared down at me with open hate. I wanted to shrink back, but I was frozen. I could only stare in terror as my life crumbled.

"I don't know you won't hurt us," my best friend said. "But I do know that you're not one of us. You're an enemy."

I stumbled back away from Daire as Fox and Cap stepped into the light. They stayed at a distance apart from each other, so the three humans formed a triangle around me. Cap seemed emotionless, but I could tell by his posture he was ready to fight. Fox's crossbow was lowered, but loaded. He pointed it toward the ground with both hands as his soft brown eyes met mine. He said nothing, but just looked at me. I knew he didn't want to shoot me. But I also knew that he would if he thought he had to. They all stared at me like a dangerous animal, and I could do nothing but search each of their faces for some sign of mercy. I found none.

They all took a step toward me, and I searched wildly around the courtyard for some place to run, a last-ditch effort to escape. I was gearing up to make a run for it when I felt a hand on my shoulder. Daire, of course, knew me well enough to see my plan. He anchored me with that hand, cutting off any hopes of escape.

"Daire." I turned to him, challenging his glare with my pleading tone. I was scared, more scared than I had ever been. I hoped that he would see that and understand. He had to understand. "Please."

For a heartbeat, I saw the green in his eyes soften. His grip on my shoulder loosened and I thought, just for a second, he would be my friend again.

But then the pain and anger returned, blocking out any hope of understanding. When I saw him pull his arm back, I forced myself not to flinch. Something inside me broke before Daire landed the knockout punch on my stomach. But the pain of getting hit was nothing compared to the feeling of my heart ripping in two. When darkness washed over me and carried me to unconsciousness, I was grateful.

33 ALMYRR

THE KING GAZED out the window of the round room, resting his palms on the windowsill. His cape hung discarded over a chair, and his coat was half open so the winter sunlight caused his undershirt to glow white. He had an air of contemplation about him, which put everyone else in the room on edge.

I stood at his side, on guard, while the master of espionage and two footmen knelt by the door. We all waited for the silence to break.

"Stand, Odyra. Repeat your report," commanded the King.

"The squadron stationed in the American state of Montana has reported that two soldiers have gone missing, sire."

"Deserters?"

"Unlikely, sir, due to the harsh and unfamiliar landscape."

"I see. No cause for concern now."

Odyra bowed low and started to leave with her guards.

"Wait. Stay." Erenvyr turned from the window, catching the spymaster and the footmen in his sweeping gaze. "All of you."

Odyra and I shared a glance. We were thinking the same thing: it was unusual for the King not to send out common soldiers during important business. The footmen knew this too, and shifted with discomfort and fear.

"Master of espionage," Erenvyr began, "Odyra. You're a brilliant soldier. You're unfaltering and relentless, and your reputation is widespread. Not to mention, you're half my age. Therefore, you're perfect to succeed me when I retire."

I watched the spymaster carefully, but not even a flicker of emotion passed across her stoic features.

"However, I am naming Almyrr my successor."

Even I blinked in surprise. The spymaster dropped her head a fraction in disappointment...or perhaps to hide a flash of anger.

"Am I to remain in my current position then, sire?" Her voice betrayed no emotion.

"Yes. Don't misunderstand, I am not punishing you. You're a superb warrior and I quite like you. But..."

He crossed the room in a few strides to stand before her. I moved my hand to my knife, fearful that Odyra would strike out, but the King seemed completely unafraid.

"When I refused to name you my successor, you did not ask why," he continued, staring down at an unflinching Odyra. "We both know why. Your ambition is all-consuming, much like mine was at your age. If I named you my successor, there's no doubt I would soon find my throat slit in my sleep. Don't deny it, Odyra. I admire your strength. But I also value my life, so my choice is Almyrr."

I cleared my throat in preparation to speak. "But sire, if I may protest—I have no desire to lead."

"I know. All the more reason for you to keep me alive, my friend. Now, Almyrr, would you be so kind as to escort the master of espionage and her guards to my generals? I should like them to relate what I have decreed. And do try to keep those footmen alive. They'll serve as witnesses."

"Right away, sire."

"One more thing. Odyra, I don't want you to get discouraged. I have big plans for you. Someday, I will have to switch my successor, and if you keep performing the way you have been, the job will be yours. Keep that in mind, and I'm sure you'll live up to my expectations. Now you may leave."

I bowed, as did the others, and left the room. The sound of heels clipping the floor echoed unbearably through the hallway. I figured this would be a very long and unpleasant walk if I didn't make some conversation.

"Half the King's age, hm?" I said. "I never realized you were so young. I figured you were in your late twenties."

"I'm fifteen." Her voice was even and once again free of emotion.

"Fifteen? Shouldn't you still be in the academy?"

"I graduated early."

"That's quite an accomplishment. How did you manage that?"

"I killed a hundred humans. The last twelve with my bare hands. And I brought their severed thumbs to my commanding officer."

I recoiled. "Your CO told you to cut off the humans' thumbs?"

"No. I just wanted to show how...eager I was to excel. Since I graduated in record time and moved up the ranks to be master of espionage, I'd say it worked. I've found that the best way to get ahead is to, as the humans say, 'get one's hands dirty.' Don't you agree, sir?"

"Yes, but was it necessary to be so...barbaric?"

"Necessary? No." She was looking at me from the corners of her impassive pink eyes. "But it was enjoyable."

A long and unpleasant walk it was.

34 TYLOS

IN A WAY, isolation is to the mind what an open wound is to the body. Without treatment, without someone to talk to, ailments fester and blood gets cold. Loneliness can eat away at a person, force them to rethink everything and cast the world in a negative light. Wyrforra were solitary creatures, but I always had to have distractions. I rarely had to be alone with my thoughts. It wasn't until I was left with only my thoughts as company that I discovered I was not well equipped to deal with loneliness. I felt crushed by all the time to think. That's what did me in. The thinking.

Arianna hadn't come to see me in two days and I could not reach the other inhabitants of my prison. The other soldier was in a cell at the far end of the basement, but judging by his periodic screams and loud babbling, it was for the best that he wasn't near me. The hooded woman was here, to my great surprise, and close enough to speak to. But she had still not woken after being carried in unconscious by an unhappy-looking man the previous night. So for the moment, I was cut off from anyone I could talk to.

That's when I found out just how loneliness grows. It boils and burns until it becomes anger, a disdain for the world and people who left you to rot. Then the anger breeds fear, and from that comes a hardened grief, self-pity, and finally distrust. And the changes can happen so fast you don't even see them pass. I felt sorry for myself, and I was so angry at everyone else that I failed to realize I had let my emotions get out of hand—a rare and dangerous thing for my kind.

Finally, she came. This time, she was dressed casually in loose-fitting pants and a sleeveless shirt. A large bandage could be seen on her side where her shirt lifted as she moved. She carried with her a basket and an air of mild disinterest.

"Tylos," she said as she sat once more in front of my cell. "How are you?"

I fixed her with a suspicious glare. "Why do you care?"

The change in her body language was immediate. Her back stiffened and she leaned away from me, and her hands clenched the tiniest bit. The carefree expression faded from her features and was replaced with indifference. She had been happy to see me and I responded to her excitement with disdain. I could tell that she was hurt. But at the moment, I didn't care.

"Perhaps I shouldn't," she said. "I came here to ask you some questions and make sure you were alive. I suppose I could also give you this food."

"I don't want it," I lied. "You humans have probably drugged it or something."

"Suit yourself. I'll just leave it here, within reach of your cell. Take it or leave it, no skin off my back. But if you don't answer my questions, I'll take literal skin off your back."

I reeled back in horror, but she only laughed. "Relax, Tylos. You should understand my dry humor by now. The only one crazy enough to torture someone is Truman, and all the trouble he's been causing has got him on a tight leash. Now, onto the questions. First, who is your leader?"

"King Erenvyr."

"Where is he?"

"I don't know."

"What do you want?"

"To be let out of this cell."

"No, not you, Tylos. The Wyrforra. What do they want?"

"To drive back humanity and dominate the world."

"Oh. Lovely," she said. "And why do you want that?"

"We need the space, and we deserve it. We're better than you." I drove cruelty into my voice.

"Really, now. You're better than us." Something flashed in her eyes, and it felt like emotions colliding. I sensed hurt giving way to resentment. She leaned in close to my cell, and I swear the air felt colder as though she was an oncoming storm. "Remind me again, which one of us in a cell, and which one is free."

"You won't be for long. You're losing the war."

She dropped all sarcasm and nearly jumped to her feet. I followed suit to loom over her, bringing my face close to hers and grabbing the bars with both hands.

"I saved your life," she hissed.

"And I saved yours."

"Why?" Her pain leaked out through gritted teeth. "Why'd you help me if you think you're so much better than me?"

"Because I—" I faltered, unsure. My anger was melting away, and being replaced by shame. "I don't—"

"You don't know." She stepped back, looked away from me. She wrapped her arms around her body. "I need more rest if I'm ever going to heal. Someone else will be interrogating you from now on."

"Wait, Arianna." My heart dropped to my knees, but she wasn't looking at me anymore.

"Who is that?" She stared at the hooded woman in the next cell. "Robin? Is that you?"

35 ROBIN

I WAS FLOATING on a pitch-black sea that was somehow cold and hot at the same time. I could see nothing and feel only paralyzing terror. The sound of waves reached my ears and, after a moment, it was joined by a voice.

...Little girl ...Little girl!

...Are you...wake...little...

...Robin...

"Robin!"

I jolted upright as the voice from my dream melded with something else. Someone was calling me. *Arianna?*

I opened my eyes to see a figure rushing to my cell door. I sat up quickly and was rewarded with a pounding headache. I took in my surroundings as quickly as I could before despair set in. I was in a cell in the basement, in the dungeon I had helped to build. In the next cell over stood a Cat with short-cropped hair and a familiar face. His yellow eyes were trained on Arianna, who was attempting to open the door to my cell.

"Robin, are you all right?" she asked, pulling on the bars when the lock failed to open. "There must be some mistake. Don't worry, I'll get you out of there. I'll go find the—"

"Wait, no." I struggled to my feet, trying to push the pain away. Being knocked unconscious is not without its consequences. "Arianna...stop. I'm supposed to be in here."

"What? Why?" I had never heard her sound so serious—or so hurt. I had to swallow past my heart to answer her.

"I— I'm one of them, Arianna."

"What the hell does that mean?"

I reached up to pull back my hood, only to discover that my hands were tied together. A wave of nausea hit me, and I had to put all my concentration into reaching my head. My friend gasped as I drew back my hood and light flooded over me. I couldn't meet her eyes.

"I'm sorry," I said. I couldn't say exactly what I was sorry for. Lying? Hiding? Or just existing? It didn't matter. I could see her trust vanish and suspicion take its place. Betrayal was scrawled across her face, and for the first time since I had known her, she seemed close to tears.

"You're a Wyrforra." She stepped away from me. "A Cat."

"Yes. I'm sorry." It was more and more difficult to speak with pain blocking my throat.

"How did you trick us?"

"I'll tell you everything, I swear."

"No, not me." She backed away some more, moving down the hall. "Apparently, I can't even trust my own judgment."

"I—"

"No! I trusted you and you betrayed me. I thought I had a friend, but you..." Her eyes flickered to the Cat in the next cell, and I got the feeling she wasn't talking only to me. "I... I need time to process this. I'll make sure more food is sent down." Without another heart-breaking word, she hurried for the door.

36 MADRYL

SPECIAL TREAT, special treat! I found something! It broke off from the wall and now it's mine. It's for Madryl! But what is it?

It's a rock, of course.

No, it's a knife.

No, it's a pen! Yes, a pen! Oh good. I liked to draw, back when I was—*what was my name? I don't remember.* Madryl! It's always been Madryl. That's what my mother named me. Or was it my father? No, it was a bird.

What should I draw with my pen? *How about a nice self-portrait, you crazy fool?* Yes, perfect. That will be difficult with my hands bound unless the pen is sharp enough to saw away at the ropes until...*there we are*... I break through them. Now I'm free to draw. But where? The walls are already covered in blood, and they don't like being drawn on, no. So where?

I'll draw on my arms. Yes, and I'll start with my eyes. One curved line, two, and a circle, and a line for the pupil. Perfect! Now for the next eye, and the next one, and the next one, and the next one...next...

Wait—someone is looking at me. How did I not see them before, the hundreds of red eyes staring right at me, into my soul! Who's there? Who is staring? Why won't you look away? *What are you?*

"He's gone insane! Hold him down, I have to bandage him before he bleeds out!"

Strong arms pinned me to the ground and others wrapped white cloth around my eyes, blocking them from view.

"Oh, thank you, friends!" I trilled. "You've saved me! Tell me, what was it? A djinni, or a hydra? How did you blind it? Will it—will it come back?"

But they left. I shouted my thanks after them, but then the walls demanded silence as I was too loud. I obeyed, and looked for my pen. I desired to write down my name again. My name, Mad—Mad—what was it again?

37 ODYRA

"OH, GOD NO! PLEASE STOP!"

I leaned against the mirrored wall in the strange room. It was filled with an odd assortment of strange devices, long bars and heavy disks and machines with purposes I could not even guess at. We had discovered this room in a multi-story dungeon near the capital, which we had adapted to hold captives. It was a confusing building, but useful, and it held many humans. The sign outside of this particular room read "Prison Weight Room." A human, bloodied, battered, and bruised, cowered in a corner. She flinched at every footstep as I crossed the room to her. I leaned down and held an object before her wide eyes.

"Let me ask you again. And this time, please, try to help me understand," I said. "What is the purpose of this device?"

"I-it's a five-pound barbell." Her voice shook. "You're supposed to lift it to make yourself stronger."

"This tiny thing is for training? You're lying to me."

"N-no! I swear, I-it's—"

"All right, say I believe you. Stop stammering, you're embarrassing yourself. Now what's this machine over here?"

"Th-that's a treadmill. You run on it."

"Why?"

"For, um, exercise."

"Now that's ridiculous. Why would you have a machine to run in place when there's plenty of room to run outside?" I abandoned the treadmill and walked over to a contraption that supported a bar with disks on the edges.

"That's f-for weightlifting. It's a 45-pound bar—" Her eyes grew even wider as I casually lifted each of the disks off and tossed them aside. "With 100-pound weights."

I rolled the bar back and forth in my hands, admiring its metallic smell. "Now sit up straight and tell me what this is called."

"It—" She was interrupted by a wet squishing sound as I launched the bar into her chest. It flew arrow-straight, pinning her against the wall and embedding itself in the concrete. The human tried to speak for a moment, which I found to be quite amusing. I turned away as her blinking eyes grew milky.

"Send the next one in," I called, and another human was shoved into the room. He landed on his knees, and began a stream of expletives in a voice that sounded different than most of the humans I had met. But when his view shifted to the dying woman, he fell silent and the defiance in his eyes was replaced with fear. *Good.*

"*Dios mio,*" he whispered.

"English, please. Or Latin, if you prefer."

"You monsters. Even when I've seen what you can do, you devils always surprise me. Every one of you relishes the blood on your hands."

"You've seen lots of us in action, I assume?"

"Yes. Even your King delights in killing. I know this firsthand."

This captured my attention. "What do you know about King Erenvyr?"

"I met him when he first came here, ten years ago. He landed in my town. He was different then, but there was still evil in his soul. I barely escaped the slaughter."

"He was different? Tell me how he changed." I dropped to my knees and lowered my voice. This was a potentially dangerous conversation. "If you give me useful information I might be able to help you."

The human's eyes lit up with hope. "I did not know him well, so I can't tell you what happened to him. But I know where you can find your answers. He was close to a woman named Rosa in my home-town, Santa Barbara."

"A human?" This made no sense to me. "You're saying that the King was close to a human?

"Si. She is rumored to have been kept alive during the culling. She'll know the whole story."

"I see. Thank you." I offered the human a reassuring smile and put a hand on his shoulder. "You've been very helpful. You're free to go."

"Really? I can be free?"

"Yes." I moved my hand to the back of his neck, dug my fingers into his skin and snapped his neck in an instant. He tumbled to the floor, a hopeful smile still on his face. "Thanks for your help."

I pushed past the corpse and rose to my feet. "Send in the next one."

38 ARIANNA

NOT MANY PEOPLE, even my friends, know where I live. Most of the Resistance lived in the Fort, and I was no exception. But I didn't live in the makeshift barracks in the parking garage. I tried when I was a child, but I could never sleep so far from the stars.

There was an old canvas tent set up on the roof. It was patched and weathered, beaten and battered, but it held years' worth of memories and knickknacks. I had a reasonably comfortable sleeping bag, suitcase full of clothes, and my sister's old leather jacket. Really, it was everything I needed. But the best part of living on the roof was that there was plenty of space for my bike.

I went there before interrogating Tylos. The stars were just coming out, and I thought that seeing them would help clear my head. But tonight, clouds blotted out the constellations. I could barely make out the Little Dipper pointing to the North Star—when the wind shifted and covered up the guiding lights. Bad omen or just bad weather?

Either way, it was time to face my demons. I donned my sister's jacket for extra support, glanced a final time to the stars, and headed to the basement, tightening the jacket around me as I went.

"Later, gorgeous." I blew a kiss to the Suzuki on my way out, but I couldn't hold my smile.

Port was leaning by the prison door. He nodded to me in that quiet, understanding way he has. I moved past him and pushed open the door, shutting it softly behind me. The crazy Cat in the corner was cackling to himself, but I moved past him to Tylos's cell. He was sitting on his cot, bent over with his head in his tied hands. He looked...well, not good. *Tylos*. He looked lost, and broken. I almost felt sorry for him. After a moment's hesitation I wrapped my knuckles on the bars.

Tylos jumped and shot to his feet. His yellow eyes were wide when he rushed to the bars.

"Arianna! You're here," he breathed, with relief in his voice.

"I am," I said, keeping my voice cold.

"I didn't think you'd come back." I could almost hear him say, *"I'm glad you did."*

"I didn't plan to." I sighed. "But my commanding officer needs some information and he thinks I can get it from you."

"Are you..." To my surprise, he ducked his head. "Are you going to waterboard me?"

"Actually, I was thinking of strapping you to a grate and putting bamboo under you so it grows up through your skin over the course of a few weeks. But I figured I'd try talking first." Was I joking? Was this my dry humor?

He thought so. Which it was. "Talking is good. There are some things I want to tell you." His expression was, for the first time, free of suspicion.

"I hope what you want to tell me is what your squad wanted and why they were here."

He frowned. "They never told me what was at the objective. But I can give you the coordinates."

"That will be helpful. Thank you. What else did you want to tell me?"

"I'm worried about your friend." He dropped his voice and

glanced to the next cell over. "I think there's something wrong with her."

Robin was sleeping, or almost sleeping. Her eyelids were fluttering and occasionally she threw her head from side to side in her restless daze. Her lips were moving, but I couldn't hear if she said anything.

"I'll see if I can have some medicine or something sent down." I sighed. "There's really nothing else I can do. Can you...keep an eye on her for me? Let me know if she's sick or something?"

"I will."

"Thanks."

We were both quiet for a moment. Something was different about Tylos. But it didn't matter. He was the enemy, I reminded myself. It didn't matter if he was sorry. I couldn't be soft with him.

"I'll go get you a pen to write down those coordinates." I left, forcing myself not to look back.

39 ODYRA

ONE, two, three. I ran the knife across my head in long, easy strokes. I didn't hesitate as the blade skimmed my scalp, leaving the sides of my head smooth. I kept the thick red hair in a wide strip at the top. It was getting long, now nearly down to my waist. I considered cutting it all off, for practicality's sake, but I liked it. I gathered it all in a loose ponytail and tied it off, then repeated the process a few times farther down my hair, tying it all together in a series of bands. It looked... intimidating. And that was very useful.

I checked my armor in the mirror. The silver chest piece gleamed dimly, clean but not polished, and the shoulder strap was strong. Underneath, my simple black clothes would keep me warm and serve as dark camouflage if needed. The leather bracers on my forearms and legs were light, allowing for movement, but still tough enough to provide protection. I slipped on my boots, belt, and back sheathes for the short swords. I was almost ready.

I was reaching for my backpack when a knock sounded at my chamber door. Instead of answering, I retrieved a dagger from under my pillow.

"Are you there, spymaster?" a voice asked. I cursed under my breath.

"You may enter, sir." I tightened my grip on the dagger, but hid it behind my back.

Almyrr pushed the door open. He took a step forward, but remained in the doorway. I did not move to greet him.

"I came to check up on you," he said. "I heard that you were going away, and I can see that you're all packed and ready to leave. You are going to investigate something, right?"

"Yes, sir. There have been rumors of suspicious activity in California, so I'm going to have a look."

"You don't need to call me 'sir.'" He frowned. "Do you have everything you need for your journey, then?"

"Yes, I am fully prepared." I paused a moment, waiting for him to respond. "Is that all, sir?"

"Please, Odyra, you don't need to be so formal with me. I consider us to be peers. I...well, I have come for another reason. I would like to apologize for how I treated you a while ago. It was inappropriate and rude. I hope I can earn your forgiveness."

"Of course." I curled my lips in a smile. "Consider yourself forgiven, sir."

I put no effort into making my words sincere, and they had the desired effect. Almyrr stepped backward, and his eyes dropped to the floor in a subconscious gesture of fearful submission. I scared him.

"Thank you, Ody—um, Ms. Warringgate. I wish you luck on your journey." He closed the door. I listened to his footsteps retreating down the hall.

I smiled to myself, celebrating my small victory. Almyrr may have had all the power in the beginning, but now he held the demeanor of someone who realized they had made a very powerful enemy. He was regretting every action he had taken against me, and his fear would only continue to grow. All I had to do was feed it, and it would drive him to take direct action against me—a confrontation I would win—or destroy him from within. Either way, I would soon have the assassin out of my way. I was one step closer to the throne.

But for now, I would leave him to his own devices. It was time to go. I slung the short swords across my back, seized my pack, and went to find a vehicle.

40 FOX

I WAS SMOKING IN BED, just as everyone had told me not to. Watching the smoke tendrils twirl up toward the ceiling in graceful spirals was soothing. The sharp scent of tobacco was meant to distract me from my troubles, but it only made me focus on them more. There was no escape from my thoughts.

"I don't think that she's against us," I said. "Robin, I mean. Yeah, she's a Cat, but she's fought hard for us. She's saved my ass countless times. I see no reason to believe that she's an enemy. But Daire...well, he don't see it that way. He's a great guy and my best friend but he's got a real 'us vs. them' mentality. He's got a hard time seeing shades of gray, ya know?"

"Yeah, I get what you mean," said Port. He rolled over from his place next to me on the bed and placed a comforting hand on my chest. "But he's adaptable. He'll come around. Give him some time to mope, and he'll come back to the light."

"I hope you're right." I sighed. I stubbed out my cigarette on the nightstand ashtray. "But even if he does, I can't see a way for this to end good. How can we get Robin back on our team? The Fort will never see her the same way they did."

"Maybe everyone just needs some time to adjust to the idea. I think it's kinda cool that we have a Cat on our side. It's like having a secret weapon. Of course, that only counts if she is actually on our side..." Port trailed off.

"Do you think she is? Never mind she's my friend, you can tell me the truth."

"Yeah, I think so. She never gave me a reason not to trust her, except her species. But I can't let that determine how I judge her, you know? I don't think it would be fair."

"I wish everyone else saw it that way. But with how it is now...no matter how this thing ends, it's gonna be bloody."

"We'll just have to see, I guess. Who knows? Maybe we'll all get a happy ending."

Port rested his head on my chest and I wrapped my arm around his shoulder, hugging him closer to me. I tried to take comfort from his warmth, but doubt and worry hung over me like a tobacco cloud.

"Yeah," I said. "A war story with a happy ending."

41 ROBIN

ROBIN... Wake... Robin

"Robin!" a low voice hissed. "Wake up!"

I opened my eyes and tried to understand what was happening. It was the middle of the night, and the other prisoners had gone to sleep hours ago, even the crazy screaming one. But someone was calling me...someone was standing right outside my cell.

I was awake immediately, focusing on the person and trying to figure out whether I should call for help. My eyes adjusted to the dim light, and I began to make out a large male figure. *Fox? Daire?*

"Get over here, Cat. I know you can hear me."

It wasn't Fox or Daire. I rolled to my feet and assumed an attack position. Whoever this was, he didn't sound friendly.

"Who's there?" I said, quiet enough not to wake Tylos.

"Relax, it's only me. Truman."

"Strangely enough, that doesn't make me want to relax. After all, you've ruined and possibly ended my life, depending on what my *friends* decide to do with me."

"Yeah, that didn't go exactly to plan. They're too attached to you to do the smart thing."

"Oh, gosh, I'm so sorry." I thought about how Arianna would say things in order to make my sarcasm as biting as possible.

Truman gripped one of the bars of my cell. "That's why I'm here."

"Since your plan didn't work, you're going to kill me yourself?" I tested the ropes around my wrists once more. Still tight.

"Unfortunately, no. This militia would never accept me if I did that. Instead, I'm going to give you something."

He reached inside my cell, holding out his hand. Something very small rested on his palm. I hesitated, not wanting to get near enough to see what it was.

"Just take it, Cat," he said. "Calm down. It's not in my best interest to hurt you now."

Unconvinced, I approached with caution and snatched the item from his hand. It was small and oval, about the size of a pea, and hard to the touch.

"Is this glass?" I asked, confused.

"It's a cyanide capsule."

The object seemed to get much, much heavier.

"Listen. You're slowing this whole place down," Truman said. "You're hurting your friends and leaving us unprepared. You said that you're not a traitor and you fight for the Resistance. So prove it. You'll help everyone by removing yourself from the equation."

My hand trembled ever so slightly. I gently closed it into a fist, gripping but not breaking the capsule.

"The decision is yours." Truman stepped back from my cell. "If you have any love for the people here, you'll make the right choice and crush that between your teeth."

As his footsteps faded and finally disappeared, the tiny thing in my hand seemed to pulse with longing. I thought about throwing it, or breaking it on the ground, but something stopped me. I wanted so badly to get rid of it...but the capsule wouldn't let me. It called to me, softly and gently, and made such awful promises. After a long time, I sat down on the edge of my cot. I tucked the little thing into my sock, lay down, and didn't sleep for the rest of the night.

42 ERENVYR

I WOKE to the feel of her soft, dark hair slipping from my fingers. She moved away from me, to the edge of the bed. I did not know why she moved from my embrace, and I reached out to her.

"My love," I called, but she did not turn back to me.

I realized she was shaking. The straps of her nightgown had slipped down her shoulders as she gripped the bed and shivered. Her raven black hair rolled down her back, waving softly with the movement of her body.

"Oh, Arron..." Her voice held no trace of its usual happy lilt. There was only pain, tinged with fear.

"My love?" I was afraid now, too, for perhaps the first time in my young life.

She turned to me, and her warm coal-colored eyes caught the moonlight. Those eyes, always so gentle, streamed with tears.

"Arron—she's gone." Her voice rocked with despair, but the meaning in her words could not register.

"What?"

"She's gone."

My eyelids fluttered as I struggled to pull myself from the dream.

Even in that state between sleep and wakefulness, I knew I didn't want to relive that memory. Not again. But it pulled me under once more.

"What do you mean, she's gone?" I screamed.

Red clouded my vision like blood dripping into my eyes, and when I could see again, I was alone. Everything had been destroyed. Pictures were broken, vases smashed, clocks torn apart—even my wooden bed frame had been snapped in two. But I didn't care. I ignored the chaos, my bleeding hands, her absence. I could see only my loss.

The humans. They stole her from me. They were too weak to protect her, and now she was gone. Killed by those filthy, undeserving creatures. They were unworthy of her, so they killed her. And with her, I had lost everything.

But now...now my path stood clear. I would take my revenge on every last human plaguing this world. They didn't deserve to share this world with us. Like a great cleansing fire, I would burn them all.

And I would start, right here, with this town. I wouldn't rest until every human was dead.

Let it begin.

The dream subsided, but the anger did not. I rose slowly from my bed, dressed, and crossed to the door. I addressed the guards on my way out.

"I'll be back, gentlemen. There are some pests weighing on my mind and I won't be able to sleep until I've taken care of them."

"Rats, sire?"

"Yes," I said. "Rats."

43 FOX

I FOUND him in a dimly lit back room. He was hunched over a table, squinting at scattered papers as though trying to see past the words on the page. His tired eyes and bent back spoke of a sudden aging.

"Daire," I said softly, afraid to startle him. "Are you still goin' over our records on Cats?"

"How didn't we see it, Fox? How were we so blind all these years?"

"You know as well as I do. We didn't see because we didn't want to see. I—I think we both knew, friend, deep down. We knew that she was too fast, too strong, and just too damn good to be human. We just didn't want to acknowledge it."

His silence confirmed what I had said.

"The question now is what do we do with her?" I asked.

"I don't care."

"So we kill her."

"No!" He shot bolt upright, clapping white knuckles on the tabletop. "No."

"So we let her out and talk to her like civilized people?"

"*No.* Let her rot." The venom in his voice made me want to with-draw, but I forced myself to stand my ground.

"She's our friend," I said, not quite pleading.

"She's one of *them!*" Again he slammed his hands at the table, scattering the papers. "She's a monster!"

"Maybe she's a good monster."

"You idiot, there are no good monsters! My parents tried to fight them and I never saw them again. *They* killed my parents, and your parents, and half the country! They're murderous creatures and Robin is one of them!"

"You love her."

He glared at me for a moment longer before his shoulders slumped and the fight died from his eyes. He crumpled as though his soul was collapsing in on itself. Defeated, he brushed past me out the door, almost whispering as he went.

"There are some things more important than love." He straight-ened his back as he walked ahead of me, murmuring to himself. "Like the whole goddamned human race."

44 ODYRA

TWO THOUSAND SEVEN HUNDRED MILES. The distance between Washington, DC, and Santa Barbara. It was going to be a long trip. Luckily, the former human White House was well equipped with human vehicles, and I had my pick. And I chose the fastest. It was large, red, and the roof folded down. This car was quite a machine.

I had trained myself in human vehicle operation, just in case. I knew how to push the pedal and move the stick, turn on the lights— all the necessary functions. I was more comfortable with the vehicles back home, which had tracks instead of wheels, but adjusting to an automobile wasn't difficult.

I left before the sun rose, letting the car's lights guide the way toward California. Next to me was my backpack, weapons, and some food. The back seats were filled with gas cans. I had a feeling that the working gas stations between here and California were going to be few and far between.

Leaving the city, I found the highways open and empty. This made sense: ten years ago, the roads had been congested as fleeing humans were ripped from their cars, leaving them abandoned. But our armies had cleared the major roads for the convoys and transport trucks, old army vehicles taken from the humans. I turned onto one highway, moved on to another. There was a map in my bag, but I had already memorized my route. All that was left was to follow the road and plan how I would find the human who had been...*close* with the King when I got there. And in the meantime, I was able to survey the territory.

Outside of the city, the state was mostly abandoned. We had no use for much of the land in this area. Our efforts were concentrated on keeping the remaining humans in captivity, finding natural resources, and understanding their technology. We were mining, logging, building, and changing. Soon, this continent would be ours. But for now, aside from small military settlements, it was mostly empty– at least, empty of humans.

It had been ten years since we had swept through this land, killing most of the humans and shutting away the rest. The changes had been astronomical. The air was clearer, what was left of the cities was quiet, and nature had begun to reclaim its own. Deer gathered by the roads, lingering in the shade of overgrown trees. Wildflowers sprouted from cracks in the asphalt. The land was a blank canvas. And I knew precisely what I was going to make with it. But that was a very long-term plan, and I had to concentrate on my current route. The rest would follow.

The sun was rising when I passed a sign that read "Charlottesville, VA."

Only 2,600 miles to go.

45 ROBIN

I HEAR A CRASH...THEN the sound of metal twisting. Chaos fills the sky. I am small and afraid. I cry out. Then I am hit with a powerful scent. Something is burning. Smoke. Fire!

I was brought back to the present by a gentle shaking. The hand on my shoulder caused me to tense up at the unexpected contact, and I felt my muscles prepare to fight. My wrists again tested their bindings but the rope held firm. I was trapped, and growing fearful, when a voice sounded from the next cell.

"Hey, are you all right?"

The Cat's concerned tone put my fears to rest. I sat up as the remnants of my dream bled away.

"I'm sorry to wake you. It was just—well, you were shouting and writhing like you were on fire," he said. "Do you get nightmares often?"

"Yes." I didn't mention that my worst dreams were always memories. "I apologize for the noise."

"It's all right." He considered me with suspicious yellow eyes. "You were the one in the woods, right? With the hood? I thought you were a human."

"So did all my friends. That's why I'm in here."

"But you're one of us. A Wyrforra."

"Yes, but only in biology. I was raised by humans and I joined the Resistance to protect them. But I kept a few major details about myself hidden and now they don't trust me. What's your story?"

"I was a soldier and now I'm a prisoner."

"Gotcha."

There was a moment of silence between us. He was still trying to judge me. This Cat was definitely the suspicious type.

"My name is Tylos."

"Robin." I offered my hand—or hands, rather, as they were tied together. It took him a moment to accept the handshake.

"I'm still adapting to human customs. I haven't been here long and I've spoken to few of them."

"You seem to know Arianna."

He paled and stopped meeting my gaze. "I fought her on the battlefield. That's all."

The Cat was lying, but I decided to leave the matter alone. I had a feeling I would learn the whole truth eventually.

"So, Robin. What do you think they're going to do to us?"

"If I had to guess, Tylos," I said with a sigh, "they're going to kill us."

46 DAIRE

THE CONCRETE CEILING above my cot looked exactly the same as yesterday. The nightstand and scattered belongings stood in their usual places. My bed was just as uncomfortable as before. Nothing was out of place. But everything was different.

I had never really experienced nightmares, or any dreams much at all that I could remember. Fox said that was because I was always daydreaming. But it wasn't pleasant daydreams that haunted me as I tried to fall asleep. No, it was familiar voices, flashing images...tainted memories. I slammed my pillow down over my face but they wouldn't stop. I couldn't keep them from replaying, over and over.

Our first mission, all those years ago.

The three of us creep across the rooftop. I have a knife, Fox carries his crossbow, and Robin has only her fists. She leads the way, fearless and silent with confidence. We reach the edge and duck behind an air conditioning unit.

"Why'd we get stuck with the new girl?" Fox mutters under his breath.

"She was the only one who agreed to come. We couldn't exactly ask Cap who else was available," I say. We're defying orders and going on

our own mission, like the young and reckless teenagers we are. "Let's go over the plan one last time."

"The convoy will be here in a few minutes. Recon said there are two vehicles and ten Cats." Her voice doesn't betray a hint of anxiety. "When they're in position, I'll run out and stop them. I'll keep them distracted—"

"While I take the supplies out of one car and load them into the other, so we get everything." My voice isn't nervous either, only excited. "Then I'll drive off to the south while Robin runs north."

"And I cover your asses so y'all can escape." Fox loads his crossbow. "Then we rendezvous at the Fort. Any questions?"

"I've got one. If Cats are basically immune to small-caliber bullets, how are those arrows going to stop them?" asks Robin.

"First off, they're bolts. Second, take a look at the tip of 'em." Fox holds one up so its black point reflects the moonlight. "It's three-sided, like a trench knife, with barbs at the end, so once this goes into ya, it ain't coming out very easily. I'd like to see them Cats heal with a stick stuck in 'em."

"That's brilliant!" She smiles, and Fox blushes ever so slightly. He's warming up to her.

"They're my own design. They'll also stick to—"

"You can brag later," I interrupt. "They're coming!"

We hear the cars before we see them, and the three of us silently move into position. Fox takes his place at the edge of the roof, overlooking the street. Robin and I crouch by the fire escape and wait for his signal. After a moment, he turns to us and nods.

"Okay," I whisper. "Let's—"

She jumps from the roof. I can only stare in shock as Robin lands easily in a crouch and sprints for the street. How did she—? But there's no time to wonder. I run down the fire escape stairs and reach the street just as she's drawing the Cats' attention. In an instant, she's standing in the middle of the street, and the drivers screech to halt, more out of reflex than fear of running her over. The Cats are shouting in confusion and piling out of the vehicles.

"Hey guys, you missed a human!" Robin calls out to the crowd. She flashes a defiant smile and rests her hands on her hips.

I watch with dismay as they swarm her, but my horror turns to astonishment as she starts to fight. She's incredible. She dips and dodges, moving like a sidewinder. She sees an opening, strikes with an open hand, and a Cat falls. More surround her, but she spins and slides out of the way, leading them on a chase. She's still smiling, almost laughing. She's a mouse toying with cats.

Something shoots past me, within inches of my face. I whirl to see a Cat behind me, sprawled on the ground with a bolt through her stomach. I had almost let her sneak up on me while I was busy not doing my job. I make a mental note to thank Fox later, and dash to the first car.

The trunk is filled with boxes and I rush to move them to the other car. Robin is keeping the eight remaining Cats entertained, so I meet no resistance. I finally get it loaded and move to the driver's seat. The keys are in the ignition. I honk the horn, and the Cats all turn their attention to me. I wait long enough to see Robin start to run while their backs are turned before I throw the car in gear and drive the other way. In my rearview mirror I see a few Cats try to chase Robin and me, only to meet resistance in the form of a bolt to the gut. We make our escape without a single injury. The mission is an astounding success.

But the happiness I feel has nothing to do with that. I'm wrapped up in an obscured face, a black hood, and a smile. I am...

I dragged myself painfully from the memory. I no longer wanted to relive any of those times I loved. I couldn't think back without seeing everything I had been so blind to. Every recalled smile made the sting of her betrayal hurt even more. My happy refuge of memories was torn down.

The concrete ceiling above my cot looked the same, not a crack in the smooth gray stone. But I was broken.

47 ODYRA

I HAD JUST CROSSED into eastern Tennessee when it started to snow. It was just a light dusting, but I stopped to pull the roof on regardless. The mountain roads were steep and curved, and patches of ice hid under the powder snow. Luckily I was practiced in dealing with winter.

The wind began to pick up on once I lost the mountain's protection. My visibility vanished as the world outside the windscreen turned white. I drove slowly, but the tires were losing traction. Finally, I began to make out large dark shapes on the horizon.

A town.

It seemed like hours of slow driving before I finally reached it. The wind and snow prevented me from reading the sign, but I crawled forward, hoping to find some shelter. Eventually, I found a building with a large open garage—a mechanic's workshop. I pulled the red car inside.

The winds fought against me as I dragged the garage door down, but once I did I was able to fully take in my surroundings. It was a small room, barely enough space for me and the car. There were oil and tools cluttering racks on the walls, and everything had a thin layer of dust, turning the whole room into a shade of gray.

"Well," I said out loud. "I suppose I'm sleeping in the car."

I started to reach for my bag but froze as the faintest of sounds reached me. Movement...something rustling among the tools. The sound was so soft I could almost believe I had imagined it. But I waited for a long moment to be sure. And then I heard breathing.

I was calm as I pulled knives from my bag. I twirled them in my hands, letting the light shine off them in an attempt to scare whoever was in the room with me.

"Where are you hiding?" I said, raising my voice, friendly. "No need to be afraid. You can—"

Something moved behind a pile of crates. I readied my weapons, preparing to strike as the human crept out...

But it wasn't a human. It was a dog. A black, medium-sized, skinny, shaggy mutt. Still holding my knives, I watched it suspiciously. *Was it aggressive?*

It stepped toward me, head low, eyes wide. But it wasn't growling or showing teeth. Its mouth opened slightly and it wheezed a little. The dog took another hesitant step, its eyes regarding me with careful hope.

"I'm not giving you any food," I told it.

The dog's wheezing grew more intense and it struggled to let out a weak bark.

"What's wrong with you?" I approached it, and though it shied away at first, it let me kneel by him. I identified the problem immediately. A thick red collar was digging into his neck, so tight it was cutting off air.

"You've been on your own a long while, hmm?" I said, keeping a low voice so I didn't startle the animal. I petted it with one hand and used my other to position my knife against his neck. With a quick motion I cut through the collar. I pulled it off his neck, leaving a ring of raw skin and matted fur. His wheezing slowed into a pant, and then stopped.

I examined the collar and found a rusted nameplate. "So your name is Lucky." He licked my hand, tail wagging slightly. "Well, I suppose it's fitting. Your body heat in the car will be helpful, so I won't kick you out into the blizzard. Hop into the passenger's seat."

I held the door open and the skinny dog jumped in. I took the driver's seat and reclined into an uncomfortable makeshift bed. Lucky rested his head on the center console. His big chocolate eyes were blinking to sleep when I drifted off.

48 ROBIN

AFTER A FEW DAYS, I figured out what prison was really designed to do. It gives the inmate the one thing that can slowly destroy anyone: too much time to think. And I had such awful things to think about.

Lying on my cot, I thought for the millionth time about what I was going to do. I suppose I could appeal to Cap, explain everything to my friends, and maybe get let out of my cell—only to be despised and distrusted by the people I depended on. I could try to escape, confirm my friends' suspicions, and enter a terrifying world with nothing and no one. Or I could do nothing, and wait for them to execute or banish me. No matter what happened, I would lose everything and everyone I cared about.

Unless I could run away from it all. I could escape from all this pain and hatred and fear and just leave. I'd never have to look back, never regret, never mourn over what I lost. I could just step away from it all. And it would be so easy.

My escape was in my sock, right where I had left it. All I had to do was...

No! Fight it! I screamed silently at myself. *You don't want to go out that way! You're a warrior. You live and die on the battlefield. You don't want to go out like this!*

But the pain is too much. I'm being crushed by loss. I have nothing left to live for and no hope for things to get better. There's nothing I can do to drag myself out of this situation. I'm broken. And escape is right there, right within reach.

Come on, fight it! Think of those you'd leave behind and how devastated they'd be. How would Daire feel?

He'd be glad I saved him the trouble!

The weight of that thought hit me like a bullet. Daire...my best friend...would be better off without me. Everyone would. And the knowledge of that crushed me. After that, I lay very still for a very long time. I feared that if I let myself move at all...I would end everything.

49 ARIANNA

I'D BE LYING if I said I didn't notice the way Tylos looked at me when I came to see him. I would sit on the ground outside his cell and he would lean forward, as though sitting an inch closer would erase all distance between us. His posture would change, too. He'd sit a little straighter, and sometimes reach out toward the bars as though reminding himself that they were still there. And his eyes. They lost all the suspicion that used to haunt their yellow depths.

He told me everything he could think of about his homeland. He told me about great cities built into snowscapes, harvesting the blistering storms into wind energy, using the harsh environment to their advantage. He described how the Cats would observe us and copy our technology, and sometimes our culture. He told me how, when they learned about plans for satellites in the 1940s, they coated their buildings in white or reflective paints in case we were ever able to take pictures from space. Some territories, he said, even rebuilt their cities beneath the snow. He told me everything he could think of.

It was incredibly frustrating. Part of me wanted him to fight back, refuse my answers, curse me, anything but be so goddamn helpful. I didn't know how to respond to his search for approval, his honesty. It tore me apart.

Finally, I asked him. "Why are you telling me all this? Do you want the humans to win? Don't you have any loyalty?" I was trying so hard to make him angry.

"No, that's not it," he answered, calm and sincere. God damn him. "I don't want the humans to win. I don't want anyone to win. Do you remember what we talked about, that night in the cave?"

For some reason, I blushed and avoided his eyes.

"I don't want anyone else to die in this war, Arianna," he continued. "Maybe, if the humans can gather enough information to be seen as an actual threat to the Wyrforra...well, maybe they'll consider a truce. That's what I want."

"So you think we—the humans and the Wyrforra—can just live together, peacefully?"

"No." He sighed. "I don't. But I can hope."

"Don't be naive!" I had been kneeling, but I jumped to my feet and slammed my hand against the bars. He jumped, and I glowered at him. "That will never happen! We can never—I mean, they can never..."

Realizing my mistake, I turned to leave. But Tylos caught my sleeve in his bound hands. His eyes implored me to stay.

"Why not?" he almost whispered. "Look at us. When this is over... we could be friends. Why not humans and Wyrforra?"

My heart shook, but I kept my tone firm, unyielding. "Maybe. But we are not representatives of our species, Tylos. And we are *not* friends."

He let go of my sleeve. I turned my face toward the door so I couldn't see the pain in his eyes as he recoiled from my betrayal.

"Those days in the cave," I said, "we were only prolonging the inevitable. One day, one of us is going to kill the other. And *I* will not hesitate."

As I left, I prayed that I had been cruel enough to sever all ties. I could only hope that he hated me as much as I hated myself.

50 PORT

"Y'ALL ARE CRAZY," Fox told the group.

"I have to agree. This is a really, really terrible idea." They kept moving. "Shouldn't we at least consult the Seven before we do this? They should be the ones making these decisions."

"I agree. And there are other ways to test this," protested Dr. Hanson.

"This is the best test we could possibly do," said Truman. "It'll be fine."

I could tell by Cap's tight jaw line that he wasn't happy with this, but he led us along anyway. The five of us continued to the basement in silence.

The door guards saw the look on Cap's face and let us in. We walked until we reached Robin's cell. She was sitting on her cot, facing the Cat in the next cell over. Robin was surprised to see us but there was no fear in her expression.

"Cap?" she said, sounding almost hopeful. It was heartbreaking.

He took a deep breath before speaking. "Robin, as you know, we are always trying to better understand our enemy so we can fight them more effectively."

"Yes, of course." She rose to her feet. "So you're asking for my help to understand the Cats?"

Truman stepped up to the cell. "We're not asking."

I saw a muscle in her jaw tighten as she looked to him, and then back to Cap. "Fine. What do you want to know?"

He reached into his coat and withdrew a pistol, leveling it at Robin. Her eyes widened and she sent a panicked glance to Fox. He couldn't meet her eye.

"I do not condone this," said Dr. Hanson.

"She'll be fine. I won't kill her," replied Truman, releasing the safety.

"*You* won't shoot her." Cap took the gun from his hands. "I will. I won't hit any internal organs or bones. It'll be as safe as possible."

"That don't make this right," said Fox. "There are two other Cats in here. Why does it have to be Robin?"

To everyone's surprise, the Cat next to Robin spoke. "My injury has healed. You can shoot me. And the other guy is too loud to have been seriously injured."

"He's sick," I told the Cat. "A few days ago, he got hold of a sharp rock and carved pictures of eyes into his arms. I don't think we should be taking chances with him. And you may have healed a lot but Dr. Hanson says you're still at risk. Really, we shouldn't be shooting anyone."

"I said they're *all* at risk. Cap, come to your senses. We *cannot—*" Dr. Hanson stopped as soon as she saw the look on Cap's face. Earlier, he had explained to me and Fox privately that this matter was outside of his control. Truman had been gaining influence. Apparently being proved right about Robin had earned him some clout around the Fort. There was a *petition,* signed by a staggering number of people, which threatened action if this "experiment" didn't happen. Cap had made it clear to us that he didn't want this to happen, but wouldn't be able to keep people from rioting if it didn't. Either way, he told us, there was going to be blood.

"It's okay. I'll be fine, really." Robin stood straight, balled up her fists, and braced herself. "Go ahead, Cap."

"Please don't," breathed Fox.

"We *have* to," growled Truman.

"Shoot me instead!" insisted the Cat in the next cell.

"Are you ready, Robin?" Cap asked. He raised the gun.

"Yes."

She didn't even flinch at the gunshot. Blood began to weep from the lower right side of her stomach. For a moment, no one said a word.

"Let me see!" Dr. Hanson pushed through the crowd and knelt at the bars. "It looks normal...except the bleeding has already slowed! How does it feel?"

"It pinches a bit." Robin had paled considerably, but she held a stoic face through the pain.

"The wound is closing itself, healing at a greatly advanced speed. It's got to be the platelets!" the doctor exclaimed. "You must have supercharged platelets that clot and close wounds far more effectively than a human's. I bet they're helping your internal organs in some ways, too."

"But how?" said Truman, half wonder and half frustration. "How did they become immune to bullets?"

"They're not immune to bullets," answered the doctor. "It's a natural defense against some kind of extreme environment. If I had to guess, I'd say the Cats come from somewhere with high winds and rugged terrain. Their ancestors probably had to deal with many things that would cut their skin, like sharp rocks or hail, so the Wyrforra developed this natural defense."

"Great." Truman was getting more and more irritable. "Now we know for sure why bullets seem to be useless against Cats. So how does this help us?"

"It doesn't. And I could've found that out by doing a blood test, you buffoon!" Truman gaped with shock as Dr. Hanson stared him down. "Now all of you, get out so I can patch this up. All of you, go! Now!"

We obeyed, rushing from the room like the wrath of God was on our tails.

51 ODYRA

IN THE MORNING, I decided to take the dog with me.

Including my slow blizzard driving, I had been on the road about twenty hours total. But the weather had cleared up by morning so I could see the road ahead of me again. However, it was still covered in a thin sheet of ice and snow, so Lucky and I were forced to cross into Arkansas at a crawl. I stopped a few hours past the state line as my car was running low on fuel. I let Lucky out, half-hoping he would wander off. But after doing what he had to, the dog waited patiently as I emptied the gas can into the tank.

I paused to lean against the car. The wind had picked up again, and I couldn't see or hear anything past a few feet away. In an effort to save food, I hadn't eaten yet. I had slept for a few hours, but it was anything but restful. The trip was, thus far, surprisingly easy. I hadn't had to kill anyone yet, or sneak around a large group of enemies, or set any huge fires as a distraction. I was starting to get bored.

Then Lucky started growling. For a moment, I thought the dog had turned hostile. I carefully brought my hand to the back of my belt and gripped the small knife resting there. When I turned to the dog, he was crouching low. His fur was standing on end and his ears were laid back, his teeth bared. They looked sharp, and he was a rather large dog. I tensed as I saw his muscles flex, but there was something off about him. Then all at once, I realized it was his eyes.

They weren't looking at me.

I sensed the creature before I heard it. It had moved quietly, hiding in the snow, so by the time I was aware of whatever it was, it was close. I forced myself to stand perfectly still as I tried to figure out exactly where it was. And then I felt hot breath on the back of my neck.

I whirled to face it, but it caught me mid-spin with some large, black blunt weapon. I was thrown sprawling across the ground. I sat up immediately, reaching again for my knife, but the sight of the thing nearly pulled the air from my lungs.

I had never seen one before, so I didn't know then that I was facing an unusually large black bear who had probably been hibernating nearby. What I did know right then was that a seven-foot-tall monster was looming over me, about to smash his huge paws into my skull.

I rolled away from the impact and sprung to my feet, finally locating my knife and holding it in front of me. The bear roared, revealing menacing teeth that were longer than the pocketknife I was relying on. The thing surged at me again, quick for its size, and again I was forced to throw myself to the side. His jaws closed on open air and I readied myself to run. But from the looks of it, there was nowhere to go except the car, which was behind the huge creature. He lumbered toward me, and I examined my options.

I could fight, and definitely die. If I had my short swords, I might stand a chance, but I had left them in the car.

I could run, and get chased down, and die. The bear was quick, in its native element, and the snow would slow me down. Besides, as far as I knew, there was nowhere within miles to run to where I would be safe.

That left me with making a break for the car. If I got in and managed to start it without the bear eating me, I could drive away faster than it could run. It was a great plan, except that the car was on the other side of the bear.

"Fight it is, then," I said.

The beast roared, rose up on his hind legs and took a step toward me. I prepared myself for what would be my final fight. The bear raised one paw to swipe at me.

Something flashed past, and instead of knocking me off my feet, the bear found himself motionless in confusion. I could only blink in surprise as a medium-sized, underfed, shaggy dog latched onto the monster, crunching down on its leg. The bear shook and roared but Lucky refused to let go. Blood welled from the skin between his teeth and he growled, brave and righteous. Finally Lucky let go of the animal and moved to stand in a protective stance between the bear and me.

I was amazed with the dog's bravery as the two growled at each other. Tentatively, I took a step back. But the bear was focused on Lucky, and didn't even seem to notice me any more as I edged away. I stepped farther and farther away as the two stared each other down. Lucky lunged and snapped at the bear's snout and he roared in response. I took that as my cue to run for the car.

The bear looked to me in surprise as I sprinted past it, but the dog snapped again, reclaiming the bear's attention. I threw myself in the car and started the engine, which thankfully rumbled to life. Without hesitation, I stepped on the gas and sped away.

The road was curved, and I quickly lost sight of the bear in my rearview mirrors. Without really thinking about it, I slowed down. I watched the mirrors more than the road ahead, slowing to only two or three miles an hour. *Come on,* I thought, *come on.*

A shaggy dog appeared in the mirror, sprinting toward the car to make up for the distance. I smiled to myself as I stepped on the brakes and leaned over to open the passenger-side door. Lucky caught up with me and barked happily as he jumped inside. I stared at the dog as he stared up at me, panting happily. His bloodstained tongue lolled from the side of his mouth. I shook my head and reached behind me, retrieving a box from the back.

"All right, Lucky," I said. "I'll share my lunch with you this time. You've earned it."

He barked happily as I tossed him a chunk of meat. "But don't get used to it."

52 ROBIN

THE SOUND OF WAVES...GENTLE...DARK...

A warm, loving embrace...Mother's? Father's?

Being rocked into comfort by caring arms...or the ocean... Sweet whispers...strange words...peace...calm...

Then the crash.

Screams, running, chaos. What did we hit? We're sinking. Rocks? No one said the coast had rocks. Why didn't the humans—

Rushing cold water. The screams crescendo. Being carried out the door, down the hall, to the deck. Pale light amplified through a sky of gray. The light and smoke hurt my eyes. Smoke?

The sea is on fire. The tainted air holds the scent of salt and burning bodies. I see those who tried to swim begin to float, facedown, before my eyes are covered by a wet jacket.

Take this, little one, and hold on tight.

I am given a plank of wood.

Let the waves take you. Don't try to swim. Keep your clothes wet. Watch for fire.

I feel myself being lowered to water. I'm floating on the plank.

Let God protect you, my child. Be safe.

The voice fades, all sounds become distant, quiet. All except the waves. I'm rocked for hours, maybe days. I lose track as my world becomes only the rocking and the cold, unfeeling water. Everything goes black.

Then the world stops moving. The sudden stillness is frightening. Strange sounds assault me...like the sea bird's cry, only melodic. Pleasant.

And twigs breaking. Footsteps. Someone's coming. I freeze in terror, but can't control my shaking body. What do I do? I'm so scared. The footsteps approach—and stop right before me. I can't move. I can't look. Help me.

Are you all right?

A young voice, full of concern. Sincere. A child? I peek out from under the cloth. I meet a pair of kind brown eyes.

Are you okay, little girl?

Am I? I wonder. Am I okay? I want to answer the boy, but my voice doesn't seem to work. Perhaps it never has.

Little girl?

CLANK!

Though I was startled out of my dream, I kept myself from jumping. Instead, I remained laying calmly against my cot and slowly opened my eyes. A large man stood just outside my cell. I didn't know his name, but he looked familiar. He had probably fought beside me at one point. He probably thought I was a hero up until a few days ago.

He stared at me, and kicked the cell bars again, resulting in another painfully loud *clank*. He looked heavily muscled, but I was more worried about the set of keys dangling from his crossed arms. He probably took them right off the hook on the wall. There would have been no one to stop him if the guards hadn't.

I was still in pain from getting shot, but I mustered all my remaining patience. "Can I help you?"

Wordlessly, the brute unlocked my cell door and swung it wide.

He stepped inside, and his huge form blocked most of the light from outside, casting me in shadow. "I'm gonna enjoy this," he said, cracking his knuckles for extra effect.

I took my cue to get up, leaning on the wall for support as I got unsteadily to my feet. Normally, I wouldn't blink at fighting a guy like this. But I was hardly in the best condition, due mostly to a recent bullet wound, and on top of that my hands were literally tied. I didn't like my odds.

I raised my bound hands, palms outward, in a gesture of peace. "Hey now, let's take a deep breath." I kept my tone low, attempting to diffuse the situation. Getting him to realize it wasn't worth it was my best chance at avoiding a beating. "Getting your hands bloody won't solve anything. Not to mention, you don't want to beat up an already injured person."

"It'll make me feel better."

"But is it worth dealing with Cap and everyone? They won't be happy. And seriously, you'd hit someone who just got shot?"

He snorted. "Are you kidding? You're the Cat that lied to us. The whole Fort wants to kick your ass."

"Okay, fair enough, but think about all I've done for this place. Does me being a Cat cancel out all the work I've done?"

"How do we know you haven't been spying on us this whole time?"

"Uh... I pinky promise I wasn't?" I said, holding up my hands and smiling in what I hoped was a disarming way. In my defense, I was far too tired at that point to think of something more clever to say.

Apparently he didn't appreciate my gesture. He reared back and threw a right-handed punch. Even with my only weapons—my hands —basically unusable, I still had my superior speed and cat-like, or Cat-like, flexibility. I was slowed down a bit by my injury, but that still left me faster than my opponent. I ducked under his punch easily, sidestepping to the other side of the cramped cell.

"You're gonna have to be a little faster. Try putting more weight on the balls of your feet." I was having fun with him now, but he didn't seem amused. He roared, throwing another punch in my direction. I danced aside, and his hand connected with the concrete wall. There was a loud crack that sounded like knuckles breaking. He screamed in pain.

I hoped that getting hurt would send him running, but it only made him madder. His face was red and contorted with rage. I stopped smiling. I backed away from him until I was cornered against the cell wall. I considered making a dash for the exit, but there wasn't nearly enough room for me to get around him. I was cornered.

I kept light on my feet, ready to spin away the second he made a move. But he was getting smarter. He pulled his right hand back into a fist, and I watched it. He feinted, and I jumped to the left. I didn't notice when his left hand snaked out and grabbed my shoulder, getting a firm hold of my shirt and pinning it to the wall. *Shit.* I was really stuck now.

The man smiled maliciously at me. I squared my shoulders, raised my chin and met his sneer dead-on. I did not show any fear. He once again raised a fist, but this time I didn't let myself flinch. I had tried reasoning and fighting. There was no place to run. There was nothing left but to take what was coming.

His fist connected solidly with my face. I could taste the blood from a cut in my lip, and I'd have a nasty bruise around my cheek. Silently, I turned my head and spat out blood.

"Here's a tip," I told him. "An open hand does a lot more damage than a fist." I didn't let any pain show. It hurt, of course, but I had experienced worse, and I didn't want him to think he had won. I wasn't down for the count yet.

"I don't need any advice from you!" he shouted, even redder than before.

"Yeah, you do," I said honestly. As much as I wanted to have fun with the guy, I knew I shouldn't antagonize him any more...but hey, what the hell. I wasn't in a healthy mindset, and I figured if I was going to get my ass kicked anyway, I might as well deserve it.

"Trust me, pal. You need all the advice you can get." I grinned wickedly. "You hit like a bitch."

Now *that* set him off. He looked like he was about to explode. He dropped my shirt, rearing his whole body back for his next punch. I could see he was putting all of his body weight into this one. I considered dodging now that I was free, but I thought better of it. Maybe if I let him land this one he'd leave me alone.

The monster roared, and I braced myself for what would be a devastating impact. He raised his fist...only to have it caught before he could swing. We both turned to see a man with dark hair standing in the shadows, one hand locked over my attacker's wrist.

"Who—" my assailant snarled.

The man punched him hard right below the ribs. The attacker released me as he doubled over in pain. He reeled backward as the shadowed man brought his knee into the attacker's face, audibly breaking his nose. Then, with one well-placed punch, my attacker was thrown to ground, moaning in pain.

The other man stepped into the light to examine him, making sure he wasn't about to get up and fight. Then, my hero's dark, shaggy hair swung in front of his eyes as he turned to look at me.

"Daire." Even as I said his name, I felt my stomach drop. *Had he forgiven me? Or did he still hate me? And if he did, why save me?* I took a step toward him, but only one. He said nothing.

"Daire, thank you," I said. "If he had landed that hit, I would've been..."

I trailed off, unable to continue. The look on his face...I had never seen it before. He stared at me, and for once his eyes looked cold—indifferent. I took a step back as the force of his gaze shot through me. Hatred I could take. But I never thought he would ever look at me with such chilling apathy. That look hurt a thousand times more than any punch.

Daire shoved my attacker out the door and stepped out after him, pulling it closed. But as he closed the door, he froze, staring at me. I was about to ask him what was wrong when I felt blood drip down my chin from the cut on my lip. It was nothing, a minor injury at worst, but it seemed to shake him. When he saw the blood, something I didn't quite catch flickered through his eyes. For a moment, his expression softened into...pain? Regret? But in an instant the emotion was gone. Daire finished locking my cell door, slipped the keys into his pocket, and left.

"Wait!" I called after him, rushing to the door. "Let me talk to you!"

But he was gone.

I resisted the urge to curl up in a ball and cry. I was a fighter. I couldn't let myself cave to self-pity. Instead, I held my head high and tried to forget the way my best friend had looked at me. Not that he was my friend anymore.

"Robin, are ya all right?" A familiar figure approached from the opposite way that Daire had gone.

"Yes, I'm okay. Thanks, Fox."

"Thanks for what?"

"Caring. Did Daire tell you what happened?"

"Not exactly." He looked down at the attacker, still on the floor. Fox nudged him with his foot, but he just groaned. "I was worried something like this would happen. Looks like he got you pretty good. You say Daire was here?"

"Yeah. He got here right after that guy landed his lucky shot. Wait, how did Daire know to come down here?"

"Well." Fox gave me a bashful smile. It was nice that someone was treating me the same as they had before. "I might've mentioned to him that some mean-looking fella was making his way to the basement for some reason. The guards will let anybody in here if they're not paying attention."

"Why not come down yourself? You could've taken this guy."

"I think we both know the answer to that, Robin. But it looks like I should've intervened sooner."

That was true. I understood why Fox had hinted to Daire that I might be in danger. It was an experiment, to see what Daire would do. It was comforting to know that he chose to come and help me. That maybe...maybe a part of him still cared about me.

"It's all right. Thank you, Fox."

He nodded. "I'll be at the guard station by the door. I won't let anyone else near ya. Just holler if you need me."

"I will. Thank you."

53 ALMYRR

GENERAL HELLMAN WAS PROBABLY the friendliest person I had ever met. He had set up his station in a building called "Casino" just outside the capital. He seemed to like the brightly colored machines and billboards, though for the moment they were shut off and shoved to the sides of the room. A single hanging floodlight illuminated a circle over a soft green table.

The general's dark gray mustache quivered as he lined up a long stick with a white ball on the table. He leaned down far enough for his beard to touch the table and the light reflected off his bald head.

"It's called pool," he said, striking the ball. "Would you like to try, Almyrr?"

"No, thank you, sir," I responded, hearing the stiffness in my own voice.

"Call me Byrron. Besides, as the High King's personal bodyguard and hit man, I'm pretty sure you outrank me."

I resisted the urge to dispel my discomfort by pacing. Byrron Hellman was unusually informal for a Wyrforra. Talking so openly about rank and position was considered impolite, as was playing games during a business meeting.

"So he made you his heir," he said. "I figured he'd do something like that. The other generals bet that he would marry that spymaster, Warringgate. But I knew he wouldn't get married. No, not Erenvyr."

This piqued my curiosity. "How did you know?"

"I've known the King for a very long time. He'll never marry, not even to have a biological heir. He's just not the type."

"Well, that's not unusual." I had to force myself not to say "sir."

"Not many of us are. Is there a reason you thought the King would marry?"

"When he was young, he used to talk about building a kingdom, starting with his own heirs. He had grand plans. But I suppose we all change over time."

His eyes crinkled, deepening the lines. I sensed he wasn't telling me the whole truth.

"Did you know..." Byrron's tone was suddenly cheerful as he changed the subject, "that most humans married for love? Earlier in their history, matrimony was predominantly for business or alliance, like us. But it became an arrangement for two infatuated people, regardless of social standing. Can you imagine entering into a legal agreement for something as fleeting as emotion?"

I forced a broad smile. "Humans are such impulsive creatures."

General Hellman laughed. "Indeed they are! So, did you come here just to tell me of your new position or is there something else?"

"There is, actually. The High King requests your presence."

"Oh well. This can't be good. But there's no sense in delaying, I suppose. Let's make haste to the White House."

54 PORT

DAIRE HAD BEEN quiet for the past few days. But then, all at once, he was very, very loud.

"You *shot* her?" He was practically screaming. It was unclear whether he was directing his outrage at Cap, Fox, Truman, Dr. Hanson, or the entire room. Either way, it was an uncomfortable situation.

Cap refused to back down. He stood tall, arms crossed, staring right at Daire. I was not so brave. I half hid behind Fox, refusing to make eye contact with anyone. Dr. Hanson seemed agitated to be dragged away from her work. Truman, to his merit, managed not to look too smug. Daire had taken an aggressive stance, and the air was charged with tension.

"Yes, I shot her," said Cap, fearless. "I shot her in order to better understand the Cats. I shot her in a place that even a human could survive with a bullet wound. She'll be fine."

"Why do you even care about that?" asked Truman. "If she dies, the doctor can do an autopsy and learn even more. It'd be a win-win."

There was rage in Daire's eyes when he turned from Cap to Truman and back again.

"Why didn't you tell me?" he spat through gritted teeth. He wasn't shouting anymore, but somehow his quieter voice was more intimidating.

"You would have fought with me about it," replied Cap, his words like ice. "And besides, you didn't need to know."

"Didn't need to know? She was my—!" Daire exploded at Cap, grabbing him by the shirt. Everyone stepped forward to intervene but before we could, Cap had gripped Daire by the arm and slammed him face first into the wall. He pinned him there, twisting his arm behind his back. Daire hissed in pain but knew better than to struggle.

"You forget yourself." Cap's voice dripped with implied threat. "I am your commanding officer. I value your opinion but you will not speak disrespectfully to me. Don't make me tell you again."

"That's enough, both of you. There's been too much internal fighting. We need each other, especially right now." Dr. Hanson spoke with a calm tone that carried absolute authority.

Cap released Daire, who had calmed down enough to at least keep his mouth shut. He stormed out of the room, and I had a feeling he was going to go punch something. Fox sighed, and I sensed his painful empathy for his friend. But he also seemed...almost frightened of him.

"I've never seen Daire like that," he whispered to me, or perhaps to himself.

I reached forward and held his hand, offering comfort and support. He ran his thumb over mine, gratefully accepting the gesture. But I could still feel his fear. He was afraid of the fighting, and the Cats, the future, and whatever fresh hell would surface next. There was serious tension building in the Fort, and it was only a matter of time before something came of it. We were all afraid, and we had every reason to be.

55 ROBIN

A SHARP PAIN woke me in the middle of the night. The last of the morphine that Dr. Hanson gave me had finally worn off, and the full force of the bullet wound hit me like a brick. I rested a hand lightly across the bandage and felt a painful heat emanating from the wound. Super platelets or not, taking a .45 round to the gut wasn't agreeing with me. I had gotten a good look at the wound the last time the dressings were changed. The wound had closed itself but it still hurt, and the internal damage had yet to fully heal. It would undoubtedly leave a scar.

My face was throbbing, too, and the painful bruise had made it hard to fall asleep in the first place. Hopefully the bruise would fade before I woke in the morning.

If. If I woke in the morning.

Daire's eyes flashed through my mind. A different kind of pain—no less physical—flooded every surface of my body. The way he had looked down at me...I had never seen such loathing.

My pain faded momentarily as I was filled with a righteous anger. *He* was the one who had betrayed *me!* I had saved him so many times and he still thought I was against him. Did all those times I proved myself mean nothing? Did all those years of friendship mean...?

But the anger vanished just as fast as it had come. *How long?* I asked myself. *How long have I been lying to him? To all of them?* Despair crept through my veins, weighing me down. I wanted to blame Daire, or Cap, or some god, or anything. But I kept circling back to my own guilt.

What could I have done differently? Could I have told them on my own? No, the same thing would've happened. Could I have been upfront from the beginning? I would have been killed without hesitation. So what could I have done?

Nothing...except being born human.

In that moment, I hated myself more than ever before. I hated myself for things I could not control. I hated every feature that set me apart. I hated myself with such intensity that the force of it caused my wounds to ache.

Self-loathing left me with the sensation of feeling hated by forces internal and external. My whole life I had never felt such strong emotions. I was a warrior. I was used to fight or die, kill or be killed. Never before had I faced an attack from within. How do you defend against yourself?

I sat up slowly. I reached to my ankle and retrieved the capsule. And then I carefully lay back down, resting my head against the pillow.

Every movement was silent and deliberate as I placed the capsule between my teeth. I didn't bite, didn't move.

And I lay there, perfectly still, for that long night.

56 FOX

DR. HANSON HUNCHED OVER PAPERS, feverishly scanning medical reports and data just as she had been all day. As the hours passed, she had begun to mumble to herself.

"Platelets...yes, makes sense. But that doesn't explain the reduced organ damage or increased muscle efficiency...maybe a blood sample? No, not the right equipment."

Daire was leaning against a wall. His arms were crossed and he was staring at the ground. He certainly wasn't listening to the doctor. He was drifting in his own thoughts, and from the cloud that hung over him, I guessed they weren't happy ones. I sensed he was still seething about his confrontation with Cap, though he was most likely angry with himself most of all.

I was caught between Dr. Hanson's mutterings and Daire's silence. I cleared my throat in an effort to ease the uncomfortable silence.

"You know, Doc, there's somethin' that's been bothering me about Robin."

From the corner of my eye, I saw Daire flinch when I said her name. Dr. Hanson finally lifted her gaze.

"When we first met her," I continued, "we tested her to make sure she was human. I was there, with Daire and Cap. I remember it."

I could see Daire recoil at the thought. He would remember it too, of course. It was the first time he had seen her face.

"We shined a light into her eyes and her pupils stayed round. They didn't shrink into a line like the other Cats' eyes did. That's how she convinced us."

I could see the gears turning in the doctor's head, but she was turning up empty just as I had. She shook her head and returned to her work.

"There might be an easy way to figure that out," she said. "You two, go ask her about it. I've got to get back to my research...find a way to..."

She trailed off, losing herself in thought. All of Daire's muscles had tensed when the doctor asked him to talk to Robin. His facial features seemed to darken and I felt an intense fear of an impending confrontation between Robin and the unpredictable Daire.

I hobbled over to him as he turned for the doorway. He looked quizzically at me as I stopped him with a hand on his shoulder.

"I'll go. You gotta get on that scouting mission for Cap. Ain't that supposed to leave soon?" I asked. "I'd be less than useless in my current condition, so I'll stay behind and talk to her."

He stared at me for a moment, then nodded, turning away. He had relaxed, though only a little. He didn't have to say he was grateful; I already knew. I felt that there was something he wanted to tell me, but I decided to wait until he was ready to say that out loud.

57 ODYRA

I RAN COMPLETELY OUT of gas at the Nevada border. Winter was coming into its own, and the desert was relatively cold. Fortunately, the car sputtered to a stop near an abandoned town and I was able to find a few stores that hadn't been completely looted. There was no hope for food, of course, or decent medical supplies, but I was able to find a clothing store.

The sign was so caked with dirt that I couldn't make out the large red letters. Wooden boards spanned the door, doubtless the human shopkeeper's last-ditch attempt to protect his property. But the glass storefront had long ago shattered and a decade of wind and sand had smoothed the remaining shards. There was plenty of space to jump through.

"Come on, boy," I told the dog, then vaulted into the store. His nails skittered across the tile as he followed me, panting happily.

The store was dim and dust-caked, and it was hard to breathe without coughing on the stale air. Lucky's ears perked up as he scanned the store for danger, or maybe snacks. I approached a clothing rack with an assortment of odd, thick pieces of cloth arranged in colorful triangles. The rack was labeled "bikinis." The dog stared at the collection with a tilted head.

"Don't ask me," I told him. "I studied the humans' military tactics, not their...fashion."

I abandoned the "bikinis" and headed to a sign at the back of the room that read "Winter Wear." To my distaste, this section had been stripped mostly bare, probably by whatever Wyrforra squad had cleansed the town.

I found a black knitted cap that the tag called a "beanie." I pulled it down over my ears, pausing to rub my hands over the dark red fuzz beginning to grow on the previously shaved sides of my head. I tugged the hat over that, too, leaving only my long banded ponytail swinging free. After an exhaustive search, I found a pair of gloves, which turned out to be useless, as the material was cut off halfway up the fingers. I shrugged and put them on anyway. Better than nothing.

I felt a pressure against my leg and looked to see Lucky, leaning on me and wiggling his whole body in delight when I showed some attention.

"Hold on, boy. Just one more thing."

It didn't take me long to find what I was looking for. The store had a wide selection of accessories, and I selected a white bandana. I called the dog over and knelt, fastening the cloth loosely around his neck.

"There. That'll protect the raw spots where your old collar bit into your skin."

Lucky's tail slapped the dirty tile as he licked my cheek. Now that I had begun to show him some care, he rarely left my side and practically shook with excitement when I patted his head. But besides the incident with the bear, he had yet to prove himself very useful.

"All right, back outside." I hopped through the glass and he followed, surprisingly graceful for his size.

It was no longer snowing in the street, though the sky held its haunting gray. It was midday, but the clouds overhead were so thick that the sunlight seemed sparse as it was diffused through the air.

The wind teased at my hair but wasn't fierce enough to whistle through the buildings. The quiet was unnerving.

"Well," I sighed, setting off down the street. "Next stop, gas station."

Lucky padded along beside me, content. His tail swung lazily side to side, and his tongue hung from his mouth. He kept pace with me easily. It seemed he wanted to run ahead in playful bounds, but was reluctant to leave my side. He was more than happy to walk through the powder-snow carpet toward...well...at the moment, I didn't really know.

Then, Lucky's demeanor changed. His tail stopped moving, and he closed his jaw tight. I watched his ears swivel, and his hackles rose.

"Shhh, boy," I whispered, looking dead ahead. "I hear them, too."

The stranger showed himself, stepping casually from around the building. Lucky and I stopped, standing about thirty feet from him. I saw immediately that he was a Wyrforra, with a torn and dirty army uniform a few years out of date. His hair was shaggy and matted, and he hadn't bathed in a long while. He smiled a wide lopsided grin, and his teeth shone white against the dirt on his skin. *Deserter.*

"That's a real pretty animal you got there," said the man. "What's its name?"

Lucky bared his teeth. "Killer," I answered.

"Can I pet him, or does he bite?" He started toward us.

"*He* doesn't."

"Oh, I see. The pretty girl is scary." He chuckled. I reached for my knives.

Pain exploded in my head as something shattered against the back of my skull. My vision flashed white and I succumbed to darkness.

When I woke up, I was facedown on the ground, with the broken remains of a brick scattered nearby. Another Wyrforra pressed his knee into my back, and he had just managed to free my knives and throw them out of my reach. My first reaction was to push myself up, but my attacker grabbed my wrist, twisting my arm behind my back. The threat of a spiral fracture forced me to stay still. I craned my neck to get a look at the one holding me down—a large, muscular Wyrforra with bad teeth.

Barking drew my attention away from the man, and I looked up to see the other deserter trying to contain Lucky. He was gripping the dog's scruff and trying to subdue him, but Lucky squirmed and fought, snapping at the man, looking for purchase in his flesh.

That stupid dog inspired me, and I thrashed about as much as I could, attempting to throw the man off my back. But he wrenched my arm tighter, and I figured I'd need a better plan. I gave it a few more convincing wriggles, then lay still as if exhausted.

"Given up, eh? Good, it'll be easier for you that way." He half-whispered, close enough for his breath to burn like acid on my cheek. His grip loosened ever so slightly.

"Hey, could you give me a—*ah!*—hand here?" called the other one, amidst Lucky's barking and growling. The man gasped in pain when the dog's teeth finally found his hand, as he struggled to maintain control.

"I'll be done in a minute!" the one on me shouted, turning his attention to his friend. "I just need to get her—"

I used the distraction to get my remaining arm under me and brace the balls of my feet against the ground. He was cut off as I sprang upward, threw my weight back, and sent both of us flying. I had planned our trajectory so he landed hard on his back with me on top of him. The momentum more than doubled my weight, and I heard the breath rush from him as he got the wind knocked out of him. He released my wrist in surprise, and before he could regain his bearings, I was standing over him. I pressed one thick boot into his neck.

His eyes bulged, first from pain, then from shock as he finally noticed what I was wearing.

"That armor—you're from the King's elite spy unit." He coughed. I pressed harder on his throat.

I leaned toward him, bending my knee and putting even more pressure on his windpipe. "I'm their leader," I told him.

Footsteps drew my attention to the other Wyrforra. He had dropped Lucky and run, sprinting as fast as he could away from me. The dog gave chase, snapping at his heels.

"If you don't kill me, I can show you where the nearest human resistance camps are," the Wyrforra pleaded. His voice shook. "P-please, ma'am, let me up. I'll draw you a map—I'll lead you there!"

I stared at him for a second before carefully removing my foot from his throat. He smiled with relief, and started to thank me. But before he could finish his statement, I swung my leg up and brought my heel down right where it had been. This time, I felt the cartilage in his trachea break under my heel as his windpipe collapsed. I left him gasping for air, scrabbling in the dirt, growing weaker and more panicked by the second as he fought for breath. I didn't look back when I heard him stop struggling and lay still.

I followed in the direction Lucky had chased the other Wyrforra. I found them only a block away, as the dog had trapped the man in a dead-end alley. Lucky growled, snapping whenever the terrified Wyrforra tried to get past him. I patted the dog's head as I walked to the man. He pressed his back to the wall, as though he were trying to escape through the bricks.

"Please," the pathetic man stuttered when I drew close. "Don't tell the King."

I almost laughed. Instead, I moved right up to him, leaning in to whisper in his ear. He drew back, but held his breath, afraid to move.

"He's not the one you should fear," I said simply.

With that, I grabbed a fistful of his hair and slammed his head against the wall. Once, twice, third time's the charm. When he collapsed, the alley was a scene of bright red graffiti, dripping down the brick. I didn't have to check to see if he was dead.

"Well done, Lucky," I said cheerfully. He wagged his tail, looking at me with brown eyes full of affection. "Let's go find some gas now, hmm? And a treat for you, too."

58 FOX

IT WAS A LONG, quiet walk down to where Cap wanted to meet. I was moving much better now, healed enough to walk without a limp. Dr. Hanson had patched me up good. I had to remember to thank her again.

I hadn't seen Daire since he left, and I was still waiting on an apology for what he said a few days ago. But I knew I only had to be patient. I knew Daire. He would make things right again.

The halls of the Fort were strikingly silent. Or rather, they weren't. They got quiet when I approached, as the people who used to greet me heartily stopped talking as I passed. Their eyes followed me. I could feel their questioning and scorn, but I didn't meet their eyes. I looked straight ahead, trying not to frown or show any emotion. Best not to give them another reason to stare.

After an uncomfortable walk, I met up with Cap. We were at the entrance to the Fort, right inside the outermost door. My attention was drawn to the floor, where a pile of metal and wood sat in a heap. The light was dim, and I couldn't make out the individual shapes until I squatted to look closer. At the top of the pile rested a machete, dulled with time but undoubtedly still effective. It shared space with combat knives, brass knuckles, bloodstained crowbars, and a score of other makeshift weapons.

Cap was staring with disgust at it all. His arms were crossed, and he seemed to be waiting for me to draw my own conclusions. But unfortunately for him, I was at a loss.

"Okay, I'll bite. What's with the weapons?"

"They were left behind," he said. My stomach dropped. At that point, I knew what he was going to say, but I had to ask anyway while I hoped against hope I was wrong.

"By who?"

"Soldiers. Ten of 'em. They decided that they couldn't stay anymore, so they took off. Left most of their weapons as a sign that they meant us no harm."

I straightened, rocking back on my heels. "No one's ever left the Fort before. Not for good," I said, mostly to myself.

"No one's ever wanted to." He rubbed his worn hands over his face. "They said they don't feel safe with a Cat here."

"It's only ten people."

"Yes, but how many more next time? We have to do something." He sighed. "Fox, what do you think we should do? I'm out of ideas."

"Well...we're still a democracy."

"You're right. We have to summon the Seven."

A moment of silence passed between us. When the Fort's governing body was needed, it was never for a happy reason.

"I'll go find Anna and Naveen," Cap said. "Tell them to spread word of a meeting, tonight."

I nodded. "I'll tell Arthur, Chris, and Aris. So that's six, counting you. We're missing—oh."

Silence descended again. The seventh member wouldn't be attending, I realized. She was locked in the basement.

Cap cleared his throat. "Tonight, just after sundown."

"Right."

59 DAIRE

FINALLY, we left on the scouting mission. I welcomed the adventure, longing to stretch my legs and explore. And maybe, if I was lucky, I would get to fight something.

We left at night. We kept the numbers small, in order to move quickly and quietly. There were five of us: Me, Port, Truman, and two others I didn't know personally. Kiana and Ladan, sisters who were originally from Iran. They were young; they had been only five years old when they had come to the United States, and the invasion had occurred a year later. But despite their age, they were quick, tough, and lethal. They were also quiet, but not just on the battlefield. Kiana and Ladan rarely spoke, and never to each other. They didn't seem to need to, as though there was some unspoken connection between them. They worked as a unit and fought as a team. If I had to guess, I'd say their cooperation was what made them so effective. I looked forward to seeing them in action.

We had only walked about three miles before nearing the coordinates the Cat had given us. When we closed in on them, the five of us stared at the building in disbelief.

"A bowling alley?" said Port. "This is the cache?"

I clenched my fists, letting my anger fight against the barriers I had been trying to construct. "That damned Cat. He's fooled us."

"Now hold on. Have you checked this place on any previous supply raids?" asked Truman.

"No," answered Port, thoughtful. "It's an unusual place to look. Which might mean...it's the perfect place to hide something."

Kiana and Ladan held eye contact with each other for half a second, then nodded to us.

"All right then," I said. "Let's go."

The door was locked, of course. Port suggested we try to find another way in, but I had a much more...satisfying idea. I could've kicked in the glass door, but I chose to punch it. *Robin would've said... well, that didn't matter. She wasn't here now.* A few quick jabs, the glass shattered, and I could reach the handle on the inside. My hand stung from a few small cuts as I unlocked it, but the blood on my knuckles felt good.

Naturally, it was dark inside. With the light from the doorway, I could just make out the shape of the lanes and the faded posters reading *"Bowling is a blast!"* The light barely showed that a decade's worth of dust hung over every surface, muting colors and painting the room a faded gray. No one appeared to have been to this place in a long while.

Truman was the first to step into the room, but Kiana grabbed his arm and pulled him backward. She gestured to the floor where he was about to walk, and I bent to see where she was pointing.

There, almost hidden under the dust, was a small cluster of nails sticking up from the floor. They were angled heavily toward the door, so that stepping on them would trap an unsuspecting shoe like a curved snake's fang. The nails were long enough to hit feet through sneakers, and though they wouldn't cause any serious wounds, they would certainly hurt. These were obviously meant to force us to make more noise than we intended and slow our escape, so nearby Cat patrols would be able to catch us.

"Traps. So we are in the right place." I rose back to my feet and addressed the group. "Good eye, Kiana. Everyone, split up and search but watch your feet. We have no clue what they're hiding here."

We fanned out across the room. Our feet left footprints in the thick dust, following us as we explored. But there wasn't really much to look at. The bowling alley was basically all one room. There was nothing unusual about the whole place.

Except... The wood paneling on one lane was the wrong type of wood. It was subtle, but to a trained eye there was a difference. I walked over to the lane and rested my hand against the wood, felt it move as I pushed it. I managed to get my fingers under the edge and the whole lane lifted easily, revealing a descending staircase.

"Bingo."

With Kiana and Ladan standing guard, I motioned for the other members of my group to follow, and led the way down the stairs. It got real dark real fast, but we had all packed flashlights. Or at least some of us did, while Truman muttered to himself and squinted. The stairs led to a small underground room, unfinished and coated in cobwebs. Against the wall, there were boxes full of...

"What is this?" I asked, rifling through strange metal and glass contraptions.

"Let's see." Port rubbed his chin thoughtfully. "Pipettes, beakers, needles... Looks like medical equipment. I bet Dr. Hanson will be thrilled to have all this!"

"This is good. We can get a few more people out here to help us move the..." But no one was listening to me. They were all staring at the opposite wall, away from the medical supplies. There was...something else there. Lots of somethings, actually. Hundreds of small, square rectangles stacked on top of each other like building blocks. The sheer number of them took a minute to register before I even began to consider what they were.

"Are those what I think they are?" I asked.

"You bet your ass!" said Truman. He had picked up one of them and turned to face us, an almost manic smile on his face. "Enough plastic explosives to take out a whole city block!"

60 FOX

I SWORE under my breath as I trudged through the Fort, wondering just how often I'd have to go searching for that jerk. Eventually, my search took me outside, high up on the walls in the lookout point where, not too long ago, Daire and I talked about girls. And there I found him, his old coat open, staring into the winter sunset. I hesitated before I approached. After a moment I cleared my throat, but he still didn't move.

"There's gonna be a meeting tonight in the Parliament Room. Just wanted to let you know early so you could get a seat." I immediately turned to leave.

"Fox, wait. Please." His voice was quiet.

"What is it?"

"I'm sorry. For what I've said and—how I've been lately."

"Sorry for what exactly? Be detailed," I said, in a lighthearted fashion. "I think at this point you owe me more than a simple apology."

"You're right." He took a deep breath. "I've been yelling at or avoiding all my friends, and well...I've been a real dick. Especially to you. And I'm sorry about that."

"Knew you'd come around. You're forgiven."

"Thanks for sticking around and trying to help me. It really means a lot."

I didn't really know what to say to this, so I just clapped my hand on his shoulder. I hoped he would smile, but he hung his head. The circles under his eyes were dark as coal. He didn't have to tell me that his struggles were taking a serious toll on his health and happiness. He hadn't slept, or eaten, or enjoyed a sane moment in some time. His dark hair hung loose and tangled over his eyes. His hand, braced against the railing, shook. My heart twisted for him.

"Come on, man. Let's get you some food before the meeting." I patted his shoulder, hoping to share some comfort. "Or whiskey. Whatever will help more."

He didn't move.

"What do you think will happen, Fox?" he asked. "What will they decide?"

"They'll probably do...something with Robin." I sighed. As much as I wanted to comfort him, I knew he'd prefer the truth. "Exile, maybe. Or continued imprisonment. Or..."

I had to swallow past a lump in my throat to finish. It hurt to think, but it killed me to say it.

"Or she could die."

Daire's hands stopped shaking as they clenched into fists. Something deep in the forests of his eyes sparked back to life.

"I won't let that happen," he said.

I almost smiled. *He's back.*

61 PORT

THE PARLIAMENT ROOM was one of the few places in the Fort where people gathered aboveground. It was an old ballroom room in the hotel, slightly altered to serve our purposes. Seven small tables stocked with pens and papers were arranged in a circle in the center of the room, and all the lights were directed at them. Rows and rows of seats circled them. Though it would be impossible to get all of the Fort in one room, we managed to squeeze four hundred in this one—enough to have representation from all families and groups. It was called the Parliament Room because it was where we made decisions in the most practically democratic way we thought possible.

That job of decision-making belonged to the Seven. They were supposed to be the wisest, most experienced people in the Fort, specifically chosen to represent all demographics of the Resistance. They were elected, and subject to exile if they failed to put the best interests of the Resistance at heart. The Seven contrasted each other, arguing all sides of a point to get the best possible answer. They debated until they reached a conclusion that everyone agreed was in the best interest for every person in the Fort.

Cap was one of the Seven. He asked me to accompany him to the

Parliament Room, and I followed him closely, so as not to get lost in the flood of people making their way to the seats. We waited for the rush to subside before heading in. I sensed he was gathering his thoughts and preparing for what would be a difficult conversation. He paused before swinging open the enormous double doors.

"Listen, son," he told me. "Take the closest seat you can get. Pay close attention to the politics of what happens. Try to see the hidden motives. Then report to me what you find."

I nodded. I didn't ask why he wanted me to do this. I had an unhappy suspicion about his plans for me and possible future leadership for the Fort. Cap had always said that those who shun leadership roles are often the best for them. I didn't want to lead, which was precisely why he was setting me up to take over for him.

He turned to the doors, straightened, and entered the room. The center was so brightly illuminated that it almost hurt to look at it. A murmuring came from the darkened seats surrounding it, and I hurried to find an empty spot near the front. Cap strode with confidence to the center desks, most of which were filled. He took one of the two empty seats. My eyes were drawn to the other one, the chair reserved for the one most unique viewpoint in the Fort. That was where the human ambassador/double agent was supposed to sit. Without her, the seventh chair seemed like a glaring beacon of betrayal.

The woman next to Cap stood and spoke, her voice silencing the room. "All right, everyone's here. Let's get started."

That was Aris Wisteria. She was a mysterious woman with a shaved head and skin darker than Cap's. She had fought in the initial attack, helping refugees right in the thick of the first battles. Rumor had it that before she joined the Fort, she led a large group of survivors across the country and managed to keep them all alive against impossible odds. She saved hundreds of lives at great risk to herself, and became one of the Fort's first heroes. Aris was famous for her incredible resilience against the enemy and mercy for those in need. They said she never turned away from a person in danger even if it seemed the odds were against her. She wore white cloth as a tight tunic and leggings.

"Yes. Let's get right to the point. I think we all agree that something needs to be done." Chris Sakata spoke next. He was raised in Japan but had lived in America for a decade before the invasion. Chris was a harsh man who was always seen frowning and never seemed to comb the nest of black hair that swung wildly about his face. He dressed in battle fatigues with long set patches and faded bloodstains worn like medals. In the eyes of the Fort, he was an unforgiving person that often called for harsh, but necessary, action.

"Definitely, the sooner the better," Anna MacCain answered, crossing her arms over her high-collared black jacket. She had tried to tame her red hair, but pulling it into a wild ponytail only made it seem bigger. She hailed from New York City and was well known for her explosive temper, which was usually seen in combat when she fought with a furious, almost reckless passion. Many said that was what made her so effective on the battlefield. Those who didn't like Anna claimed that she was too quick to anger. Others said that her fury turned the tide in many battles and saved human lives. Consensus was that she was a great asset to the Fort, but it was best to avoid crossing her.

"I think we all agree that we need action," said a calm voice. "But to decide on the right action, we need to think carefully." Naveen Gamir was the voice of reason, always calm and thoughtful, sometimes too hesitant. The bearded and bespectacled man had moved from Baghdad just before the Cats got here, and his wisdom had saved the Fort many times before. It was Naveen who came up with the creative solutions that saved the Fort in times of need. His tweed jacket and khakis made him look like a college professor, though he never really explained what he had done before the war, or even why he had moved.

The last member of the Seven remained silent. He hunched over in his chair, supporting his weight on a weathered cane. It was common knowledge that he was the oldest person in the Fort, and he listened carefully during meetings but almost never spoke. When he did have something to say, however, it was almost always the last word on the subject. The Seven didn't have a leader, but his judgment was always seen as the wisest, and no one in the history of the Resistance could remember him being wrong. He was known only as Arthur.

Chris began. "The people are angry. And rightly so. One of them, one of us, one of their *heroes* turned out to be the enemy. It's a scourge and an embarrassment! And until we find a way to settle things about Robin, the Fort will be divided."

"It's simple." Anna spoke next. A blue fire burned in her eyes. "We do the American thing and put her on trial. And if we agree she's guilty, she'll be executed for treason."

My captain raised his voice. "Put her on trial for what? Being a Cat? She can't refute her species, so she'll be found guilty and killed?" To everyone else, Cap sounded confident and confrontational, but I heard the weariness in his voice. From here, the voices came so quick that they almost blended together in a heated frenzy. It was difficult to keep up with who said what, but I tried my best.

Chris: "That's right! It's the best thing for everyone."

Cap: "How many of our lives has she saved? Even if she is one of them, she doesn't deserve to die! She's done nothing but help!"

Naveen: "Cap is right. I believe that, even if she is a traitor, there is much she can teach us. Killing her wouldn't help us at all."

Chris: "It would bring us together as a people again! You know what they say about a house divided."

Anna: "I agree. The people want blood. Hell, *I* want blood! And after what we've been through, we deserve it!"

Aris: "Now hold on a moment. Rushing to violence is never the best option. Even if it brings us together, it'll be a pact signed in the blood of a former comrade. That is not how the human race should rewrite its history."

Naveen: "Yes, fighting fire with fire only causes more burns.

There must be something we can do to regain our camaraderie without murdering a friend."

Anna: "You *still* consider her a friend? After how she lied to all of us?"

Cap: "*I do*, dammit! The only thing she's done wrong was been born one of them. She has helped us."

Chris: "She *is* one of them! She's one of the creatures that have devastated our country and killed *millions* of humans. She's a Cat, and we can't trust her! I say we execute her and be done with it!"

Aris: "We will not decide who lives and dies so easily!"

Chris: "We need action *now* before things get more out of hand. The Fort is angry, Aris, and they won't be satisfied until they've had revenge!"

Naveen: "Revenge is the absolute last thing we need. It's a dangerous road, and a very slippery slope. And Cap is right. Robin has done us no real harm except concealing her identity. Killing her can't be the right option."

Anna: "Don't you see? It's the *only* option. We need closure on this matter, and that will only come with that lying Cat's death!"

"That is enough."

A voice, old and tired, silenced the room. All eyes turned simultaneously to stare at the bent old man in the center of the room. He raised his soft gaze from the floor and addressed the room, seeming to speak to the heart of every individual.

"The answer is, as it always is, a compromise," said Arthur. "Anna and Chris are correct: the people thirst for blood. It will be an unfortunate, but necessary show of solidarity. The people feel they have been wronged, and they deserve retaliation for the lies they have been told. Without some action to show everyone that crimes against the Fort will not be tolerated, their trust in us will wither and fade.

"But the others are right, too. Robin was our friend. Ending her life would be a small death to each and every one of us. Furthermore, executing Robin would cause a rift among us, between those who believe we did the right thing and those who feel it was a great injustice. We, as an alliance, cannot survive such a division. That is not the answer."

The entire room held its breath as Arthur paused.

"However...we have two other Cats in our possession," he continued. "And one of them is a soldier and a high-ranking officer. A dangerous foe that must be dealt with—keeping him captive for a prolonged period is an avoidable drain on our limited resources. But his imprisonment may be of use to us yet. It is his death that will bind us together as a community again. We will remind the people that we are strong, and though we lack superior numbers or supplies, we are a force to be feared. With one life, we will show the symbolic death of our enemy and give our people something to believe in again. I propose...a public execution. This Cat will be our scapegoat, and his death will allow us to heal."

The audience stayed silent, waiting to see if one of the other five representatives would make a rebuttal. But one by one, they locked eyes with each other and nodded. It was decided.

62 ROBIN

IT WAS early morning and the sunrise was filtering through the stale basement dust when they came for me. I was awake, laying on my cot and staring at my ceiling, rolling a little red capsule between my fingers when I heard their footsteps. I sighed, closed my eyes, and waited. I didn't know who it was, but at this point, I doubted anyone could have anything good to tell me.

I didn't move from my bed as they approached. I half-hoped they would pass me by, but I knew better. I tucked the pill into my fist, keeping it safe and easily accessible. Just in case things took a turn for the worst.

The footsteps stopped. "Robin," a voice called from my cell door.

Truman. Great. Showing that I was in no hurry to address him, I rolled out of bed to face the door. He stood, flanked on one side by the twins Kiana and Ladan, whom I knew from my days in the field. I had fought with them before and knew them to be quiet and effective and easy to get along with. I liked them.

On his other side was Daire. I took a long second to look into his eyes and to my surprise he looked back, unflinching. I had to tear my gaze away. I walked up to Truman, showing I was unafraid.

"Are you here to take me to my execution?" I asked.

"Unfortunately, no. But we are here to take you. Come with us." He unlocked and opened the door, gesturing for me to fall in line behind the twins and in front of him and Daire. I complied, because I saw no reason to resist. They would carry me if they had to, and I chose to walk with all the dignity I could muster with my hands tied.

They led me through the Fort, into the upper levels. It was early enough that we didn't meet anyone on the way. Eventually, we came to a far room, one with a makeshift door of wooden planks. Port guarded it, leaning on a wall and looking overworked. My heart went out to him, but I didn't have time to dwell on it as I was pushed through the doorway. The room was white from floor to ceiling and suspiciously devoid of furniture. Two chairs were set apart from each other, and in one sat a bearded man in a tweed jacket.

"Naveen," I said in greeting. That was a good sign. Naveen was a pacifist—when dealing with humans, anyway—and didn't generally engage in violence when he had the choice.

"Robin, my friend." He gestured to the other seat, and I took it. Kiana and Ladan moved to stand behind him, while Truman and Daire took positions on either side of me.

"They are for my protection," Naveen told me when he saw me glance at the men. He waved his hand at the twins beside him. "And these two are for your protection. That way everyone is safe. We all know how tensions can sometimes run high."

"I understand." That actually made me feel a little more at ease. "It's good to see you."

"Yes, it's good to see you, too. And after all this time, it's nice to finally see your face." He smiled, tugging thoughtfully at his beard. I returned the smile gratefully.

"So why am I here?" I asked.

"I was finally granted permission to talk to you. I want to know your story, Robin. How you, a Cat, came to be here."

I smirked. "So you're not going to torture me for information?"

"No, of course not. I merely want to know more about you.

And..." He leaned toward me and lowered his voice, as though sharing a secret. "I want to give you a chance to prove your innocence. Prove that you're actually on our side."

"I see. So where do I begin?"

"First you can tell me who you are."

"You know who I am. I'm Robin."

"Full name, please." He asked it gently, apologetically. "For formality's sake."

"All right, fine. My name is Robin Wake."

"And now, start from the beginning. As far back as you can go."

"Okay. My first memory is on a boat, off the coast of Oregon. I was three or four years old."

I let myself slip into memory, recounting as I went...

The boat rocks upon impact. There's the fire, the awful smell, and the arms around me. Someone wraps me in a jacket and lowers me to a floating board. I drift far from the boat, for some long hours. I finally, finally wash up on shore and then...

"Are you okay, little girl?" a voice asks, curious and concerned. I gather the courage to peek from under the jacket and I see two wide, brown eyes staring at me. I blink in surprise when I see that they belong to a little boy. His knees are skinned and scarred below his shorts and his T-shirt is stained with ocean salt. He's a bit older than me, probably around nine, and much bigger. I'm terrified.

But his concern reaches me. He sees my fear and steps back to give me room. Kneeling to be on my level, he smiles at me.

"Little girl, where's your mom and dad? There's no one else here and I haven't seen anyone on the beach for a long time. Are you lost?"

I pull the jacket tighter around me, beginning to shake with cold and fear. I'm soaked to the bone with seawater and starving, too afraid to move. Tears well up at the corner of my eyes. The boy's expression softens to serious concern.

"Come with me." He extends a hand slowly. "My house is just along the beach, only a few minutes away. My mom will make you hot chocolate and call your parents. We'll get you home, don't worry!"

His patience seems endless as I remain hunkered under the jacket. Finally, I reach out and grasp his hand. He smiles. The boy helps me to my feet and leads me along the sand, walking slowly so my short legs can keep up.

"You'll love my mom," he says. "She's great with kids. She's a foster parent, though we don't have anyone with us right now. She makes great food too, and..."

The boy talks nonstop until we reach a small house at the top of a large hill overlooking the ocean. Long grass, waving gently with the ocean breeze, frames a dirt path to the driveway. The door is a soft blue and the roof is dark gray, like the house is mimicking the ocean tones around it. The white shutters are thrown open, giving the house a feeling of a warm invitation. A small garden rests off to the side, with spring leaves just starting to bloom. Beyond the house lies a wide forest with dark trees.

He leads me up the front steps and through the door. I'm trembling with fear as I step through the entryway, and the little boy squeezes my hand again.

"Mom, come quick!" he calls.

A lean woman emerges from around the corner. She's drying her hands on her apron as soft brown curls float around her face. She's quite beautiful. She shares her son's kind brown eyes and seems to emanate a comforting warmth. Those eyes open with shock as she catches sight of me.

"She was alone on the beach," the boy says as the woman rushes to me, kneeling and glancing over me for injuries. "I think she's lost."

"Sweetheart," is the woman's first word to me. "Where are your parents?"

I don't answer, don't know how to answer.

"Do you know their phone number?"

I shake my head, confused, tears returning to my eyes.

"Oh my." She turns to the boy. "James, make her some hot chocolate and toast." He nods and rushes off. The woman rests her hand on my forehead, checking my temperature. She looks me over again, and I can almost see her heart breaking for the poor half-drowned creature in front of her.

"Honey, come into the kitchen with James. He'll get you whatever you want. I'm going to call the police and they'll find your parents. Don't you worry. You'll get home soon."

And she does call the police. When they come, they can't figure out who I am. Of course there were no missing children reports. I'm a mystery. The police try to take me to the station for the night, but the woman won't allow it.

"She'll stay here. I have an extra room. I'm a registered foster parent, for God's sake. I'm not letting that little girl sleep in some police station."

I stay there that night, in a soft bed with a pink quilt. The bed is so comfortable and I am so exhausted that despite my terror, I fall asleep as soon as I get settled. When I wake up crying in the middle of the night, there's a soft knock on my door and it cracks open. I hide under the covers.

I'm shaking as I peek from under the quilt to see the boy, holding a teddy bear.

"I heard you crying," he whispers. "When there's a foster kid here, sometimes at night, they cry too. But sometimes having something to hug makes them feel better. So I let them borrow Roscoe. Do you want him?"

The bear looks worn but soft. It's probably seen decades of love. I nod.

"Here you go, then." He hands me the bear, which I take gingerly. James heads back down the hall. "Good night, little girl."

I hug Roscoe softly, then tighter, taking comfort in the feel of his fur. He soaks up the last of my tears as I fall asleep.

I wake as sunlight creeps through the window. I slip from the bed, leaving Roscoe behind. This new house is too much for me, and I feel the need to look for something familiar. I creep through the house until I find the back door. Still afraid, I slip into the backyard, closing the door behind me. My bare feet slide through the dew, carrying me past the garden and to the forest. The trees look inviting, so I walk toward them. I am mystified by the amazing amount of green. Forgetting my fear, I grab at every plant, clutching the leaves like treasures.

Eventually, I come across a little flower with three white, triangular petals. I reach for it but stop, realizing that if I pulled it, I'd damage the petals. Instead, I plop to the ground and gaze at the plant as sunlight glitters off its leaves.

From behind me comes crashing, hurried footsteps. Fear seizes me until I hear a familiar voice.

"Little girl? Little girl! Little g—oh, there you are!" James runs up to me, obvious relief on his face. "We were so worried!"

I hang my head. I feel awful to have made these kind people worry.

"Oh, it's okay," says the boy. "I didn't mean to make you feel bad. And I'm sorry I keep calling you 'little girl.' Do you remember your name?"

I shake my head. The thought that I have a name hasn't occurred to me.

The boy scratches his head. "Well, I have to call you something."

An epiphany strikes me, and I point feverishly at the flower that had captivated me. James considers it carefully, then turns to me.

"You like that flower?" he asks. I nod.

"Well, that's a wake-robin. I guess Robin is a girl's name...so we can just switch it around. How about Robin Wake? Is that a good name for you?"

Again, I nod. Then, I smile. James returns my smile, encouraged by my happiness. He grabs my hand and urges me gently back toward his house.

"Come on, Robin. My mom is looking for you too, so we gotta let her know you're safe. And I bet she'll love your new name!"

I go back to that house. I end up staying there for a long, long time.

Obviously, the police never found my parents. I become a ward of the state, but James's mother signs the paperwork to make me her foster child. She sends me to the nearby public school, and my new foster brother walks me to the bus stop every day. The woman searches relentlessly for my family, checking every lost child report she can find, even after the police have given up.

After a year, I begin to call her "Mother."

After two years, she formally adopts me.

By the end of the third year, there is no doubt that they are my family. My mother helps with my homework, makes me my favorite foods, sews me clothes, and does everything else I need. James calls me his "angel sister" because he claims that the reason I washed up on a beach is because I fell from heaven. Every so often, he goes into the woods and collects a bouquet of wake-robins for me. Roscoe shares my bed every night.

James is an amazingly smart boy. His keen observational skills are matched only by his kindness. One day when he is fourteen and I am eight, we go to gather vegetables from the garden. He begins to talk to me in an uncharacteristically serious tone.

"Robin," he says. His voice is quiet. "Listen. I know that you're different. I can see it in how you move and react, and in your eyes."

Of course he notices. He is wise far beyond his years, and he understood something about me that I had only begun to sense about myself. For a moment, I am afraid.

"Don't worry, I won't tell anyone. As far as I'm concerned, you're my little sister and that's all that matters. But don't you tell anyone, okay? People are afraid of what they don't understand, even if what they don't understand is something wonderful. So we'll keep this our secret."

"Okay." My voice shook with emotion. "James...do you think I'm bad? Because I'm different?"

"Of course not, little sister." He smiles. "I've always said you were an angel, and angels are a little different too."

His words comfort me, and I use them as a way to deal with my differences. I'm not a freak, I think. I'm different, but different can be good. Of course, I don't know what I actually am until three years later, when foreign ships start landing on US soil. The Invasion rocks us as it does to everyone, but we hole up in our little house and stay hidden. Rumors of terrible devils with paranormal reflexes and beast eyes float through the radio, until the cell towers are invaded and the broadcasts go dead. A flyer makes its way through the nearby town until it reaches my family. "Beware" it reads, over a picture of a man with eyes like a cat. Eyes like mine.

Only a few days later, we see them approaching. James, Mother, and I watch from the kitchen window as the huge metal ships inch closer to our beach. At this point, we know it's too late to run. The surrounding towns had already been attacked, and ours was most likely taken over. With no place to go, we could only hope the invaders would overlook one small house. So we wait.

"I'm a demon," I whisper. We are huddled together in the kitchen, having been hiding out for days as the Cats ransacked the coastline.

My mother rushes over to me, takes my face in her hands. "No, no. You're not one of them."

"But I am!" I cry.

"Robin, your species doesn't matter." She knows, of course, that I am one of this strange new people. She figured it out as soon as she had heard of them and their differences. But her soft eyes held mine, showing her unconditional love. "These things are murderers. You, Robin, you are an amazing, kind-hearted child. You're not them."

"Mother." James is at the window. His voice is quiet, calm, but urgent. "They've landed on the beach."

"Robin, your humanity lies in your heart, not your blood." A tear rolls across her cheek. "Never forget that. You're my daughter, and your spirit is what really matters."

"They've seen the house. They're headed toward us." James, only seventeen, is a child himself. But he has the calm resolution of a natural protector.

"Come here, children." My mother ushers us to her, encloses both of *us in a hug. Her tears run into my hair and I cling to her. After a long moment, she breaks off.*

"James," she says. "Take your sister into the woods. I'm going to lead them in the wrong direction."

"No!" I lunge toward her, but my brother holds me back.

My mother opens the door. She stands, framed against the pale light, looking back at us with tears in her eyes.

"I love you both," she breathes. "Now go."

Before I can protest, James has picked me up and run for the back door. He holds me tight to his chest as he sprints into the woods. We make the cover of the trees before we hear shouting. Then screaming.

I shut my eyes tight against the sounds and press my face into my brother's shirt. He does not falter, but keeps running. He runs until it seems impossible for anyone to run so long while carrying a child. But fear for him and for me drives him, and he presses further and further into the trees.

The sun is just starting to set as we hear them. They're tracking us, following James's footsteps. We both know they're behind us, and it will only take minutes to for them to catch up. I look to James with uncertainty, too frightened to cry. To my surprise, he sets me down. His arms are shaking.

He kneels, once again fixing me with his brown eyes. "Robin, listen very carefully. They don't know there are two of us, and you can move much more quietly than I can. You need to run as fast as you can in the opposite direction than I go. Head to the hills outside of town and hide until they leave. They won't be looking for you, so you should be able to wait until they go to sleep for the night. Then you can run."

"I want to go with you." I am barely able to whisper.

"I'm going to draw them off. You need to escape."

"No!"

"Shh." James wraps one arm around me, pulls me close, and kisses my forehead. "I love you, little sister. Good luck. Now prove you're an angel, and fly!"

And with that, he runs back the way we came, his failing strength renewed in his desire to protect me. I have no choice but to do as he says and run toward the hills. I'm faster and quieter than humans, so the Cats don't hear me. But I hear them.

"There he is! Don't let him escape!"

Blinking back tears, I run on. The ground flies under me and around me the trees are thinning. The voices get fainter until they fade altogether. But I don't need to hear them to know what will happen. I know what they've done to towns, cities, and maybe the whole country. I know what they've done to my family.

I break the trees and find myself at the foot of the gigantic hill. I start the climb without pausing. The sun has just set.

The orange and pink sky is giving way to darkness by the time I reach the top of the hill. I am panting, gasping for breath, sobbing. I am almost afraid to look back, but I have to. From this height, I can see all the way to the ocean. And I can see my house, my home, illuminated by towering orange flames. The whole house is ablaze with a fire bright enough to reach the heavens. I watch it burn, and with it my only memories, my family, my garden, my haven, and Roscoe. Eleven years old, alone in the world, I weep for everything I have lost. I weep for the only mother I can remember.

But when I think about James, I find no tears. This sadness, this grief, does not suit his memory. For a moment, I don't know what I feel about my brother.

I watch my house burn, taken away from us by those monsters. They killed him. They took everything and left my life as ashes.

Suddenly, I understand the emotion. I think about James, letting the feeling build, until I cannot contain it and I scream my rage into the night.

"I'll destroy you!" I scream to the Cats. "Every! Last! One!"

"And that's—that's my story," I told Naveen, still feeling the echoes of my memory fade.

He leaned back in his chair, clearly at a loss for words. After a moment, he found his voice.

"That's quite a story," he said. "Now, I know this is a lot to ask, but just so I can remember all the details, can you tell it one more time?"

"All right." I suppressed a sigh. "My earliest memory was on a boat..."

63 ALMYRR

I OPTED to ride back to the White House with General Hellman. After I saw what he would be driving, I immediately regretted my decision.

He had a foot soldier actually drive the vehicle, leaving the General and me bouncing uncomfortably in the back of the ancient Jeep. How he had maintained the antique vehicle was beyond me, though the relic seemed to be a matter of pride for him. The torn canvas roof was not protecting us from the cold or the wind, so the ride was noisy and cold. On especially large bumps in the road, my head hit the ceiling, and my jacket whipped around in the cab. For the first time, I wished I had cut my hair short.

General Hellman seemed to be enjoying this heinous ride. For the past three hours of the five-hour ride, he had been staring out the window and whistling a happy tune. The sound nearly drove me mad. I began to wish that the car would hit a pothole big enough to make him accidentally bite his tongue off. When I thought the damn whistling was going to make me snap, I forced myself to make conversation.

"So, General, I was wondering-"

"Please, Almyrr. Byrron."

"Right. Byrron. I was wondering about the initial invasion. I heard you were there, on the first boat."

"Yes, I was. That was ten years ago now." He stroked his beard, apparently reminiscing.

"And the King was there too, right?"

"Indeed he was." He tried to hide the change in tone, but I could tell that he was suddenly guarded.

"So what was he like, back then?" I asked. "Just out of curiosity."

"He was—well, he was different. Younger, obviously, but also more idealistic. He had such high hopes for the war."

Had? He had taken over the country and installed himself as King. Yet the general's tone made it seem like he failed somehow.

"What kinds of hopes?" I asked. He eyed me carefully before responding.

"His motives back then were a little different. He thought that the humans, with some extreme conditioning, might be assimilated into our culture. I know, it sounds crazy. And he quickly realized the fault in his plan. After we discovered that humans were even more inferior than we thought, we decided to conquer rather than just introduce. And Erenvyr was the spearhead of this invasion."

I had always been told that we were meant to kill the humans from the start. This mysterious hidden beginning of the war was intriguing and rather confusing, to be honest. *Why did they want to simply greet the humans? And why did that change?*

"So it was King Erenvyr who decided that peace wasn't viable?" I asked.

"Well, yes and no. He wasn't King back then, only a general. But he rose to power very quickly after the invasion, and led the effort to wipe the world clean, staring with this country."

"How did he manage to rise to power so quickly?"

"He was popular and enigmatic. No one could deny that he was the most driven and powerful Wyrforra in charge. Not to mention, right as Erenvyr reached the peak of popularity, our previous ruler suddenly died."

The implication of the word "suddenly" was not lost on me.

"What a lucky coincidence," I remarked. "What happened?"

"We had a Queen back then. She was a war hero and had been ruling for a long time, and it was she who sent the first boat over. But just a few months after we landed, she was visiting with the troops when a human snuck into her dwelling and murdered her."

Impossible. A human would *never* be able to sneak onto a military encampment, get past the Queen's guard, and then somehow kill a war hero. There was no feasible way for a loud, clumsy human to do this. Our ears would have picked up a human's footsteps easily, making it practically impossible for them to get to our most heavily guarded political figure. Which meant that a human was framed, most likely by someone who could gain directly from the Queen's death. Which meant that Erenvyr didn't just *rise* to power.

"How interesting," I murmured.

"Isn't it? Oh, Erenvyr was quite torn up about it. He was good friends with the Queen, you know."

General Hellman was a very smart person. He was well aware that I understood the real story he was telling. Which meant he wanted me to know. But why?

"He has become a great King," I said. I had a theory, and though it would be a risk to voice it, I felt as though I had to confirm my suspicions. "It's curious how such a great leader can follow such a tragedy, like the Queen's murder."

For just a second before he answered, the general met my eye and offered the slightest smile.

"It's curious indeed, how often a great rule only comes after... tragedy." He laughed and patted me on the back with a tad too much force. "We have such a colorful history. Remind me to tell you some old war stories sometime. I've got some good ones!"

Hellman returned to his whistling, clearly indicating that the conversation was over. We both knew that we had shared a potentially dangerous conversation and he gave me some information he could be killed for. But there was an unspoken understanding that it was never to be mentioned again. We would both pretend there was nothing unusual about the King's political gains.

And then there was the rest of what Hellman told me. Did he mean that I should guard the King carefully, as there would certainly be an attack on his life from someone seeking power? Or was he telling me that I could gain the throne by murdering the King? It seemed to me that he was implying that I could "inherit" the throne the way that Erenvyr had...

But why would he tell me that? What could he gain by having me seize power?

So many questions. Fortunately, I had a long car ride ahead of me, and plenty of time to think.

64 ROBIN

NAVEEN INSISTED on bringing me back to my cell—alone. Somehow, he convinced Daire and Truman to leave, letting him escort me through the Fort himself. When we reached my cell, Naveen opened the door and I stepped inside. But then he paused.

"Thank you for telling me your story," he said.

"Of course."

"My old friend, do you remember how we met?"

"Yes, all those years ago. It was during a supply run, right?"

"Yes." Naveen smiled to himself. "You found my band of survivors in the woods outside of the city. We had been on the move for months with little food or rest... We were almost dead. But you found us, and promised to lead us to safety. And when we were attacked, you fought the Cats off almost single-handedly. My group made it to the Fort, thanks to you."

I remained silent as Naveen locked my cell door and swung it closed—but not quite closed. I eyed him questioningly as he stepped back from the door.

"You saved my life that day, you know," he said, his voice soft. "Best of luck, my friend."

And with that, he left, whistling down the hallway. I stood motionless, one hand on the cell door, marveling at how simple it would be to push it open and escape. Something inside me fought to leave, to run as fast as I could, make it outside and just keep going. But the weight of this choice and its implications were not lost on me. I was frozen, willing myself to consider everything instead of succumbing to one instinct or another.

"You can leave." The whispered voice nearly made me jump, but it was only Tylos. "You're faster than the humans. You can get out."

I thought for a long, silent moment.

"No," I said with finality. "This place is my home, and these people... Despite what's happened, they're still my family. I am, and always will be, part of the Resistance. So no matter what happens, I'm seeing this through until the end."

I pulled the door shut, letting the lock slide into place. To be honest, there was a stab of regret when I considered how I had probably just signed my own death warrant. But I also felt certain that my choice was the right one—for my friends, but more important, for me.

I sat on my cot, once again feeling the weight of my decision on my shoulders. But presented with the same choice, I would always choose what was best for the humans, because it would haunt me if I didn't. My sense of betrayal would be a fate far worse than imprisonment or death. And with the Cat in the next cell, I had the distinct sense that things were revving up. The scent in the air told me that something was coming, and I wanted to be around to see it, and to fight for my friends if I had to. Somehow, I still had confidence in my cause. I would not abandon it.

When I was sure that Tylos was no longer focused on me, I reached into my sock and pulled out my tiny red escape. It was warm, having rested against my skin for days. I turned over the thing, letting it roll across my palm. My choice reminded me of my determination. And in my determination, I regained my strength.

"I'm seeing this through," I repeated, softer than breath, "to the very end."

I dropped the capsule to the floor and crushed it against the concrete.

65 ARIANNA

BEFORE THE MEETING, I had found myself beginning to wonder. I turned over Tylos's words again and again, thinking about his ideals. Peace between the Cats and the humans. Coexistence. It was a beautiful but impractical thought. Part of me knew that it could never be done. Our two species were on an unstoppable warpath. We had both committed atrocities, done things that could never be forgotten. Humans and Wyrforra had been fighting for a decade, and not once had there been talk of making a truce. We could never reach a compromise.

And yet...despite what I had said to Tylos, we had something... special. He cared for me, I knew. And if I let myself, I cared for him too. And I still wanted Robin to be my friend. Shouldn't that prove that humans and Wyrforra could get along? The more I thought about it, the more I came to wonder if maybe peace could be achieved. If we proved that humans and Wyrforra could live with each other, that we could be equals, maybe we could convince everyone to stop fighting. Maybe...just maybe...we could end the war.

Those nights in the cave showed me that very different people could be brought together. Or perhaps it showed that our people weren't as different as we thought. Tylos showed amazing compassion when I needed it, and when I opened up to him, even if it was in a state of mortal dread, he accepted me with...well, with humanity. I'll admit that the situation probably caused us both to be more open than we ordinarily would have been, but in that openness, something connected. I know he felt it too, with how he had tried so hard to help me. He had changed from the suspicious, aloof warrior who almost killed me a couple times to someone who might be my friend. Maybe even more.

And that connection had refused to disappear, even when I attempted to sever it. Despite my efforts to distance myself, there was a bond between Tylos and me. It didn't feel like a bond between a human and a Wyrforra. It was a bond between people.

Before the meeting, I felt my shoulders grow lighter. I pondered the idea of Tylos and I showing the world that peace was an option. If we could convince just a few humans and Wyrforra at a time, we could gain support from both sides. Maybe we could get the whole world to follow our example. As I took my seat at the meeting of the Seven, I resolved to tell Tylos about this as soon as I could. He'd be so happy.

After the meeting, I didn't feel much of anything. Some sort of internal delay kept away all the pain that followed those words "public execution." I could only let my feet carry me away, not thinking about where I was going until I ended up on the roof. There was my bike, my tent, and the stars. And my thoughts. And right then, alone, was when the full force of those words hit me.

I dropped to my knees, hugging my arms around me chest and letting my hair fall in a protective curtain around my face. I gasped, fought off tears, knowing I didn't have time to let myself fall apart. As hard as it was, I couldn't stop to cry just yet. I had to be the one to tell him. I forced myself to regain composure. I let the cold night air wash over my face, and closed my eyes against the clouds. After a long minute, I gathered my strength and headed back inside.

The walk to the basement cells was longer than usual. My feet felt like water, melting into the floor with every step I took. I probably met some people I knew on the way, but I didn't see anything except for the halls around me. I stared straight ahead and tried desperately not to let myself think, or feel, but it was impossible. My head swam as I walked, and the dark thoughts ricocheting around my head seemed to cloud everything I saw. When my feet stopped moving, I looked up to find myself at the door to the basement. It took a lot of strength to push the door open, and I felt lightheaded as my feet carried me to Tylo's cell where I stood, stupefied.

"Arianna?" He sounded surprised to see me. The concern in his voice nearly tore me in two.

He was sitting on the floor, so I knelt to be on his level. He moved closer to me, and I couldn't meet those yellow eyes. There he sat, so close to me, cross-legged and almost touching the bars, face crinkled in worry. Not for himself, though. He was worried about me. I could tell, from how his hands were lifted slightly as though he were about to reach for my hand. I finally found my voice, and I fought hard not to let myself waver. It was the most difficult thing I would ever have to say.

"You've been slated for execution."

Tylos drew in a sharp breath, then let it out. I stared at my own feet, too afraid to see his reaction. I noted with surprise that I had started shaking.

"I'm sorry, Tylos." This time I couldn't suppress a quiver in my voice.

"It's all right."

I looked up to him in shock, and I found him gazing back at me. He must have seen how confused I was.

"I knew that this was a possibility when I was captured. I figured something like this would happen when I joined the army. Dying in war...it's a sad reality. But I'm... I'm glad it's here. I'm glad I got to see the humans, and see both sides of the war. I'm glad I wasn't just another soldier. I am...sad it had to end this way. I was hoping I could change something."

My hands trembled as I listened. I wanted so badly to tell him that though he didn't change the war, he did change something. He changed *me*. And I would never be the same.

His wrists were tied, but he managed to fit them through the bars and rest his hands on my face. His battle-scarred palms felt as comforting as the softest blanket and I found myself locked in his gaze.

"Please don't cry," he whispered. I hadn't realized the tears had managed to escape, but he wiped them away gently with his thumbs. And that was when my composure broke down.

"Tylos, I'm so sorry," I cried. "I wanted what you wanted too. I thought we could bring peace, together. I thought we could..."

"Me too."

Tears traced my face and ran down his fingers. I reached up and rested my hand against his, feeling the warmth and drawing comfort in it. In that moment, I could feel the remaining walls between us crumble. I wanted to share everything with him, and I wanted to listen to everything he had to say. I wanted to build a future with him. And I truly believed he wanted to build one with me.

It was a closeness I had never felt before. And it killed me to know that it was going to be taken away from me before I could learn to accept it.

"You actually care about me, don't you?" he asked.

"Yes."

"Then I'm sorry. This is going to be harder for you than for me. I'm sorry I got attached. I didn't want to hurt you."

"I know. But as much as this hurts, I'm glad that we saved each other."

He took my hand in his and lowered his head, resting it against the bars. I leaned forward and pressed my forehead to his. Our tears fell together on the concrete.

66 ROBIN

WHEN I WOKE, I was surprised to see that Tylos wasn't alone. Arianna sat on the floor, leaning back against the bars and against the Cat, whose position mirrored hers. The two were locked in whispered conversation.

Oh, no.

I moved to the far end of my cell to give them some privacy. I felt for my friend, though I considered it a stupid idea for her to get so close. But seeing as how I was in a cell next to the Cat, I didn't really think I could judge anyone's decisions. And perhaps she would be a friend for me, too, when I inevitably shared Tylos's fate.

The sound of footsteps broke me from my reverie. It was Fox, cigarette in hand, who greeted me with a sad smile.

"You're walking much better. You're healing well?" I remarked.

"Mm, almost back to shipshape." He exhaled smoke, glancing in Arianna's direction. "How long've they been like that?"

"All night, I think. What happens next...isn't going to be easy for her."

"Yeah, but it's a good thing she's doing. No one should be alone, in the end."

"I suppose you've come to tell him when it's going to happen?"

"Tha's right. It'll be this evening."

"So soon?"

He shook his head. "Not my decision. Truman is demanding it be done as soon as possible, or he'll raise more hell. You should hear how he convinced Anna MacCain to 'fortify' the Fort. But I'll tell you about that later. I gotta go break the news."

Fox ran a hand through his sandy hair. He took a long drag from his cigarette before stubbing it out to the ground. I got the feeling he was gathering his strength.

"I gotta go tell someone that he's gonna die at sundown." He sighed as he walked toward them.

67 ODYRA

LUCKY'S NOSE led us to the deserters' hideout. There we found food and fuel and were able to continue on our way. As we passed through Nevada, the snow became a rarer and rarer sight, until it disappeared completely. In these conditions, from there, we made it to our destination in just under twelve hours.

Santa Barbara was a Wyrforra army stronghold. Several hundred troops were stationed in a small gated part of the city. I was met at the entrance, and immediately given an escort. My position was finally working for me.

I ordered for my car to be refueled and the trunk filled with enough fuel canisters to get me home. I did not have to ask for provisions; my car was stuffed with rations. I was offered any food they could prepare, and Lucky happily received water and fresh meat. I, however, denied their offers and asked the nearest soldier if there were any humans around.

He paled visibly. "Yes, ma'am, there is one. But we're under strict orders to leave her alone."

"Orders from whom?"

"No one knows, exactly. My CO just says they're 'from the top.'

The human is under our protection."

"Where is she?"

"A restaurant near the edge of town. I'll lead you there." He hesitated, fidgeting. "If anything happens to her, ma'am, we face...harsh consequences."

"Soldier, I could slaughter everyone in this base without repercussions. However, I promise no harm will come to her."

I was brought to the building. With strict orders to the soldier to keep Lucky outside, I approached.

The restaurant's double doors were heavy and hard to open. When they swung out, they sent up spirals of dust reflected in the light from the dirt-stained windows. A human woman bent with hardship but not age was sweeping. She didn't seem to be looking at the broom, or the floor, or the empty tables, or anything in particular. Her mind seemed far away, as though her thoughts were swept up with her hair in its tight bun. She seemed intent on cleaning, but I doubted she had gotten any more dust to clean up in a long while.

This was the first time I had seen a human in its natural habitat. I approached her, cautiously, but she didn't so much as glance up. Not wanting to frighten her, I called out softly.

"Are you Rosa?"

"Yes, but you can just call me 'rat' or 'filthy human.' " Her voice was not spiteful, but tired. "That's what most of your kind calls me anyway. Have a seat. Technically, we're closed, but I know better than to refuse business to a Wyrforra. I suppose you want me to cook you a 'traditional human' meal, like the others."

"I'm here for information." I crossed to a table and gestured for her to take the other seat. "I hear there's a story that only you know."

"Oh, I know lots of stories. Humans are storytelling creatures. But which one do you want to hear?" She leaned backward in her seat, resting the broom against the table. I got the impression that she was glad to get off her feet.

"The story I'm interested in is of one of the first landing parties that hit ground not far from here about ten years ago. I'm told you had contact with them."

"I did."

"I'm also told that High King Erenvyr was part of that crew."

"He was."

"And you knew him."

"Yes, I did. I knew him...quite well. But if I tell you that story, he'll kill me." She sighed. "But if I don't tell you, you'll kill me. And I suppose you're the more immediate threat."

I chose not to acknowledge her accurate fear. "So what happened?"

"You know the first part. Erenvyr and a small group of soldiers landed here and took over the city. But most people don't know that he wasn't the King then, just the highest-ranking general. Back then, he had a very different view on humans. He thought that humans and Wyrforra could coexist peacefully. He even considered us his equals."

It was difficult to hide my surprise at this, but did not interrupt her story.

"He even took on a human name, to better interact with us locals. I knew him as Arron King." Her gentle laugh was sad, and completely human. "He had high aspirations even then. He was young, in his early twenties, and he came to me asking for a guide. I agreed to show him how things worked in the city and teach him about our way of life. We became close."

"You were friends?" I asked.

"At first. But then...well, I was young too. Only nineteen. And I'm sure you know how charming he is. I fell for him."

"And he rejected your advances?"

Rosa's smile crinkled her brown eyes. She was really quite beautiful, for a human. "Not exactly. I know it's hard to believe, but he loved me. He promised me that he would bring me to wherever he established a capital and build us a home. He promised me the world. He thought that our love would be the start of warm human–Wyrforra relations everywhere. And when...when I got pregnant, he was the happiest I had ever seen him. He said that our family would bring humans and Wyrforra together and create generations of peace. It was his dream come true."

"What happened?" I had to ask.

"I lost the baby." Her voice was a course whisper. "He was...well, devastated isn't the right word. He withdrew into himself, disappeared for a few days, and then...he lost his mind. He killed almost everyone in the city. He told his men that humans were weak and inferior...worthless. And then...you know the rest. He rose to power and set the human race toward extinction. And I'm partly to blame. So is that the story you wanted to hear?"

"Yes," I said, rising. "Thank you. And don't worry about your safety. I can assure you that Erenvyr does not know I came here."

"I'm not worried. I don't actually think he'd hurt me. After all, I'm still here. No one has killed me or herded me off into some prison cell. Not a single Wyrforra has bothered me, aside from asking for some of my cooking, so I think I have some sort of protection. Maybe Arron still has some affection for me, even after all these years. I almost—no, never mind. Is there anything else you need to know?"

"No, that will be all. Thank you for your time, Rosa."

"Of course." She stood slowly and resumed her sweeping. "If you have any other self-incriminating stories you need me to tell, you know where to find me."

The lethargic sounds of the broom faded as I walked for the exit. The door seemed lighter as I closed it on Rosa and her memories. Briefly, I considered killing her, just to tie up all possible loose ends. But she was harmless, and I doubted anyone else would come looking for her. Not to mention, it was entirely possible that the King had set up some local protection for her. Besides, Rosa had helped me more than she realized. Finally, after all this time, I saw Erenvyr's vulnerable throat. I had the information. All that was left was to wait for the time to use it.

68 TYLOS

SHE REFUSED to leave my side. For that, I was incredibly grateful. But when the sky began to show orange, I knew that I'd have to urge her to leave. It killed me to let go, but I dropped her hand.

"Arianna," I said, keeping my voice low, gentle. "You need to go home."

"No, I'll stay until... Maybe I'll be able to change their minds."

"I don't think you can. These humans are almost as stubborn as Cats. Also...I don't want you to see it."

"I understand."

"Thank you."

The sky was coloring more and more by the second, painting the clouds. An eagle called in the distance.

Arianna choked back tears. "You goddamn stupid Cat. I'll miss you."

With my bound hands, I brushed her hair behind her ear, watching a tear trail down her cheek. Those sad storm-cloud eyes locked with mine, and I tried to think of a way to tell her all the things I couldn't say. That I didn't blame her for ending up here. That she was the best thing to ever happen to me. That even if I would have lived a thousand years, I would have given it all to spend another second with her.

But as always, my words failed me. Footsteps echoed down the hall, and I knew my time was running out. I reached into the breast pocket of my shirt and closed my hand over the small crinkled thing I had stuffed there. I closed the item in a fist and gave it to her. As she took it, I took her hands in mine, folding it into her palm.

"I love you," I whispered.

That's when they reached my cell. Two large men and one smaller one approached me, all respectfully silent. The small one helped Arianna to her feet and then unlocked my door.

"It's time. Come with us," he said in a heavily accented voice. He offered a hand to me as well, and pulled me up gently by my tied wrists.

Arianna looked as though she were about to protest, but I shook my head and offered her a weak smile. *Let me go.* Her brown hair silhouetted her face, and the dying sunlight cast her like a beautiful, fierce angel. As terrified as I was, that image gave me strength. I hoped that she could find strength in something, too. As strong as she was, loss is never easy. It's the ones left behind who suffer the most.

That was why turning away from her was the hardest thing I've ever done. I left behind the only person who had ever shown me any care. And as the humans fell in line beside and behind me, I walked with a straight back, strong shoulders, and broken heart. Arianna was left standing alone in a ray of light, watching as I was led away from her and to my death.

69 ARIANNA

IN MY HAND, crinkled and worn, was the ace of hearts.

70 ALMYRR

THE HIGH KING set up a dinner for us. I was aware that the occasion was mostly for General Hellman, but I was invited too. And when I moved to my usual position standing behind the King and watching for threats, he asked me to sit. I was apprehensive when I took my seat, as it was highly unusual for me to attend royal events as anything but a bodyguard. But apparently, the occasion was for me as well.

We ate in the White House's formal dining room, which was ornately decorated and almost uncomfortably large. The table was also too big, so the three of us seated at one end made the rest of the room seem oppressively empty. I was aware that there were guards positioned outside every door, but it still felt as though the three of us were alone. For me, it was incredibly awkward.

Luckily, the general and the King got along famously, meaning that I didn't often need to talk. I occupied myself with the food—it was quite a feast. A huge roast fowl of some sort sat at the middle of the table, and the vegetable called squash, which I found much to my liking, filled a bowl the size of a hubcap. Then there were tiny little green soft balls called peas, orange and red fruit, and something called cider that was served warm. After all that, something dark brown and square was brought out, covered in a thin red drizzle. At this, I couldn't help but ask before I tried the dish.

"General Hellman," I began.

"Byrron, son, my name is Byrron!" He chuckled. I gritted my teeth.

"Byrron, what is this...dessert, you called it?"

"It's chocolate! It comes from a bean grown in the tropics. It's got raspberry on it. It's a delicacy for humans. Give it a try!" he urged.

I did, and I was not disappointed. But the sweetness turned bitter on my tongue as I realized what was happening, and why I had been invited. Like a farm animal, I was being fattened for something. Erenvyr was giving me this feast because he was planning something. At best, I was being bribed, and at worst, I was being fed for slaughter.

The High King cleared his throat. *So which is it?*

"Byrron, there's a reason I called you here," said Erenvyr. The general nodded politely and listened, for once shutting his walrus-like mouth. "There's a squad in Montana that reported losing several soldiers some time ago. Now at first, I attributed that to desertion and didn't think much of it. I ordered the squad to report their numbers daily after that. But I have not received any messages from them at all. It's as if they disappeared."

Hellman rubbed his beard in thought, considering the possibilities. "You think something happened to them?"

"Yes, I'm quite sure. It's not like my soldiers to forget to send a message. So I think they may have stumbled across a human resistance camp. That's why I want you to take a small contingent of troops—say, two hundred or so—and go to Montana to investigate."

"Absolutely. I'll gather the troops first thing in the morning." He beamed.

"And Almyrr." The King turned to me. I felt my heart speed up, and I resisted the urge to check my weapon. He could easily call every guard in the building and have me torn to shreds on a whim.

And with his recently erratic behavior, I had plenty of reason to be worried.

"I want you to go with Byrron," he said. I nearly sighed with relief. *A bribe, then.* "I haven't sent my assassin out for blood recently, and I don't want anyone to think I've gone soft. So I want you to kill as many humans as possible."

"Yes, sir."

"Good. And have fun." He smiled that broad, charismatic smile. His eyes were almost pink with levity as he clapped his hands, summoning the serving staff.

"You two will take the trucks and leave tomorrow. But for now, more desserts!"

71 ARIANNA

WHEN I MADE MY CHOICE, I'd like to think that I wasn't ruled by emotion. But isn't everything we do determined by how it'll make us feel? Every decision, big or small, is made based on what the outcome will do to us. It might make us feel temporarily happy, or it might allow us to avoid guilt, or maybe it'll help someone we care about, thus saving ourselves. So I will fully admit I let my emotions guide me to this. But, I argue, they were the right emotions.

As much as I cared for Tylos, it wasn't affection that drove me. Love is a powerful motivator, but not my goal. No. What I did, I did for my morals. I did it because I knew that it was the right thing to do. And I did it for peace, because maybe, if I could show everyone that we didn't have to kill each other—maybe they would follow my example. If I could show them that instead...we could coexist. And someday, we could care enough to die for each other.

As I was fully prepared to do. I hoped I would be able to avoid it, but there was no guarantee for that. But it was well worth the risk.

All my friends, my family, would hate me for what I was about to do. And that hurt, very much. But I wasn't about to stand by and let something terrible happen. Not when I could stop it. I hoped that someday, they would forgive me. I hoped that I could forgive myself.

In the end, I didn't do it for Tylos. I didn't do it for the Fort, or the Cats, or the war.

I did it for peace.

And I did it for me.

72 TYLOS

I WAS glad that the execution was outside. The setting sun painted the clouds an array of beautiful colors, and the air was crisp and fresh. The humans probably thought it was cold, but to me, it was perfect. The pink and red tinted clouds looked like they held snow. I hoped it would snow. That would be a pretty sight.

The humans led me into the forest outside their stronghold. My bare feet snapped branches as I walked with my escort, crunching bark and frozen dirt into the ground. I enjoyed this sensation, though I suppose it's easy to enjoy anything when faced with impending death. Or perhaps I focused on these physical feelings so I didn't have to face my emotional ones. I let my mind loose in the world around me, so long as it didn't reach forward to the gallows. I found that it was the best way to deal with the walk. And besides, I had always been at home among the trees. It felt like a welcome reunion as their branches reached to me like comforting arms.

I was led to a meadow, a relatively small clearing about a mile from where we started. The ground was soft under my feet as I crossed the wet grass. There were about twenty people there, most arranged in two half circles on either sides of a wooden post that stuck up from the ground like half of a cross. Directly across from the post stood three humans, dressed in formal military attire and holding long, bending human weapons. Bows, I believe they were called. *So that was how they planned to do it.*

My guards led me to the post. They untied my hands and brought them behind my back and the post, then retied them. It was far too tall for me to slip my hands over it, and the rope was too thick to break. But with all the armed humans, there was no chance for escape even if I could free myself. I could only wait for panic to set in.

The human with the accent took a place a short distance from me as my other guards joined the audience. Another human with no hair and darker skin moved to stand on the other side of me, opposite the first one. I took a moment to appreciate how perfectly symmetrical it all was, with the three humans across from me, the two on either side, and the ones around us all. I had to hand it to the humans—they knew how to turn a death into an occasion. There was a pause in the ceremony, as if no one knew how to continue. I wondered if this was the first time they had done this. This seemed an odd concept to me. In the Wyrforra army, executions were fairly common. Finally, after a few seconds, the bald one spoke.

"We are here today because this Cat, or Wyrforra, has been sentenced to death." He cleared his throat before continuing, enunciating clearly to everyone in the clearing. "The method of execution will be by firing squad. In the Fort, those who make decisions are responsible for seeing the actions carried out firsthand. As such, the archers will be Chris Sakata, Aris Wisteria, and Anna MacCain."

The three humans with the bows all nodded as their names were called. They held a look of grim determination, and I took pleasure in the fact that they did not seem to be enjoying this.

"Since bullets wouldn't be effective, they will be using specially designed three-edged arrows. It has been determined that three arrows to the thoracic cavity would be the..." He almost seemed to stumble here. "...the most humane way to do this."

It surprised me that they had my pain in mind when they designed this. *They were really worried about making it humane?* And for many of them, it seemed they didn't want to do this in the first place. I suppose that Arianna wasn't the only human with a kind core. More than ever, I wanted so badly to show this to the Wyrforra, so they could take this kindness to heart and let it touch them as it touched me. There was more to life than survival and domination, and I wished desperately to prove this. And to the humans...I wanted to make them see that peace was possible. Not all of us are heartless. Maybe...maybe we could get along someday.

"As another member of the Seven, I will be giving the commands. Archers, ready your bows."

But today was not that day. And it was dawning on me that I would never see it. I would never see another full moon...or spring melt...or gray storm-cloud eyes.

"Draw."

I hoped my life wouldn't flash before my eyes. I knew exactly what I would see. Years and years of lonely, monochromatic uniforms and then a brilliant flash of color and warmth at the end. And then nothing.

"Aim."

I was proud enough to lift my head in my final moment. I would face death with my head held high and my heart strong, and whatever came next could not possibly scare me. I stood against that post with my shoulders back and my face lifted toward the ones who would end my life. But I lifted my eyes farther, turning to the sky's dying colors. Just then, a cloud opened up and began to gift the world with tiny, perfect snowflakes. They spiraled down like a veil, and when I closed my eyes, I felt as though my last sight was something truly beautiful.

I whispered, quieter than death, my last word.

"Arianna."

And as the man drew breath for the final command, I was ready.

But he never got a chance to finish, as another sound filled the clearing. I opened my eyes and searched in confusion, to find that all the humans were doing the same thing. Every pair of eyes there was trying to pinpoint the location of the sound, which was getting louder by the second. It was a familiar sound, too, but I couldn't place it. As whatever was making it rapidly approached us, it became more and more clear. Something began to glint in a break in the trees. It sounded like—

An engine?

A red motorcycle roared into view, popping back on one wheel as it entered the meadow. Riding it was a figure clad in black clothing and a red helmet, so they were completely hidden. My heart nearly jumped out of my chest as panic gripped me for the first time. *If that was...then she was in danger!*

The rider raced toward us, covering the small clearing in seconds. She—I guessed it was a she—reached behind her and drew a machete, holding it straight out like a knight with a sword. The humans began to panic, finally grasping the situation. Then, several things happened at once so fast that my mind had to parse out the events to understand what was going on.

I was still in a dream-like state when the rider reached me and set the bike into a slide around the post. The knife in her outstretched arm—because it had to be a woman—swiped at me, and I jumped back in fear only to realize that I could move my hands—she had neatly cut the ropes. I was free.

At the same time, one of the archers shouted "Fire!" My heart screamed in protest, worrying for her. To my surprise, someone else actually did scream in protest.

The man on the other side of me, with the accent, seemed to recognize the rider. He stepped forward as the bike continued to swing around, dust flying sideways from the tires.

"No!" He shouted. "That's—"

And that was just enough to get the archers' attention. Their arrows had been aimed at my heart, but the interruption had sent their aim haywire so only one flew dead at me. Unfortunately, it would still hit my chest and tear through. It was too late. I was dead.

Or I would have been, if the rider hadn't drifted the bike around the post, coming to a stop right in front of me.

And just as she did, the arrow struck. It made a dull *thunk* as it embedded itself into her back. The body that shielded me took the impact without a whimper. She let go of the handlebars, leaning forward in pain as weakness began to overcome her. I was frozen, staring, afraid that if I moved she would crumble before my eyes.

But then the faintest, most beautiful, familiar voice came from within the helmet.

"Drive."

And time returned to normal. The humans were beginning to gather themselves and Arianna was seriously injured. I wasted no time jumping into the driver's seat. As she wrapped her arms around me, I was infinitely glad she had explained exactly how to drive a motorcycle.

There's the throttle...and the clutch...

"Notch another arrow! They'll get away!"

When the bike actually responded to my commands, it felt like a miracle. I felt Arianna cling tighter to my back as the motorcycle took off, speeding away from the post. The sounds of confusion from the humans faded as we broke away from the clearing. I should have slowed down once we got into the trees, but I sped up instead, dodging the vegetation with adrenaline-fueled reflexes. The bike swerved and leaned and I was glad that the snow-riders back home were so similar. I pushed the machine even faster.

Arianna was shaking. Fear mounted in me as I considered the ramifications of a human hit with a weapon designed for Wyrforra. I hadn't seen how deep it had gone in or where exactly it struck, but an arrow sticking out of flesh is never a good thing.

"Don't worry!" I shouted over the roar of the bike, not knowing whether she could hear me. "There's an army doctor a few hours from here."

She clutched at me, and I wondered if she had a few hours. I knew right where the house where the doctor was—my squad had stumbled across it by accident a few months prior. We were going to kill the old human, but he fixed up some of our wounded so we let him stay. It seemed my generosity was coming full circle. I revved the engine higher, hoping to make it there soon, before it was—before she couldn't hold on any longer.

But it would be a long ride. I could only pray that we would both make it.

73 MAD CAT

A SILVER WIND spiraled into my little room, carrying with it a very distinct sound. *Shh, walls. I'm trying to listen. Is that—? Yes, it is.* A heartbeat, strong and hopeful. A heart that thought it was out of beats, but somehow survived to love another day.

I lay on the floor, back against the soft stone, arms and eyes splayed around me seeing and feeling the wind. The walls hummed with happiness, and I was inclined to sing along. A botched killing. A crisis averted.

But the wind carried with it a sound from much farther away. I sat up and leaned closer, trying to hear better. *Shh, shh. Was that? It was.* Angry, marching footsteps.

Another crisis on the way. This one would not be so easy to avoid. Not nearly.

Shh, now. There's danger in the wind. I can already taste the sweat and the tears and the...oregano?

74 ALMYRR

IF THERE'S anything I could credit General Hellman for, it's efficiency. He had two hundred troops with weapons, vehicles, and supplies completely prepared to leave by sunrise. The convoy formed a neat line of activity on the White House lawn. King Erenvyr met us before we set out.

"How soon will you be there?" he asked.

"It should take us about three days," the general answered with certainty.

"Across the country in three days? How is that possible?"

"As you know, sir," Byrron said, beaming, "my technology department has been working on blending human and Wyrforra technology for our purposes. We've recently developed modified human vehicles that can not only go through deep snow, but actually move faster in it."

"So the terrain will play to our advantage. Excellent!" He gestured for the two of us to lean toward him and lowered his voice. "Officially, your mission is to locate the missing squadron. Unofficially, find any humans in the area and eliminate them. Every one."

"Yes, sir," we said in unison.

"Very good. Report back to me when you return. I'll expect you in about a week." He sent us away with a salute.

As we left through the front of the White House, Hellman slapped me on the back in a way that was all too familiar. He led me through the lawn and into the bustle of several hundred soldiers. Men and women in white-speckled olive drab ran every which way, loading things onto vehicles, double-checking weapons and ammo, and locating squad mates.

"Almyrr." Hellman brought me toward the front of a long line of vehicles. "Just wait until you see these trucks. They're incredible! Quite a feat, if you ask me. Look, they're getting this one ready now!"

We stopped before the first truck in the line. It was huge and square and beige. The sharp angles and tiny windows gave it the look of a true moving weapon. The plow fixed to the front seemed needlessly sharp, narrowed to a polished point. I counted eight giant studded wheels on each side, and two long planks of metal with upturned ends ran out in front of the truck. It was intimidating, but it seemed heavy and cumbersome.

But as I watched, it began to change. Two soldiers hustled to the hulking machine, carrying an incredibly long strip of sectioned metal. They began to loop it around all of the tires, fixing it into the studs for security. It was a track, I realized, like for a tank or a snowmobile. I noticed what appeared to be nails sticking out in patterns from the track, no doubt meant to dig into the snow. The soldiers fixed the two ends of the track together with some sort of locking mechanism, completing the loop. With that done, they stepped back and the truck made a loud gear-turning noise. To my surprise, the metal planks began to lower. The truck brought them all the way to the ground where they rested against the snow, forming enormous skis. General Hellman noticed my awe.

"If you think that's something, wait until you see how fast she goes!" He laughed. "Now all aboard! We're riding point."

75 ODYRA

FOR DAYS STRAIGHT, I drove. When snow drifted over the road, I drove slow, but I kept going. I could do without sleep. When Lucky whined in hunger, I remembered to feed us, but I only ever turned off the car to refuel. But on the way home, I had plenty of gas and food, so I drove with little interruption.

And every second I drove, I planned.

Erenvyr had thought that a child—his child—could bring peace and maybe even change the world. But he had lost the baby, and reacted by starting a war. This was all interesting, but how could I use that? The King believed that humans were too weak to carry Wyrforra children, so these halflings could never exist. But was that true? In his grief, perhaps he had never considered that what happened to Rosa was a tragic accident. Perhaps a human–Wyrforra hybrid was possible.

But how could I *use* that?

Lucky panted happily from the passenger seat. I couldn't help but scratch him behind the ear.

"We'll be home soon, boy," I told him.

I turned my thoughts back to Erenvyr and how to use his past against him. But no solutions presented themselves. Yet.

That was probably for the best. He was at the height of his power at the moment. It would be far wiser to wait for his decline before I put some plan into action. So for now, I would wait as long as I had to. I was in a good place, after all.

And I had the information I needed. And when the time was right, I would use it.

76 DR. HANSON

MY SUPPLIES WERE DWINDLING. Most of my pills were gone, and the only gauze and bandages left were old and torn. And I was down to my last bottle of morphine. To say it was a sorry state of affairs was an understatement. And the equipment that Daire and Truman had brought back for me wouldn't help at all. Or at least, it wouldn't be of any medical help. But it was useful in a different way, a way that might save some people a lot of hardship. So I gathered up some of the old stainless steel—mostly syringes—put them in a satchel and headed for the basement.

Robin was doing pushups, but with her hands together due to the binding. I don't quite know what I was expecting, but it wasn't that. She had stripped down to her cargo pants and a sports bra—for all the running and fighting she did every day, it didn't surprise me that she always wore one. The bandage I had put on her bullet wound was white, showing no signs of blood. She didn't notice me as I came closer, and I stayed silent so I could hear what she was muttering under her ragged breath.

"388," she said. Sweat dripped from her nose as she pushed herself from the ground again. "389."

I coughed as I got to her cell, drawing her attention. She paused mid-motion and looked up to me in surprise.

"Can I have a moment?" I asked.

"Of course." She rose, stretching her arms. "What do you need, Doctor?"

"Pull your cot over to the bars here and have a seat," I instructed. She reached for the bed, and I noticed a faint purple circle around one eye.

"What's that?" I asked.

"Oh, the bruise? It's nothing. There was a minor incident a few days ago, but I'm almost completely healed now. You should see the other guy." She did as I asked and pushed the cot against the bars and sat on it, facing me.

"So what can I do for you?" Robin asked, a hint of nervousness in her voice. Her purple eyes were hopeful but not entirely trusting.

"I'd like your permission to run some tests. All I need is a blood sample. I think I might be able to figure out what the Cats are exactly if I had a little data."

"Absolutely. Do whatever will help," she said, extending her arms.

I smiled my thanks as I prepared the needle, alcohol wipes, and blood collection tubes. With my fingers, I felt for a vein and then wiped the spot with the alcohol. I took the needle and positioned it just right.

"This might pinch a little, but I'll be quick. I'm a practiced phlebotomist," I said, and pressed the syringe into her arm—only to have it snap against her unusually tough skin and send half the needle flying, leaving her skin unblemished.

"I should've known that would happen," I grumbled. "I forgot that Cats have thick skin. I have another needle but I don't know how to get past your skin without cutting you open."

"How about this?" Robin asked, tapping at the bandage on her stomach. "It hasn't healed all the way yet. Could you get blood from under the scab?"

"Yes, I should be able to. But it'll probably be deeply unpleasant for you."

"That's fine. Go right ahead."

She peeled back the bandage, showing a round mass of dried blood. It seemed to be healing well, and much faster than a human would have healed. And right at the edge of the scab was a soft spot between the skin and clotted blood. I prepared another needle, but I hesitated.

"Are you sure about this?" I asked her.

"Yes." She pointedly looked away from the syringe.

I tried not to think about what I was doing as I plunged the needle into the wound. Robin drew in a sharp breath and winced, but didn't pull away. I got the blood as quickly as I could and pulled the syringe away, much to both of our relief.

"Well, you were right about that being unpleasant. But if it helps, then it was more than worth it." She sighed. I began to gather my supplies, but she asked me in a soft voice, "Dr. Hanson, how are Daire and Fox doing?"

"Fox is...well, who knows. He's too quiet to talk about his feelings and too smart to let them slip. But I think he's all right. He's tough. But Daire...he's more lost without you than even he knows."

Robin seemed to crumple a bit at that. She hugged herself, folding inward slightly at the waist. She was worried about him.

"He'll be all right," I assured her. "He just needs more time to process. He'll come around."

"Thanks, Doc." She smiled at me with tired eyes.

"Of course. Send for me if you need anything." She nodded as I turned to leave, but seemed too preoccupied to answer.

77 FOX

WE WERE LEFT in a state of angry confusion as the motorcycle vanished from sight. I wouldn't admit it, but I was secretly glad that we weren't able to go through with the horrendous affair. But I was afraid of what this would mean for the Fort. Even now, people were starting to shout angrily at each other. Would we have a riot on our hands?

"Captain!" I called, panic rising in my voice. "What do we do?"

He didn't have to think—he had already strategized. He marched up to me as people began to crowd around us.

"Go after them!" he ordered.

"But that was—"

"I know." He didn't let me finish.

Truman had already gathered a few followers, ready for blood.

"We'll never catch them on foot!" he growled.

"I know," Cap repeated. "Follow them, see if they leave tracks as the snow falls."

Truman and a small posse took off in the direction the bike had gone, but we all knew it was useless. They would be long gone by the time the snow was deep enough to leave tracks. Cap ran a hand over his bald head, worry showing in the crinkles of his eyes. He locked his gaze with mine and I knew we were both thinking the same thing. *What would a botched execution mean for the already failing morale of the Resistance?*

†

By the time I got home, it was completely dark. Truman and his men were still in the woods, but the light of the moon wouldn't be enough for them to follow. They would give up and return to the Fort soon enough. I could barely see as I trudged into the basement, dragging my feet with weariness and a low-burning fear. Unsurprisingly, Robin was still awake, and she moved to the edge of her cell as I approached.

"Fox," she said. "How did it go?"

"It didn't."

"What?"

"The Cat was rescued and managed to escape."

Genuine shock flitted through her features. *So she hadn't been in on it.* That was comforting at least.

"How many Cats came for him? Was anyone else hurt?"

"Just one, and we didn't see their face so we don't know if it was a Cat."

"One? How?"

"They just showed up and whisked him away. On a red motorcycle."

Robin drew a sharp intake of breath. I could see the gears turning in her head as she decided exactly what she should say.

"So, what you're saying is..." she said carefully. "The Cat was rescued by someone who stole Arianna's bike."

I almost smiled. Some bonds are too strong to be broken, no matter the damage. And despite everything, Robin always protected her friends.

"That's right," I said, going along. "Whoever did it probably attacked her too, since we haven't seen her since. I bet she's been kidnapped. I doubt we'll find her for a long time."

"I hope that, wherever she is, she's all right."

"Me too."

I ran a hand through my hair. I could see my fears and worries echoed on Robin's face. If there was anyone I could confide in, it was her.

"It's all goin' to hell." I sighed. "Now two of our best fighters are inoperable and people are getting restless and unhappy."

"We—or rather, you—still have almost a thousand fighters."

"No, we've got a thousand people. Almost a third are too young or old to fight. About half of what's left have no experience with the Cats. That's only about three hundred."

"That's not too bad. We could still fight off a big attack."

"Except the average Cat is five times deadlier than the average person. If there were more than a few of them we'd be done for."

"But we've got some incredible people," she protested. "I've seen you take out ten before they even knew you were there. And Kiana and Ladan coordinate so well that they're great at separating and confusing Cats. And Cap, Anna, Naveen, Aris, and Chris are all legendary fighters. Not to mention Daire. He's the best."

"No, *you* and Daire are the best. Alone, he's just...off-balance."

"Off-balance? I don't understand."

"Never mind that. The thing is, if we have you two as a team, we have a chance no matter what the fight is. But now—I'm scared, Robin. There's something comin', I feel it."

Robin and I nearly jumped as another voice screeched from across the room.

"Something coming! Something coming!" howled the crazy Cat in the corner cell. "The fox eats Cats, the puma eats the fox, the bear eats the puma!"

"That Cat's lost his damn mind," Robin muttered. "Fox...don't worry. Our fighting power is diminished right now, but we're still strong. We're the Resistance. We stand, we endure, and we fight back. We can survive whatever will hit us next."

"Your faith is inspiring, friend. I hope you're right with all that. I really, *really* hope you're right."

78 ARIANNA

IT WAS the blood loss that would get me. The arrow had missed my spine, but it was shaped perfectly to take a big chunk out of my back. I prayed it wasn't deep enough to reach my lungs. But whatever else it did, I was losing a lot of blood.

I barely had the strength to hold on to Tylos. I passed in and out of consciousness as the night got darker and darker and the cold reached through my jacket. Somehow I managed to stay on the bike as Tylos pushed it faster and faster. He was a quick learner—incredibly fast. But Cats had good reflexes, so I guess it made sense. He dodged every tree and rock, swerving the bike over the snow. To my surprise, he seemed to have a clear destination in mind. I think he told me where we were going, but my memory of the past few hours was getting fuzzier by the minute. My whole world was becoming endless snow, dark trees, and Tylos.

A few hours into the trip, I felt us slow down. The snow was picking up, whipping at us and making the drive almost impossible. But he pressed on, taking the worn bike slowly but deeper into the forest. Wind and momentum tried to tear me from Tylos, but I used my fading strength to dig my fingers into his clothes. My mind grew fuzzy, consciousness becoming too hard to hold...

And then I must have blacked out. When I woke up, we had stopped. I was no longer on the bike and for a moment I thought I was floating. Slowly I realized I was being carried, Tylos's arms wrapped around me with frightened tightness. He was carrying me toward a large house that must have been at the edge of the woods. A rather fat old man was standing at the door, holding a lantern up to see us. It took a moment for sound to return to me, but then I realized that Tylos and the man were shouting back and forth.

"...Have to help her!" Tylos's voice fought the wind.

"No! Take her somewhere else! Dealing with the Resistance is too dangerous!" argued the man.

"She won't make it anywhere else!" Tylos pleaded. The man considered for a long moment, before opening the door. I felt Tylos shake with relief.

"Bring her to the back room and lay her down with her wound facing up," the man ordered as Tylos brought me into the warm house. I felt myself being carried and placed on a frigid operating table. The man hurried to tie on a white apron and grabbed for his instruments.

"Thank you, Doctor." Tylos sighed.

"Go hide your motorcycle. There will be people following you and I don't want them stopping here," said the man.

Tylos hurried back to the front door, but the doctor called to him right before he left.

"Wait! What's her name?"

When he answered, he wasn't looking at the doctor. His brilliant yellow eyes were fixed right on me, conveying deep fear for me but also a fierce hope.

"Arianna."

"Tylos," I responded, using the last of my strength to reach out for him.

And then I finally succumbed to unconsciousness.

79 CAP

SNOW FELL SOFTLY as we left the clearing. But it was just a light dusting. By morning, there would probably be only a few inches left. It used to snow so much more here. I would know. I had been in this area for a long, long time. But the state was different now. Things always change.

In a few short days, I had lost two of my best fighters. And though I'd never admit it, my best friends. And Daire was so far gone I didn't even know where to look. It was tough to watch someone like that fall to pieces. I had known him since he was a kid, and his father had been a good friend. The kid would pull himself together eventually, but in the meantime, this whole goddamn place was in chaos.

The thing that most people don't understand about the Fort, or about people for that matter, is their reliance on heroes. For some it's athletes, or models, or superheroes, or actors. Everyone has some inspiration. The Fort had 1,044 people at last count, and there wasn't a single one that hadn't looked up to Daire and Robin. They were the dream team, and they had carried all our hopes. They were beloved by every man, woman, and child. Their exploits and adventures were told and retold like legends, and they were met with admiration by anyone who crossed their path. Fox was a legend too, without a doubt, but there was nothing like a pair to draw people's attention. Robin and Daire gave the Fort a reason to fight.

And now, with Robin in jail and Daire emotionally shattered, the people had lost hope. Every single member of the Resistance had felt betrayed by Robin. The chosen team had broken up, and broken everyone's hearts with it. It felt as though the entire foundation of the Fort was collapsing. And not even what was left of the Seven could save us—the war heroes and the role models were just as distraught as the rest of us. Not even the seasoned veteran knew what to do about it. As the snow filled our retreating footprints, it felt like our morale was as dead as the human race.

80 DAIRE

THE WAR HAS BEEN over for twenty years.

I'm sitting in my living room, drinking coffee and reading the newspaper just like my father used to. I'm wearing khakis and a button-down shirt—clothes I never had an opportunity to wear during all the fighting. My house is big, comfortable, and painted soft fall colors. Early morning light radiates from the windows. It's peaceful and quiet.

An orange cat with a red collar hops onto the couch next to me. I go to pet her but she ducks away, meowing unhappily.

"What's wrong? Have you not been fed yet?"

The cat meows again, and I take that as my cue to get up. I wander into the spacious kitchen, looking for the cans of cat food. But the cupboard is completely empty. The cat rubs against my leg, still protesting her hunger.

"I can't find your food," I tell her. "I don't normally feed you. Where's—"

I trail off as I realize that something is very, very wrong.

"Where's my wife?" I ask the cat. The cat meows in response, *louder and more desperate. I raise my voice, too, feeling panic creep into it. "I don't understand you. Where is she?"*

Another cat, this one white, hops onto the counter. It stares through me.

"Do you know where she is?" I ask.

But the white cat doesn't answer. All of a sudden, the cupboard doors start to rattle. I open them, and a cat leaps into the kitchen. Then another, and another, forming an impossible wave of cats from inside that cupboard. I turn in confusion to see cats appearing from the living room and the hall, filling the kitchen with hundreds of tiny furry bodies.

"Let me out!" I say, struggling to move among all the cats. "I need to find my wife!"

I fight my way out of the kitchen amidst a cacophony of yowls and hissing. But my entire house is covered by now, cats filling every corner like air. I push past them, forcing my way through, finally stumbling out the front door and falling onto the porch.

And there I find thousands of them, running every which way, dodging and jumping over each other, like a living hurricane. Cats fill the streets and the lawns, even the rooftops. Not a single one is stationary as they do acrobatics, whipping their tails and leaping into the air.

"Where's my wife?" I call out to the mass. I get no answer. Desperation floods me and I scream to be heard over the cats. "Where is she?"

And then right before me is—a cat. But this one is sitting silently, staring right at me with green eyes. This is the only sleek black cat I can see, and the only one that seems to notice me. We stare at each other, me and this cat, for a long moment.

"Do you know where she is?" I ask it.

It stands, turns, and walks away. But its tail curves toward me, as though beckoning me to follow. I oblige, letting the animal lead me down the street. The surrounding cats thin out as we progress, until finally there's room to move. The black cat breaks into a run and I follow, sprinting to keep up. I follow it around a corner and we are alone and the moon barely lights the darkness. The cat sits and waits for me, and I walk cautiously toward it.

"Where is she?" I ask again. "I don't see her."

The cat waits a moment before it continues, leading me away from the suburb and into a secluded, gated park. Bare trees cluster the grounds, their knotted branches trying to blot out the moon. Shapes emerge from the mist clinging to the ground and I realize we're not in a park. It's a graveyard.

I follow the black cat farther and farther as the cold night air creeps up my spine. I shiver in fear, for myself and my lost wife. Was the cat really bringing me to her? What could she be doing in this awful place?

Finally, the cat stops. It flicks its ears toward me, and then jumps onto a headstone. The cat stares at me as its long tail hangs over the stone, curling around the engraved name. I'm shaking as I kneel to read the words as the cat's pitying eyes bore into me.

No. I read the words again. It's impossible! It can't—but she was—my...!

Robin Wake.

No!

My eyes flew open. I sat up in bed, trying to chase away the nightmare. As I went to rub my eyes, I found my hands were still shaking. And I realized something I had known all along.

This will never end.

81 ODYRA

IT WAS midday when I finally pulled up to the White House. I had driven for a few days straight and I was more than glad to get out and stretch my legs. I opened the door for Lucky and left the red car to the guards that patrolled the grounds. It was to my great surprise that High King Erenvyr met me at the doors.

I bowed stiffly, reminding myself that I was no longer the highest-ranking person in the area. The switch was a painful one, but I hid my resentment. The King must never know how I felt about him or everything I worked for would be jeopardized. I put on my most complacent face.

"I have returned, Your Majesty," I said.

"It's good to see you! I trust your mission was a success?" he replied with his usual booming voice.

"Of course, sir. I am pleased to report that the supposed resistance encampment in the California territory was nothing more than rumor." I was ready with the answer to any question he might ask, but I doubted he would guess I was lying.

"Really? Then what happened? I mean no offense, but you seem a little banged up." He gestured to the bandage on the back of my head where the deserter had knocked me out with a brick.

"I ran into a bit of trouble, but nothing serious. And I assure you, everything has been taken care of." It was getting easier and easier to act like a happy little soldier, and I could tell he was buying the charade. Soon enough, he'd trust me *completely*.

"Come in and tell me all about it. Oh, what's this?"

The King stared in confusion at the big, shaggy mutt in a white bandana behind me. Lucky leaned against my leg, tongue lolling as he looked at all the new people he was meeting. The dog wagged his tail as Erenvyr looked questioningly from the mutt to me.

"Just a stray, sir. I...found it to be useful on my journey."

"Are you going to keep him?" he asked, genuinely curious.

I glanced down and met Lucky's big brown eyes. They stared up at me with more affection than I had ever seen. He had gotten a little plumper just in the few days we had traveled together, and his coat was almost shiny. The once-starving mutt was really coming along. And he had saved me from that bear, risking his own life for someone he had barely known. And when that deserter had come after me, the dog had done his best to protect me. Lucky had been a more selfless and caring companion than anyone I had ever known.

"No," I answered.

King Erenvry shrugged. "Very well. Come in, come in."

I turned to follow the King into the building, but paused to speak to the guard.

"Chase the dog away," I ordered. "And if it comes back, kill it."

I saw the guard begin to herd Lucky off the grounds. The dog shied away from the strange man, turning his ears back in fear. His brown eyes locked with mine, searching for help. I closed the door.

82 DAIRE

COME ON, man. You can do this.

I repeated that again and again, staring at my haggard reflection in the bathroom mirror. My bloodshot eyes and stubble stared back, undermining my thoughts with my own disheveled appearance. I had made up my mind to talk to Robin this morning, but something kept stopping me. Namely, fear. Fear of rejection, perhaps, or righteous anger on her part. Or my part. To be honest, I was more afraid that I'd end up acting like an ass again. My emotions seemed to spin out of control lately, and as much as I tried to control them, they escaped and hurt those I cared about. I had yelled at Fox, been disrespectful to Cap, and refused Robin the slightest chance to defend herself. I felt terrible.

But at the same time, I didn't. She had lied to me for all these years. She had hidden her true identity, and to what cost? I didn't really think she was a double agent working against us, but how could I be sure? How could I be sure of anything anymore? My life had been turned upside down and it was her fault. So of course I was mad. But what good did blame ever do anyway. And what was I doing, moping around? But what was I supposed to do?

Go talk to her, I prodded. I tried to psych myself up, but my confidence failed, leaving me to glare at my shivering reflection. After a few deep breaths, I ran my hand through my hair and left, grabbing my coat. I headed for the prison with a purpose that seemed determined but were actually terrified. I tried to think about what I would say when I got there. And then I tried not to think about anything. I was almost there when I ran into Dr. Hanson.

"Daire," she called, striding toward me down the hallway.

I waited politely for her. She carried a large box, wrapping her arms around it with obvious effort. Various pieces of equipment balanced atop it—beakers, tubes, stands, empty vials, corked vials, vials filled with some suspiciously bright liquid, among other things. The delicate glassware rocked about, threatening to pitch off the box at any moment.

When she reached me, she shoved everything into my hands with an unceremonious "Here." I struggled to regain balance with everything as she selected two of the full vials from the pile and carried those herself, one in each hand. She turned in the opposite direction and hurried off. After a second of confusion, I set off after her.

"What is all this?" I asked, peering between the glasses to see the box was stuffed with papers.

"It's DNA testing equipment," she answered, not turning to look at me. "I'm testing Robin's blood against some samples to see if it is similar to anything I'm familiar with."

"How?"

"I'm separating the samples to their smallest components, comparing the blood cells and the plasma to identify—"

She looked over her shoulder and met my eyes. It was clear I didn't understand.

"Science," she said finally. "I'm using science."

"Oh."

"I'm almost done, actually. I have a hunch, and I should be able to tell soon if I'm right. I just need the tests to settle. And I'll need some help in the lab to make sure everything goes smoothly. That's where you come in."

My stomach dropped. "But I was planning to—"

"Make an ass out of yourself, I'm sure. You're not ready to talk to her yet. Wait until you're in full control of yourself."

I sighed. There was no use resisting. And besides, the doctor was always right. She was one of the few who could see right through me, and I had no doubt that she knew my state of mind better than even I did. So as I bustled off toward her clinic/makeshift lab, I figured it was for the best. I would have to talk to Robin later. I had all the time in the world.

83 ALMYRR

ON THE SECOND day of our trip we were, predictably, halfway
there. I had almost dozed off in the passenger's seat when the truck
jarred to a halt, nearly making me bounce my head off the dashboard.
I turned to General Hellman, who was riding in the back with eight
soldiers. He was preparing a rifle.

"What is it?" I asked. "An attack?"

"One of the men spotted an animal and wanted to shoot it for
dinner," he said through his hulking mustache.

I frowned at the delay but followed Hellman out of the truck to
see the poor beast. There it was, standing perfectly still on a snow-
covered berm. I recognized the shape instantly.

"It's a horse," I whispered as Hellman raised his gun.

The horse didn't move, but its head was turned right at us. I
wondered if it was waiting to see what we would do. Its ears pointed
straight ahead, and they didn't even twitch as Byrron cocked the gun.
He pulled the trigger and the air was filled with the sharp crack of the
bullet followed by a strange and confusing metallic pang. Hellman's
aim was true and it struck the horse in its chest—but the animal didn't
fall. Actually, to our extreme confusion, it didn't move an inch.

Hellman and I exchanged a glance, then stalked toward the creature with the gun raised. As we approached, it slowly dawned on us that this thing in the shape of a horse was not actually a horse.

"It's a statue," remarked Hellman. "Quite a nice one, too."

I walked up to the statue. It was about as tall as I was and made of a dull brown metal. It was dirty and old but structurally perfect. The representation was both accurate and artistic in a way that I didn't know was possible. The thick metal showed the creature's muscles in smooth, arcing lines, looking real enough that it seemed the animal could gallop off at any moment. Its mane was so finely crafted that I couldn't help but run my hand over the impossibly tiny strips of metal. Its wide back was smooth, unmarked by seams or imperfections. The legs were graceful and long, somehow both giving the impression of strength and delicateness as tiny veins ran through the bronze. I couldn't help but stroke the creature's face, almost feeling life in its realistic beauty. Though its eyes were just metal domes, I could've sworn they held a soulful warmth. The only flaw in this art was a small circular puncture in the creature's breast.

"Humans made this?" I said in disbelief.

"Oh, yes. They made pointless things like this all the time. You should see their art museums. I like their paintings, myself," remarked Hellman, already heading back for the truck.

But it took me a long time to tear myself away from the sight. The statue of the horse was among the most beautiful things I had ever seen, and it tore at me to know that it was crafted by clumsy human hands. Humans were graceless and stupid, but somehow, they created things like this. How could these inferior beings be the masters of such extravagant art?

As I climbed back into the truck, I rested my head against the doorframe but there was no chance of me falling back asleep. My mind was consumed by the statue and its creators. I kept turning this idea over and over as it gnawed at me. The humans were worthless. Nothings. *But... were they?*

84 TYLOS

I HATE it when people tap their feet on the floor. I really do. It drives me crazy. But that's not nearly as awful as sitting for what felt like days, waiting for any word on Arianna. Seconds dragged on with impossible slowness, each one tearing off a piece of my control as they passed. It was the worst torture I could ever imagine, the *not knowing* that reduced me to a sweating, foot-tapping, clock-staring mess. I could feel myself going insane.

When the doctor finally came in, the clock said it had only been twenty-four hours, but I would've sworn that years had passed. I hadn't slept, even though I was more exhausted than I had ever been. But I jumped to my feet and made myself stay silent so I could hear the news.

Slowly, the doctor untied his blood-spattered apron, placing it on a hook. He didn't speak for a long minute.

"What's the news?" I blurted out when I couldn't hold my words in anymore. "She made it, right? She's okay? She has to be, she's so strong. Really, she's the strongest person I've ever met. She is okay?"

He didn't meet my eye. "Listen, boy. There's a small army coming this way, and I hear they're looking for you. If they find you and her in the same building, there'll be trouble. Best be on your way."

"So she's okay to travel?" I asked eagerly. "Or should she not ride a bike yet? I can carry her. If we leave now we'll have a good head start." I had to force myself to stop talking.

"She won't be coming with you, son," the man said softly.

I could feel the fear rising in the back of my throat. "So she's not ready to travel. Can you hide her? You'll keep her safe until I can come back for her?"

The doctor stayed silent, staring at the floor. Panic rose inside me, and I moved around him, heading for the operating room. A hand on my shoulder stopped me cold.

"Arianna's dead."

I can't describe what I felt at that moment. In a way, I suppose I didn't feel anything at all. It was as though all my thoughts and emotions were just gone. I was saved for the moment by that small doubting voice that told me the doctor was lying. After all, Arianna couldn't really be gone. Could she?

Though I made no conscious decision, my feet carried me to the door of the room. I heard the doctor shout, "No, don't! You have to get out of here!" but it didn't register. Just a distraction. The world seemed to slow down as I gripped the handle, pushed the door open.

A white sheet marked her outline—a pure, unmarked shroud. Something clicked in my brain and I finally realized that I would never see her storm-cloud eyes again.

Arianna.

"You have to go now! They'll be here any second!" He had probably been screaming at me the whole time, but it took me a while to realize what he was saying. I didn't care if the whole army was knocking at the door. In that moment, I wouldn't have cared if they had killed me.

But I knew I had to run. I'll never know if I was running from the army or my own grief, but somehow I was able to turn my back on the woman I loved.

Then I was on her motorcycle, riding and riding. I don't remember getting the cycle and I had no idea where I was. All I knew was that the numbness was fading, retreating to a corner of my mind. The bike was slowing too, and I realized that it was out of gas. *I must've been riding a long time,* I thought. As the bike slowed to a stop, I found myself dismounting, then wandering in no clear direction.

Then, all at once, the last of the numbness vanished, and the full force of Arianna's death hit me. The pain of it knocked me to my knees. I didn't feel the cold, or the aching that must have been in my muscles. I only felt grief.

I screamed.

There, in the snow, in the middle of nowhere, I screamed. I screamed to everything and nothing. I screamed without purpose, with only a deep, unwavering pain the likes of which I could never have imagined.

I screamed, and then I found myself silent, kneeling in the snow. I stayed there for a long time.

85 MAD CAT

THE STARS WERE FALLING from the heavens.

I sprawled across the warm ground to watch them through the window. Tiny little stars floated down outside, twisting and twirling through the air as they twinkled. One of the stars managed to waft through the window. I caught it in one furry paw. It felt cold and wet and lonely, but when I opened my hand—*poof!*—it was gone. How curious. I guess stars don't last very long.

The walls loomed around me, but they no longer caused me any bother. We had made an arrangement, me and them. They would give me enough room to breathe and I would tell them stories. I like telling stories very much, and the walls were always eager to listen. It was a good deal. I told the walls about my life, or what I could remember of it, and the fairy tales I grew up with. I think they liked those the best, and I could see why. Everyone likes a good fantasy. And lucky for me, there were lots and lots of stories to tell. But no matter how many I told, the walls always cried for more.

"Not now," I told them, speaking strongly yet quietly. That is how you talk to walls. "Let Mad Cat rest."

The falling stars brought with them one of the old gods, though I could not remember her name. She had long limbs and flowing hair and she carried flowers. *Wind!* That's what it was. The stars carried a cold wind with them. It swam into my little room and ruffled my fur —my hair—and sent a chill down my spine. This was a harsh and unforgiving god. She made me shiver.

But she carried something far more chilling than mere cold. She carried a scent, but not flowers. No—the wind held the smell of violence. I sniffed hard, trying to grasp the sense and understand it, but the unforgiving wind whisked it away before I could grab it. But as fast as the wind was, she wasn't quite fast enough. I caught the most important part of the scent and in a second I realized what it was: the smell of blood not yet spilled.

The stars kept falling, drifting in tiny, multi-faceted shapes. They were beautiful.

86 DOC

THE OPERATING ROOM was cold and quiet as I closed the door behind me. Night was falling, but I was unwilling to turn on the old oil lamps just yet. Seemed disrespectful. Using the fading light from the window, I slowly gathered up the operating tools to clean them. I moved past the girl under the white sheet to the sink, but for some reason couldn't bring myself to turn the faucet on.

"Are you absolutely sure we did the right thing?" I whispered.

"No. I can't be absolutely sure," came the reply. "But I'm as sure as I can be that it was the best thing to do."

Slowly, the girl sat up, letting the sheet gather around her shoulders. She winced, and I knew that the arrow wound must hurt like hell.

"He seemed really upset," I said.

"I know." She looked as though she wanted to cry, but held back her tears. "But he'll be okay. As long as he thinks I'm dead, the army can't hurt him...and he won't get himself hurt looking for me." She sighed, and wrapped her arms around herself as though she were holding herself together.

"This is what's best for Tylos." Her voice came out as barely a whisper.

I looked down at the bloody instruments in my hands. I have seen a lot of suffering over the years, but watching pain like this never gets easy. Once again, I cursed the war for what it had done to these poor kids—and for what it had done to so many others.

I reached over and switched on the faucet. "Tylos was right about one thing."

Arianna looked over to me in surprise.

"I'm willing to bet that you're the strongest creature on Earth."

87 PORT

I CREPT out of bed as the sun began to rise through the window. I had stayed the night with Fox again, but I let him sleep, walking silently out of the room as he snored. I closed the door after taking one last look at the peaceful scene. I wished I could be so restful.

The Fort was already beginning to bustle, so I sought a moment of solitude by venturing outside. I left out the back door of the lobby and, after checking for unfriendly eyes, continued into the woods. It hadn't snowed last night, so my boots crunched down on morning frost and pine needles. I walked about a quarter of a mile until I found a square arrangement of stones—what had to be the foundations for a cottage that had collapsed decades ago. The building had probably toppled before the war, but the floor was still smooth and the fireplace stood vigil among the broken walls. There was no furniture left, but a spot next to the empty fireplace provided shelter from the wind.

This was one of my favorite places. It was a secret to all but me and Fox, who had shown me where it was. This old cottage was the perfect place for some quiet and self-reflection. I lowered myself to the floor, warmed by the sun, and sat cross-legged in the winter air. A rusted nail poked up through the floorboard near my feet. I plucked it, turning it over in my fingers as I thought.

First: Robin. That was scary. It was frightening to look up to someone, to know them for years, only to find out they weren't who you knew at all. To find out they had been lying and deceiving you and everyone you cared about. To find out they were an enemy. Or was she? I couldn't shake the feeling she wasn't as terrible as everyone thought. How many times had she saved a comrade's life? Or mine? She had orchestrated countless missions and kept us safe and fed and happy. Robin was awfully helpful for someone who was supposedly working against us. And I was secretly glad that the Seven hadn't decided to hurt her. Even if she was a Cat, Robin was my hero. I didn't want to turn my back on her.

Another thing weighing on my mind was this botched execution. The Cat had escaped, and one of our own was missing. That was worrying, but there wasn't much I could do about it now. I hoped Arianna would be all right.

Then there was Fox. So far, we had kept this—whatever it was—a secret. We didn't have any particular reason to hide, and I had little doubt we'd be accepted as a couple. We were just private people who preferred to keep things like this to ourselves. Should we go public? I didn't know. Things were working well. Best not to mess with them right now.

I was worried about the other Cat, too—the one I had interrogated. He had clearly lost his mind, and the scars all over his arms proved he might be dangerous. But what could we do? We didn't have any physiatrists or psychologists, and Dr. Hanson only dealt with physical injuries. So what to do? I suppose we'll just have to leave him and hope he doesn't do any more harm to himself or anyone else.

Problems, problems, problems...and no solutions. It was frustrating to say the least. Turning them over again and again in my head hadn't helped any, and I was left even more stressed than before. Desperate for a distraction, I took the rusted nail to the wooden floor, scratching out a rough image. I'm no artist, but I was rather proud of the little fox drawing I etched into the wood. I leaned back on my hands and let the sun shine on my face, listening to birdsong.

Only there was no birdsong. The startling silence filled me with a sudden sense of dread. I couldn't hear anything, not wind moving through the trees, not the distant calls of coyotes or elk, not even the soft footsteps of deer. The forest was utterly quiet. The lack of natural sounds was unsettling, so much so that I looked around to see if something sinister lurked nearby. I couldn't see anything, but I could feel it. This unnatural calm was more than just unsettling—it was wrong. And it felt dangerous. I followed my gut feeling and stood, moving quickly from the cottage. I almost ran home.

88 DAIRE

SMASH!

The sound of breaking glass woke me with a start. I sat up, feeling groggy and resenting the midday sun streaming glaring at my tired eyes. *Wait, midday?* I pushed up from the lab table where I had apparently fallen asleep and saw that it was, in fact, later in the day. The last thing I remembered was working into the early hours of morning with the doctor. I had been helping test the blood samples when I had passed out among the test tubes, hunched over in my seat like a tired student in lab class. I looked over and saw a broken beaker on the floor, which I must have pushed off the table in my sleep. *Yikes. Hopefully that wasn't important.*

I rubbed my eyes, looking around for Dr. Hanson, but it appeared that I was alone. After a brief search, I stumbled across a note. It took me a moment to decipher the handwriting: "Gone for food. Be back soon. Don't leave! I still need your help." Well, that was Dr. Hanson. Straight to the point. But I couldn't blame her. This work was important. Probably the most important work I could ever do. Not that I really knew what I was doing. I didn't know what half of the equipment was for, and the names were lost on me. There was the...spinny thing, and the little tube turkey basters, and the whatevers. But I did my best, and I think the doctor benefited from my help. But I had no clue if we were close to figuring out what the Cats really were. I ran a hand through my hair in frustration and stood to find something to do when something shiny tucked away on top of a shelf caught my eye.

I had to shuffle around a few boxes to reach the white object, but when my hand closed around it, I found it to be unsettlingly round and smooth. *It's a skull. Of course it's a skull. Gross.*

Pushing down my revulsion, I turned the thing over in my hands, wondering why the doctor would keep it around. When I turned it so that its empty eye sockets were facing me, I noticed something interesting. A bullet, flattened by impact, was bored into the bone. But somehow, it had failed to pierce the skull, spreading out into a star pattern but not going very deep. But how?

"That one took me a while to figure out," said a familiar voice from the doorway.

I jumped, nearly dropping the old skull, but it was just Dr. Hanson. She walked in carrying two plates with delicious-looking sandwiches, but my hunger had been temporarily tempered by the dead thing in my hands. The doctor set the plates on the table and took the skull, holding it delicately and running her fingers around the jaw.

"Cat skulls are exceptionally thick," she explained. "A lot like dog skulls. They seem to be more durable, too. That's why bullets don't really work on them."

"But if the bone is thicker, shouldn't that mean that there's less room for their brains? I mean their heads are about the same size as ours. So does that mean they have smaller brains?"

"Yes and no. I thought the same thing at first. But a few years ago, I got the chance to do an autopsy."

"Ew."

"Quiet. I discovered that their brains are smaller, but they have more folds than we do, which translates to roughly the same surface area."

"So they're about as smart as we are?"

"It's more complicated than that!" She sighed. "But essentially, yes."

"Did your autopsy explain their weird eye pupil thingies?"

"No. But I have a theory about that. So you know how their eyes narrow into lines instead of circles, just like cats. But cats—the small, domestic animals—use their eyes to see well in the dark. I think the Wyrforra use their eyes a little differently. When the Resistance started, at the beginning, we used flash grenades against the Wyrforra. But those barely affected them at all."

"Why not? Their senses are sharper than ours. It should affect them more than it affects humans."

"That's what I assumed. Until I realized that the domestic cat's eyes narrow in bright light in order to take less light in."

I stared at her. That didn't make *any* sense.

"God, I miss grad students." The doctor sighed. She picked up a wide-bottomed beaker and a test tube. "So this beaker is a Wyrforra's eyes in the dark, or a human's eyes all the time."

"My pupils aren't shaped like that."

"Shut up and pretend it's a circle. Our eyes are shaped like this so that they can take in as much light as possible. See, big circle, lots of light. Now this test tube is a Cat's eyes in the daytime. There's plenty of light so they don't need to take in so much. That's why it's a narrow line. Small line, not so much light going through."

"Okay..."

"So then I considered the flash grenades. You know what they do, right?"

"Yes, they make a blinding light to incapacitate our enemies," I said.

"Correct. But they didn't work as we intended because of the Cats' pupils. They just took in the light with their tiny pupils. *They* could see just fine."

"So you're telling me Cats can see well in the dark *and* in harsh light?"

"That's right. So tell me what that means, Daire."

"It means that... We can't fight them in bright light or darkness?"

"Yes, but that's not what I meant. It means that wherever the Cats are from, they have evolved to live with bright light and dark nights."

"Like the arctic circle! Where it's night for half the year, and the sun reflects off the snow for the other half!"

"Exactly." She smiled. "So we're one step closer to understanding the Cats. I have another idea about where they came from, but I won't know for sure until we're done testing this blood."

"What's the theory?"

"I'd rather not say. We'll know soon enough. Let's get back to work after lunch. We have a long day ahead of us, so eat your sandwich."

89 ALMYRR

THE SUN WAS SETTING on our third day when we spied the old hotel. The cold wind brushed my jacket around my feet as I stood atop the stopped truck. I had watched the building from a half-mile away for an hour with binoculars. Flickers of movement drew my attention and then finally, as the sun touched the horizon, I saw them. Light glinted off weapons in open spots of the derelict walls—lookouts. So it was an organized group of humans.

Well, look at that. There really is a resistance base here.

General Hellman emerged from the truck. He stretched, staring at me, turning to see where I was looking and back again.

"Is anything there?" he asked.

"A human camp. Probably at least a hundred of them," I answered, still looking into my binoculars.

"Very good. Should be pretty easy to wipe them out. But there's no sense in rushing in. We'll wait for the sun to go down and let the darkness hide us. I'll go inform the men."

I could hear the excitement in his words. I felt it, too. I hadn't been in a real battle for so long, the adrenaline already held me in its grip. My body itched to fight.

"Come to me, humans," I muttered. "Ride out on your metal horses. See where your artistry gets you."

†

When dusk finally fell, we were more than prepared. Every soldier knew the plan: halfway there, we would abandon the trucks and creep in on foot, climbing over the high brick walls with ropes. They wouldn't even know we were there until we started the slaughter.

Darkness descended, meaning that the humans' frail vision would betray them. It was time to set off. The soldiers were all loaded in the snow-tanks, with General Hellman and me in the forward-most vehicle. I gripped my knife in giddy anticipation as the truck began rolling. I felt the familiar bloodlust come over me as we headed toward the battle. I had been in a dozen battles, a hundred fights, and a thousand assassinations. There was no fear left in me. Just eagerness and a strange sense of...destiny.

We moved in silence toward the human base, a long string of identical trucks in our wake. Our precision was flawless, and everything was going perfectly.

That is, until a piercing alarm sounded from the base.

The trucks began to slow, preparing to drop us off. I swore, turning to the general. Byrron was stroking his beard, looking not nearly as concerned as he should have been.

"Change of plans, sir?" I asked.

"Let the soldiers in the other trucks dismount and continue on foot," he said with a smile.

The driver looked to General Hellman. "And what should we do, sir?"

"Full speed ahead," he answered.

"But the wall!" I shouted as the truck gained speed.

"The plow on the front of this is military-grade steel," he said, gripping the overhead handles and grinning like a happy child. "We can take down any wall."

"We're going to ram it," I said to myself, unbelieving.

"We're going to ram it!" repeated the driver, as a warning.

I braced myself for impact half a second before we collided. The truck was rocked violently backward, but it did the job and a circle of bricks came tumbling down, collapsing on the truck but leaving enough space around it to use as an entrance. I looked to the general, who seemed ready to giggle. I was unhurt, but thoroughly confused.

"That worked," I sputtered.

"You probably think I'm crazy," responded the general. "Here's a little tip, Almyrr: the wisest people usually are. Listen to the fools. They are often one step ahead of the rest of us."

I had no response to that. I could only stare.

"From the way he's bent over the wheel, I think we lost our driver," he continued. "But other than that, it was a complete success. So what are you waiting for, son? We've got an army to command!"

I don't know if it was the collision or the sheer insanity that had my head spinning when I stepped onto the battlefield, but it didn't matter. The smell of blood would clear it soon enough.

90 MAD CAT

WHAT A BEAUTIFUL, beautiful, *beautiful* night. Or almost-night, I suppose. The walls shone with silver pouring from the window, which dripped down and pooled on the ground. I wanted to drink it but someone told me that no, mercury was poisonous.

The sun was setting, or the moon was rising, or perhaps they were meeting somewhere in the middle. My human friends would have said that it was dark, but my face eyes and the eyes scarred into my arms could see just fine. I could see the woman, or creature, or god, across the room in her own silver cage. She slept, but dark thoughts hung above her like clouds. I could see them, so thick and resolute that they threatened to suffocate her.

I whispered to her, "Oh, your highness, you'll be all right. A warrior princess can tame the wolves inside herself." She did not hear.

The stars twinkled down into my room, reaching a million tiny antennae out onto the Earth. The stars pushed back the walls, stopped them from closing in on me. For that, I was incredibly grateful. Stayed by starlight, the bricks and the bars failed to trap me. I could sit comfortably in my room, unafraid of the tight borders. It was rather wonderful.

And then, as if it couldn't get better, the walls began to sing. It wasn't poetic, but it was music, and I loved it. Louder and louder the walls sang, until I knew that every wall in the whole building, maybe the whole world, had joined in. They all sang in joyous unison, louder and higher and louder and higher until their song reached to heaven itself and roused the gods from slumber. It also woke the little goddess, I saw.

"Isn't the music beautiful?" I said to her, laughing, as she ran to the bars in a panicked dance.

"It's not music, it's the alarms!" she cried. "We're under attack!"

91 DAIRE

CHAOS. Utter chaos.

Everyone was swarming around the Fort, racing for weapons or loved ones, fighting not to get trampled. I struggled to keep my footing amidst wave after wave of bodies surging and crushing around me. I got turned around and disoriented, pushed, elbowed, stepped on, and altogether attacked. Finally, I caught sight of a familiar bald head in the crowd, limping toward me.

"Cap!" I called. "Where's the fighting? I'll go and—"

"Escort the civilians out of the Fort," he called over the noise. "Dr. Hanson will help you. Get them all to the woods north of here and ready to run if need be."

My stomach dropped to my knees. It seemed to be doing that a lot recently.

"But I can fight!" I protested.

"No, you can't, son. You're missing your other half. Besides, this is more important. Get everyone at least a mile away from the building."

"Yes, sir."

Cap finally reached me through the crowd. He set a hand on the back of my neck and locked eyes with a soft intensity. He was trusting me with something very important, and he believed in me wholeheartedly.

"Get them to safety, Daire. And after you do, come join the fighting."

I nodded, and Cap almost smiled before turning and hustling back down the hall. He called back to me over his shoulder.

"When those civilians are safe, come find us. Just follow the sounds of dying Cats."

"Yes, sir," I said into the crowd, chin raised in pride. If there was anyone who could command us to victory, it was Cap. But everyone had a part to play, and it was time for me to do mine. I cleared my throat, raising my voice to be heard above the bustle.

"Listen up!" I called. Heads turned to me, and I put as much authority as I could muster into my words. I needed these people to listen. "Everyone who's not fighting, head to the northern exit! We'll be leaving from there as soon as everyone is out. Hurry! There's no time to lose!"

92 FOX

WHEN THE WALL broke down and everything went to hell, there were a few of us who stepped up before the alarms had died. I strode onto the battlefield as Cats began to pour through the opening, crawling three or four at a time through the rubble. As our enemies descended, I looked to my allies, lining up beside me like a football team. Kiana and Ladan were with me, staring ahead with reassuring calmness. They gripped their knives—identical long, curved blades that Kiana once told me were called *pesh-kabz*. I had asked her why they each had a matching knife, but she had told me that was a sad story she would rather not repeat.

On my other side was Truman, who I was secretly hoping would be a casualty of the fight, or at least have a minor injury. He was looking big and confident.

It hurt to admit, but I almost turned to look for Robin and Daire. I had never faced a big fight without them, and it felt off-balance not to have them here. But there was nothing I could do. Daire would come in time, but as for Robin—well, it was looking more and more like our days as the three musketeers were over. With the look of all the

Wyrforra flooding the courtyard, it was starting to seem like *all* of our days were over.

I sighed to myself, feeling the pre-battle jitters slowly get replaced with grim determination. I gripped my crossbow, loading a bolt and feeling the mechanism click into place. People—my own people—began to pour out from the Fort, filling the space behind my line. I waited, as did Truman and the twins. The Cats were grouping, preparing for their strike. The humans did the same, muttering to each other and readying whatever weapons they had been able to scavenge.

The courtyard began to fill to capacity, and from where I was standing, our odds seemed less than ideal. The Cats, probably about a hundred fifty of them, were forming ranks. We, the humble humans, were shaking in our boots. Those of us who had had military training were doing our best, but for the most part, we were just survivors. But the Seven and especially Cap had trained us well. We might not have been a perfectly organized army, but we could fight. And we would fight until the last man.

As my friends rallied around me, I couldn't help but feel some hope. If there was any chance of us winning, it lay with these people's hearts. These Wyrforra—when they fought, they risked losing soldiers. But when we fought, we risked our family. That's why we would fight harder and longer than any of these Cats. Even outnumbered and outgunned, we stood a chance. Hopefully more of a chance than any of the Cats realized.

We had another advantage, too, though that was a double-edged sword. The courtyard was huge, but it wasn't infinite. It couldn't fit all the Cats, but it couldn't fit all of us either. But we were closer. When each side ran out of space, it looked like there were between a hundred fifty and two hundred people on either side. It was a tight fit, but no one was willing to press the lines. Humans and Cats fought until both armies had to turn the excess soldiers away, forcing them outside the walls. Cats peered in from the hole in the wall, and humans appeared in the windows of the Fort. Hungry eyes, human and Cat, surveyed the battlefield, while those of us battling weren't feeling so lucky.

There was a moment of silence in the courtyard. For just a few seconds, the Cats and the humans just watched each other. Their leaders, an older man with a beard and a younger one with long black hair, stared me down. Their soldiers followed suit, turning slit-pupiled eyes to my people as we met their gaze. But every single face shared a hollow, deep-set look—the look of someone preparing to die. For those few seconds, there was a tiny moment of peace between two species who were, in each of their hearts, afraid.

And then the Cat leader, the one with the beard, pointed toward us. And all hell broke loose.

Just like that, the fighting started. The Cats charged at us, and with a cry the humans charged right back. I could almost hear the impact as the armies clashed. Humans swung machetes and baseball bats, combating the Cats' regulation army knives. I waited, feeling the rush of activity around me. Things were moving so fast as I lifted my crossbow, glancing at the loaded bolt. The moon shone off the metal tip, reflecting with an eerie beauty.

"There are so many beautiful things in this world," I whispered to my bow as I lifted it toward the oncoming slaughter. "But this ain't one of them."

I leveled it at a Wyrforra and released the arrow.

There was no going back once I joined the fight, and no slowing down. I loaded bolt after bolt, weaving through the crowd, ducking under allies' swinging arms and taking quick, careful aim at the Wyrforra. I concentrated my efforts on the most imminent threats to my friends, taking out the Cats who were about to land a finishing blow. It was difficult to kill one of them with a bolt but I knew the secrets, and I incapacitated when I could.

A Cat snuck up on Port, reaching to strike with a combat knife. I put a bolt through his forearm, pinning it to his shoulder. Cap was getting overwhelmed in a circle of enemies—but when the Cats were struck in the kneecaps, they were distracted enough for Cap to fight back. I fought, I killed, and I protected my friends. Things got gory fast, with almost immediate casualties on both sides. A young Wyrforra warrior was cut down from behind when he took one step farther than he should have. A human woman was practically torn apart when she was disarmed and surrounded. A Wyrforra met her end when she was trampled by the sheer number of humans. A human was killed on his knees when a stomach wound brought him to the ground. Death and blood and pain. It made me sick.

A piercing scream came from behind me, and I grimaced at whatever terrible grief had caused it. But I didn't turn to look until the same voice cried out a single wrenching word.

"Kiana!"

I whirled in a panic, found a circle of Cats gripping weapons and watching like wolves surrounding their prey, waiting. In the center was Ladan, clutching her sister. Kiana lay across her sister's lap, arms hanging at her sides. Blood, a horrible, impossible amount of blood, welled from Kiana's stomach. The dying woman looked up toward her sister and offered a somber smile. A red drop fell from her lips. Her hand twitched on the ground.

The Cats stepped closer as Kiana drew wet, ragged breaths. I feared for a moment that they would descend on her but they waited, watching. Ladan ignored them completely, cradling Kiana and crying. She whimpered as her sister's lifeblood puddled around them. Kiana convulsed, rocking as Ladan clutched her.

Finally, Kiana relaxed. She met Ladan's gaze, and I think they were talking in that silent way they had. After a moment, Ladan's jaw clenched. Her hands stopped shaking as she lowered her sister's body to the ground. She bent over Kiana, folding her hands over her chest, and when she straightened and stood to face the Cats, she carried a righteous fire with her—along with Kiana's *pesh-kabz*. The Cats lunged forward and Ladan shouted, not with pain but with fury, two identical curved knives in her outstretched arms. She surged forward with a battle cry, launching herself in a spinning duel-bladed attack. She whirled and lunged, slicing in long arcs. She moved too fast for the Cats to catch and in a matter of seconds five lay dead at her feet. Ladan stood there panting, fists clenched on handles slick with blood. Her shoulders shook and she stared downward. I knew she must have been torn between falling to her knees to grieve and continuing the fight. But Ladan was a warrior. She raised her head, tears streaming, and she marched back unblinking into the fray.

Kiana lay still, her now-vacant face turned toward her sister's back. For a moment, it seemed as though Kiana was watching her sister with pride. But her eyes were hollow and glazed. She was gone.

I stood quivering with my bow, driven toward revenge. But blood costs blood, and there was no room for any more hate. I would fight and I would fight hard, but I would do so to protect the ones I cared for, and humanity as a whole. I couldn't save Kiana. But there would be others. As hard as it was, I needed to continue the battle. I gritted my teeth and loaded another bolt.

93 ROBIN

BLOOD STREAMED from my knuckles as I pounded against the wall. Anger, frustration and fear fueled me as I tried to break through the brick walls with my bare hands. I kicked and punched and screamed as though the sheer force of my emotions would free me from this damned prison. But the walls were deaf to my pleading. I couldn't bend the bars on the window. I was trapped, and there was absolutely nothing I could do about it.

Outside, my friends were dying. The sounds of battle pained me, as I was forced to listen to the cries of pain and the clash of metal. This was where I should be helping. I could save the Fort and drive back our enemies, if only I could get out of this *damned cell!* I jumped and spun, landing a hard kick on the outermost wall. But the brick didn't move, and I was left still imprisoned, but now with a sore heel.

I jumped as the brick seemed to move, but it was just an impact from the battle resonating through the stone. Another scream from outside—it could have been someone I cared about being killed. I screamed in frustration, feeling the need to defend my home rock me to my bones. *What if Fox got hurt again? Or Port, or Cap, or the twins or...*

No. I couldn't even think his name. I wouldn't let the thought of him falling in battle cross my mind. If I did…I would start wishing for that red capsule again.

A cry of pain and grief sounded from outside, followed by the impact of a body being thrown to the ground. We were going to lose the battle. Everyone I cared about would be gone. There would be no hope left for humanity, just as there was no hope left for me.

I fell to my knees. I had chosen the humans long ago—or rather, I had just ended up with them. But I had never once regretted taking humanity's side. And I knew the risks. I figured that I would one day be killed, either in battle or by my own allies. But *this*—this was far worse. To sit by helplessly while my world crumbled was a fate far worse than death. I dug my fingernails into my palms until crescents of blood welled in my shaking hands. Everything was collapsing and *I couldn't save it!*

I dragged my attention away from the sounds of battle as footsteps echoed down the hall. I couldn't find the strength to look up, only stare at my hands and pray it was Wyrforra or human who wanted to kill me. I clenched my fists even tighter. The steps came closer and I waited with bated breath. I closed my eyes. They were just a step away from my cell now. Whoever was coming for me would have to—

"Robin."

I squeezed my eyes tighter. *No. Anyone but him.*

"Are you here to kill me, Daire?" I asked. All the pent-up rage helped me keep my voice steady. I was done apologizing.

"I should be," he said, his voice quiet but strong.

It carried conviction, and something else I couldn't identify. I opened my eyes and met his gaze.

His face was tired and worn, matching his battle armor. He didn't have a full set—a light chest cover, a guard on his left forearm, and thick boots, split down the side and stitched up to fit. He carried a machete in his belt. I wondered if he planned to use it on me. But… there was no bloodlust in the green depths of his eyes. I couldn't tell what there was exactly, but it seemed—gentle. His words, however, were far from it.

"You're not one of us." I flinched when he said it, but couldn't tear my eyes away from his. "You're a Wyrforra, a Cat, and a demon. And no matter who or what you care about, you will never be human."

Blood dripped to the floor. I had dug my nails further into my skin without noticing, tearing away flesh. I barely felt it. I was enveloped by another pain.

"People say you're a traitor," he continued. "And a liar. And you could never, ever be our ally."

I felt as though I had been punched in the stomach, as pain and nausea fought their way to the surface.

"They say you were born a Cat, so you could never be a member of the Resistance."

Another blow. The agony was nearly unbearable.

"They say a human and a Cat could never be friends. We can never be together."

That struck home with such force that it left me feeling almost numb. The shaking in my hands subsided, ever so slightly.

"The same can be said for your entire species. They're all evil, ruthless—irredeemable. We are good, you are bad. This war won't end until one of us kills the other. Humans and Wyrforra can never coexist. They say that your species is our enemy, and you are defined only by what you are when you're born. They say you're only a Cat, and I'm only a human, and our species are the only things that matter."

I finally had to look away, turning to stare with wet eyes at the dirt. But as I watched, something clattered to the ground right in front of me. I squinted in the darkness, confused, until I made out...*a key?* I picked it up, surprised to find that it was a key, I suspected to my cell. I turned to look at Daire.

His eyes were imploring. His voice was quiet now, and...hopeful. Trusting. Caring.

"Prove them wrong."

94 DR. HANSON

"RIGHT THAT WAY, until you find the others," I said, pointing the last group into the woods.

They set off, with a last look back toward the Fort—their home. A man, woman, teenager, and a child too young to know what the world was like before the war turned away from their refuge of the past decade and headed off into the unknown with all their worldly possessions on their backs. They also carried as much of my testing equipment as they could carry, bless them. That little family was the last stragglers left after Daire cleared out the Fort. Every noncombatant was headed to a safe zone, and Cap had ordered me to go along with them.

But there were no wounded soldiers there. No one who needed my help. Meanwhile, my friends were fighting and dying. So it was time to defy orders once again.

I hurried to the side of the Fort, a large open area that was rarely used. It was far enough from the fighting that it wouldn't be noticed, but close enough to hold people. There was open space ringed with trees, and a large wooden container off to the side. It was perfect, and thanks to some foresight on my part, it was already prepared. A canopy was rolled up and pinned to the wall, but I pulled it away easily and stretched it out, attaching it to the nearest trees with ropes. Roof, check. I ran to the container and threw the doors open, pulling out stretchers and unfolding them into makeshift cots. I only had about a dozen—it was all we could salvage from abandoned ambulances through the city, so it would have to do.

Finally, I grabbed a box from the back of the crate, closed the container, and spread out the stash of medical supplies I had hidden long ago. And just like that, the first-aid center was ready. It was no hospital, but it was all we had. I rolled the sleeves back on my lab coat and tied a thin rope around my waist to keep it from fluttering around. With that and a bracing deep breath, I headed inside the building and ran for the courtyard entrance.

I couldn't hide a grimace as I stepped into the courtyard. It wasn't the first battlefield I had seen, but it was certainly the most hopeless. I had never seen people with such fear in their eyes, but I could hardly blame them. The battle had only just begun and already gallons of blood had soaked into the earth—most of it human. The Wyrforra were just too powerful and frightening.

Our soldiers were standing to fight, but their weapons shook in their hands. They grouped in tight clusters, seeking safety with friends only to be surrounded and overpowered. The Cats were already starting to overwhelm us. Bodies dropped to the ground like ragdolls, and I tried not to see their faces as I determined the dead from the wounded, figuring out those I could save. So many people were simply too...torn apart. Their opponents were too ruthless, and even more than they damaged their bodies, they hurt our morale. Our hope was failing fast, and because of that, our fighting force was far less effective. Our odds had been slim to begin with, but now—we didn't have a chance.

"Doctor!" A voice shook me from my thoughts and I saw Port, with Cap's arm around his shoulder. Port was holding the older man up, struggling with his weight.

I rushed toward them, but a few steps into the courtyard I found myself thrown to the ground by a rushing force. A Cat in red battle armor stood over me, poised and silent with a knife in one hand and the other with fingers splayed out like claws. His eyes seemed to glow as he watched, as though trying to determine something.

"M-medic!" I cried, taking a wild chance.

The Wyrforra's eyes flickered over me, and for a second, it seemed like he didn't care. My heart jumped to my throat, but then he turned his eerie eyes away and moved on, leaping into battle with someone else. Swallowing my fear, I pushed myself to my feet and ran for Port.

"Damn Cats," grumbled Cap. He was gritting his teeth in pain but didn't seem grievously injured. "I only had one good leg left and they went and broke it."

I slung his other arm around my shoulder. "Let's get him out of here. Follow me to the first-aid tent."

"Wait." Cap's voice stopped us. "Is that—?"

Port and I couldn't help but follow his gaze to the top of the outer wall ringing the courtyard. Two figures stood, silhouetted by moonlight. One was tall and lean, with black hair that had grown far too shaggy. He was smiling as he pulled a machete from his belt and surveyed the battlefield with green eyes.

Next to him stood someone in fitted black battle armor. A hood was pulled over her head, and under it was a mask that covered the top half of her face. The mask was a familiar veneer of white and tan, mimicking the colors of a barn owl, with feathers carved into the material. The eyes of the mask cast shadows over the woman's eyes. She stood tall, and carried no weapons except a radiance of determination.

Robin and Daire! I almost shouted in joy, and my reaction echoed through the crowd as people realized who was there. Humans lifted their faces, eyes wide as they took in the sight of their old heroes back on the field. But then doubt surfaced as people remembered that Robin was...not like us. Hundreds of faces looked to her, waiting to see what side she would choose. The whole battle, maybe even the

MCKENNA MILLER

war, hung in the balance as the collective morale of the humans could fail or be revived by whatever happened next. For a long moment, everything was quiet.

Robin slowly reached for her mask and then removed it, pushing her hood back in the process. Her violet eyes shone as she raised the mask above her head, framing it against the silver moon.

"Humanity!" she cried, throwing the mask into the sky.

Her cry was taken up by every single human in the battle, until it became a resonating rallying call. The humans' efforts redoubled as hope spread like holy fire. The Wyrforra, already confused by the humans on the wall, were unprepared for the sudden onslaught. The score, it seemed, was starting to even up.

Even I couldn't hold back a smile as Robin and Daire joined the fray.

95 ALMYRR

THE NIGHT AIR was cool as it swept around the churning masses of fighting and death. The breeze carried the sharp, metallic smell of blood. The high, derelict walls of the courtyard framed the sky and allowed moonlight to rain upon the scene and bring a shine to the scattered pools of blood and gore. Screams and grunts echoed off the tension in air, highlighting the cacophony of blades smashing against metal and bones. It was a glorious battle, and I was right in the middle of it. And in this arena of devastation and brutality, I came alive.

I had killed four humans. Their bodies sprawled under my feet, soaking my boots with gore. They had charged at me, weapons held high, faces gleaming with defiance. They had been fearless until my knife cut their fragile lifelines. And now, those defiant faces were frozen in a death mask of helpless mortal fear. They were such pathetic, inferior creatures. The most any of them had done was rip my coat.

I balanced my knife in my hand as I scanned the battlefield for my next target. The fighting was in condensed groups in my periphery, giving me a clear line of sight to the scragglier picking off my troops from behind and dueling alone with those who broke from the crowd. One human stood bloodstained amid a trail of Wyrforra corpses. A crossbow hung from his back, and his bare arms showed scratches but no serious injury. He stooped to retrieve a hatchet from a cleaved head on the ground before he rose and met my eye.

There, in the heat and passion of battle, something passed between us. I stared him down like a wolf does to a rabbit, but he met my predatory stare as though...as though he was my *equal*. The human considered himself to be on my level, and with that, he sealed his fate as my next opponent.

I had taken one step before he had the crossbow pointed at me. I ducked below its range, and as he adjusted his aim I disconcerted him again by leaping high into the air. The human reared back, causing me to land right before him, not inches from his face. I shoved the arm with the crossbow down and sliced toward him with my knife. He was quick, though, and dodged under my arm. I brought the knife back but he caught it with the underside of his hatchet, biting my arm with the blade.

For a moment, neither of us moved. The other humans had been much easier to dispatch, and I had not been expecting much from this one. I bared my teeth at him, but he responded with a calm, determined expression. This infuriated me.

I had been holding his arm with the crossbow, and I dropped it and landed a punch hard against his stomach. He stumbled backward, but recovered quickly enough to spin the hatchet, cutting a large gash on my arm. I lunged forward, closing the distance between us once more. I stabbed and sliced but he deflected again and again and *again*. With a roar, I shoved the knife toward his face, but in one liquid motion he dropped his hatchet and caught my hand. The filthy human *touched* me. I was so enraged I forgot to check what else he was doing. Too late, I remembered the crossbow, as the tip of an iron bolt rested on my kneecap.

Before I could move, there was a searing, tearing pain as it was fired. The bolt tore through my kneecap and into my leg, destroying my tendons and ligaments and cracking every bone it passed. It followed its trajectory through my limb and passed cleanly out the back of my shin, leaving a blood-gushing hole. I would never walk normally again.

By all rights, I should have crumpled to the ground. That's what the human expected, as his grip on my hand loosened. He thought the fight was over. But something kept me standing. I don't know if it was determination, patriotism, or simply adrenaline, but whatever the cause, I would not fall. The human was going to die, and I was going to kill him.

I dropped my knife with my right hand and caught it with my left. And then I plunged it into his stomach.

The human did not look down. Instead he met my eyes with acceptance. I waited for the fear and pain to show in his expression, but it never did. He dropped the crossbow and stumbled back a few steps, clutching at the spreading blood pouring out of his stomach. Then, faintly, he smiled.

"*Fox!*"

With this cry, another human rushed to the dying man's side. It was an older female, unarmed. A medic. She slung the man's arm around her shoulder, holding him up, though he towered over her. She glanced at me with fear and hatred.

All at once, I remembered my decorum and respect for enemies defeated in battle. I straightened, ignoring the pain in my leg, and addressed the man.

"You were an impressive opponent, human. I will pray for your soul to rest in the afterlife."

"Thanks, friend, but my soul's just fine." The man spoke, to my great surprise. He looked to me with a faint smile, only slightly twisted with physical pain. "Best save your prayers for your own soul."

"I—what?" Never before had anyone so thoroughly shocked me. Why should this human care about my soul? I had set in motion the end of his life. And yet he wished for my peace? There wasn't a

Wyrforra alive who would converse with the enemy like this. And this morality was coming from a creature so inferior. *Or was he truly inferior?*

"Look around," said the human, his voice weakening yet confident. "Who do you think needs salvation?"

I turned to look at the raging battle. And, for the first time, I saw.

In one fight, a human soldier was knocked off his feet and sprawled on the ground. But before he could be finished off, another rushed to defend his comrade with reckless disregard for his own safety. In another fight, a disarmed man braced himself for the death blow. At the last second, a different human flung herself in the way, taking the strike and sparing her friend's life. Beyond them, a man impaled on a spear lay on the ground, but his head rested in the arms of a human who was risking his life to comfort the man in his last moments.

Meanwhile, my brethren were slaughtering these humans, sparing no thought to mercy or their own injured comrades. They ignored cries of pain from their own kind and fought relentlessly to kill, never maim, always kill. My trusted brothers and sisters would murder each other for the chance to spill more blood.

As understanding finally dawned on me, I turned back to the human I had been fighting. He was leaning on the medic, unable to support himself. When he saw the horror in my eyes, his expression softened to hope. Not for himself, for his own life was spilling out with his blood. No, his hope was for me.

"My friend," he said. "It's never too late for redemption."

Then, for the first time in my life, I fled.

I stumbled across the courtyard, dragging my injured leg. I ignored the weapons and shouts flying around my head as I hurried toward an opening in the wall. Desperation drove me on as I ran toward my escape. I kept my head down and tried to run past without seeing the bloodlust in my people's eyes.

How could I never have seen this? The humans, the ones I thought so lowly of, were one step ahead of us. I had blinded myself with thoughts of my own superiority, and all along ignored their advances and accomplishments.

There were so many things my own civilization could not achieve, and the humans held the secret. But we hated them too much to seek it. How had they survived, fought, and flourished so much? The answer had stared me in the face with kind, dying eyes. The humans cared and helped each other more than Wyrforra could have dreamed of.

So which of us was the truly superior species?

At last I broke past the fighting and through the opening in the wall. I lurched out into the night, bloody, out of breath, and alone. I scanned the area, searching wildly for any witnesses, but there wasn't a soul outside of the battle. I took a breath to calm my racing heart, and stumbled for the woods.

96 ROBIN

WHEN I STEPPED onto the battlefield, I figured that I would feel a great many emotions. Fear, resilience, the worry that my friends wouldn't take me in. But I never could have imagined the rush that filled me as I looked out over the courtyard. I didn't feel as though a weight was lifted from my shoulders. I felt like I was Atlas and a whole world was removed from my burden. I had nothing to lose, and I felt so light and flexible that I could run forever. And Daire was behind me every step. I wouldn't have to guess at his support anymore, which was useful seeing as how I'd need someone watching my back in the fighting. And there was no one better for that. We made the best team, after all. When one of us wasn't in jail.

But when I held up that mask and the entire fighting force of the Fort began chanting with me, the terrible recent events just...faded. Or perhaps I was just caught up in the moment. And in that moment, I needed to concentrate on not dying or letting Daire die. So, as Wyrforra began to scale the walls up to the lookout where I was standing, I decided to leave the past behind me. I dropped into a fighting stance, open handed as always, and felt Daire's back press against mine. That could only mean one thing—they were coming from his side, too.

"How many?" I asked, over the roar of battle.

"Two, but I got it," he responded, a smile dancing in his voice. It was so nice to hear that— *No, battle. Concentrate only on the battle.*

Two soldiers lunged at me. But space limited them to single file, so when the first swung a large knife my way, it was a simple matter to grab his arm and twist him off the wall. Screams from behind me let me know that Daire had done the same, and soon we had both toppled our assailants over the wall back down into the fray.

"I want to talk to you," called Daire. I turned to him, watching the crescent moon hang in his eyes. The flecks of blood on his face made his skin look paler than usual.

"Uh, no," I responded, turning face the next set of Cats who were scaling the walls up to me.

"Wha—wait!" Daire shouted.

I was already deep in the fighting, throwing as many as I could off the sides and pounding the remainder into the wall. My knuckles began to ache in a pleasant, familiar way as enemy bones broke beneath them. Perhaps it was the Wyrforra in me, but getting blood on my fists again felt good.

"Robin, be careful! You're injured, you need take it easy!" said Daire. I couldn't help but flash a smile over my shoulder. Daire met my gaze, and his eyes widened as he looked past me and saw the Cats I had already taken out.

"When you thought I was human, I had to act like one," I explained, not really caring if he heard me. I was more focused on the line of enemies ahead of me. "Now, I get to be myself. I don't have to hold anything back."

"Please do anyway. You're making me look bad."

Daire's back brushed against mine before he sprang forward and plunged a knife into someone's shoulder and a fist into someone else's stomach. And then I felt a tap on my heel as he nudged me with his foot—a signal. He ducked and on cue I spun over his back, launching a kick over his head and taking another Cat off the wall.

"I missed this, fighting with each other instead of—well, each other," I remarked.

A Cat threw a knife at my head, and as I dipped under it I reached back and touched Daire's hand. At the touch he mimicked my movement, flawlessly dodging the knife. But then he grabbed my hand, a signal that I did not recognize.

"I missed you," he said.

"Not right now," I said, pulling my hand away. "I'm busy."

"I need to apologize to you, too."

Another scream as another Cat fell. Slowly but surely we were taking them off the wall. It was an effective strategy as there was no possible way for any of them to sneak up behind or surround us.

"Yes, you do." I laughed between throwing punches. "But that will be a lengthy conversation with a long, drawn-out apology, so we don't really have time right now."

"Is it weird that the middle of this battle is the best I've felt in a long time?"

"Maybe, but I'm right there with you. I feel alive. But since I'd like to stay that way, let's continue this conversation later."

"Okay, but promise we'll talk? Provided we make it out of this?" called Daire, more sincere than I'd ever heard.

"Promise."

In another life, it might have been a romantic moment. But the fine mist of blood wasn't exactly perfect for a...oh, I don't know. And I didn't have time to think like that. I was in the middle of fighting Cats and protecting my friends and my home. I was fighting and somehow smiling and then everything went south in the worst way I could have thought.

First there was a dull thud behind me, then a whoosh of air. Something swirled in the air behind me, which either meant a Cat was attacking from behind, or—

"Daire?"

I spun just in time to see him topple, thrown over the wall, and tumble toward the ground ten stories below.

"Daire!"

"COME ON, Fox, come on! Keep up with me now."

Dr. Hanson was doing her best to pull me along. She was remarkably strong for such a small woman, but she was struggling under my weight. I was a lot bigger than her, after all, and by that point I had mostly lost control of my legs.

"We're almost there. Keep moving!" she urged.

I had never heard panic like this in her voice before. Poor Doc was terrified, but she kept her head, moving me with a desperate intensity. I did my best to stumble along with her. Part of me wanted to remain on the battlefield, fighting and dying with my friends. But deeper down I was glad Dr. Hanson was pulling me away. I had seen so much violence in the past ten years. I wanted some rest for the first...and last time.

We finally made it outside the battle to the far side of the hotel, where Doc had set up a medic tent. She dragged me to a cot, cooing words of encouragement as I lay back. She made sure I was secure before dashing off to a crate of supplies.

I think the cot was comfortable. I wasn't really sure, because most of my body was numb by then. My brain had shut off pain responses, and I was left with a pleasant warmth emanating from the large hole in my stomach. The knife must have fallen out somewhere along my path, but I hadn't noticed. I didn't care. It didn't matter anyway.

Dr. Hanson rushed back to my side, carrying bandages and a syringe of morphine. Her face shone with concentration as she moved to prick me with the needle. I laid a hand on her arm to stop her.

"Thanks kindly, Doc," I said through a heavy tongue. "But don't waste that on me."

With that, I told her what she already knew—that it was far too late. She had done her best, but there was no saving me.

Poor Doc. The hope drained from her face, and she set the supplies down with a dejected *thunk*. She reached out and grasped my hand, which I squeezed as much as I could. She looked like she was about to cry but held back. For a moment, she softened. I smiled up at her and she gazed down at me with an almost maternal care. Her eyes showed all the things she didn't have to say: that she was my friend, she loved me, and she would miss me.

"Fox," she said after a quiet moment. "What's your real name?"

I grinned. "Well, ma'am, the name 'Fox' was given to me by my best friend when he saved my life. What name could be more real than that?"

Dr. Hanson nodded. She squeezed my hand once more.

"I'll go get Daire," she whispered, and left.

I was happy to be left alone. My mind was succumbing to a peaceful numbness, letting a beautiful silence wash over me. I stared up at the canvas tent, but somehow, I saw the stars. The night sky reminded me of all my time with Daire and Robin, all those happy memories.

My friends—good things to remember in my dying seconds. As my consciousness slipped toward the stars, my thoughts were happy.

I closed my eyes.

And when I opened them, I was a kid again.

I wander around a dusty Montana city. My feet are blistered and my shoulders are sunburned. My only possessions are the filthy clothes on my back. I am alone.

The biting wind pushes and pulls at my tiny body, but I hardly notice. The only thing I can think of is my need for food. I can't remember my last meal, and I am so weak it's a wonder I'm still on my feet. I want to cry for help, but there is no one to hear. I am a starving child in a deserted city.

But it isn't quite deserted. At the sound of footsteps, I duck behind a parked car and peer out from around the trunk. I locate the source of the noise—a large human man in a military uniform. He carries a crate loaded with shiny metallic cylinders, which he loads into the back of a pickup truck. The man then turns and walks into an abandoned storefront, apparently for more crates.

The cylinders catch my attention, and I creep forward to get a better look. Could it be? Yes! Canned food! I steal close to the truck, creeping low to the ground and moving silently. I look around and make sure that the man is still in the shop before I reach out and grab a can.

"Hey!"

I jump, dropping the food. I spin around, ready to face the man in camo but instead see a boy. He can't be much older than I was, but he puffs his chest out and plants his fists on his waist. The boy looks angry, and I freeze in fear.

"What do you think you're...hey, wait. Kid, you don't look so good. When's the last time you ate?"

Unable to speak, I shake my head. The older boy's expression softens.

"Don't your parents feed you?"

I shake my head again.

"Where's your dad?"

"He—he's dead," I squeak. "The monsters got him."

"I'm sorry, kid. Where's your mom?"

"She's dead too. The monsters got her after she brought me here."

"Oh." *he seems concerned, but unsure of what to do.* "Hey kid, how old are you?"

"I'm eight. I'll be nine on Mar...March fourteenth."

"How long have you been alone?"

"I dunno."

"What's your name?"

"I dunno."

"You talk funny. Where are you from?"

"I dunno."

The boy examines me critically. After a moment, he stoops down and picks up the can I had dropped.

"Here, kid. Take this."

He holds it out to me. My eyes dart between the boy and the can. I wait, balancing on the balls of my feet. In a split second, I snatch the can from his hand and race down the street, away from the truck. But as my feet pound the pavement, I find myself slowing. I don't get far before the boy calls out to me again.

"Hey, kid! Wanna come home with me?"

I stand in the middle of that street for a long time. My immature mind is confused, conflicted, and afraid. I am about to make the most important decision of my life. And I make the right one.

The boy is ecstatic as I go back to him.

"You're gonna love the Fort!" *says the boy, leading me to the cab of the truck.* "There's all sorts of cool stuff there, and it's one hundred percent safe from monsters. And we can be best friends, kid!"

He turns to me, green eyes sparkling in the sunlight. "My name's Daire! What's yours? Do you remember yet?"

I once again find myself unable to talk. But this time, it isn't fear blocking my voice, but an adoration bordering on fraternal idolatry.

"Well, I can't just call you 'kid.' I know! The way you snuck over here and ran away was really sneaky and fast, just like my favorite animal. Is it okay if I call you Fox?"

I go to answer, but stop when my vision becomes black around the edges. The shadows inch farther and farther into my field of view, and though I should feel some panic or fear, there is only peace. I feel myself drifting away from the scene. As the blackness is just about to swallow me whole, I hear Daire's voice one last time.

"It's all right, Fox. Robin and I will miss you, but we'll be okay. You're done fighting now. Everything is all right."

I have one final thought before everything melts into blissful nothingness and I escape into whatever it is that happens after.

Yes, everything is just fine.

98 DAIRE

I'D LIKE to say that as I tumbled toward the ground, I fell with a serene and stoic expression and that I looked death in the face with no fear. But that would be lying. I think my life flashed before me, but I squeezed my eyes shut as I tried to control my bowels, at least until I hit the ground. I was consumed in terror as I felt the rushing wind rip my dreams away. *After everything, this is how it all ends. At least, in the end, I didn't say anything stupid to—*

I felt a bump and then I was no longer moving in a downward motion, but in a sideways motion. My eyes flew open and saw that Robin had launched herself from the roof after me and pushed off from the wall, forming a human projectile headed right for me. She wrapped her arms around me as we collided in midair, pushing us both toward the adjacent wall. It seemed like a miracle when the momentum carried us to the wall and somehow through a window—but of course it wasn't a miracle. The amazing Robin had planned it perfectly. We shattered the glass and tumbled onto the floor, rolling around in broken glass with surprisingly no broken bones. My chest heaved as I took a moment to lie on the floor, astounded.

"You saved me," I told Robin, who was already getting on her feet.

"Not really. I made you fall two stories instead of ten." She held a hand out to me and smiled. "But you can still thank me profusely."

She helped me to my feet, but her attention focused over my shoulder and her eyes went wide. She called my name as she rushed past me through the door and into the hallway. Stumbling after her, the smell of blood hit me full force, and I counted four bodies sprawled across the floor. I followed her as she knelt by the only figure still moving collapsed in the dark hallway. I couldn't make out his face in the darkness, but by the way his chest was heaving and the wet rattling sounds of his breathing, I knew that whoever he was didn't have much time left.

"Truman," Robin said.

"They're in the building." He coughed, struggling to speak. "They ran inside when we started fighting back hard. They've taken over. But there are no humans in here, which means—"

"I know." I breathed. "I'll take care of it. Come with us."

"No, I'll stay. Always wanted a Viking funeral." He found the strength to chuckle, and Robin and I stood to leave. I had a plan, but there was no time to waste.

"Wait. Robin," said the dying man. "I saw you fighting. There's something I should have said to you a long time ago."

We waited, and to our surprise, Truman brought his hand to head in an old military salute.

"It's been an honor serving under you, ma'am." He coughed. My breath caught in my throat, and I heard Robin swallow back emotion as she saluted in return.

"You've done well, soldier."

She wanted to stay but there was no time, and we both knew it. We tore ourselves away, running through the familiar labyrinth of the abandoned hotel, making for the ground-floor lobby. A Wyrforra appeared from the rooms we passed, then another and another. They followed us, but Robin turned and fought back, smashing heads against walls and faces into each other without a misstep. Finally, we reached the lobby and the entrance to the battlefield.

"You have a plan," she said, panting, as we caught our breath. "What is it?"

"No time to go into details. I need your help. Take every human and get them out of the courtyard. Make the Cats think we've fled inside the Fort. Get as many of the Wyrforra as you can inside and all our soldiers out back."

"On it." Her back was already to me as she ran back out into the battle.

I wanted to run out after her, but I had my own assignment. As she went to rally the troops, I raced to the basement door, but paused before flinging it open. There would probably be dozens down there. I was trembling in anticipation but I forced the door open slowly, listening. The concrete steps stared up at me, and I knew there was no time.

Taking a deep breath, I darted into the heart of the Fort, moving as silently as possible. I sprinted past the makeshift rooms, not stopping in any place long enough for any Wyrforra to investigate. Finally, I reached a room with a large table strewn with various machines and instruments. A Cat was pondering over them, turning a strange item over in his hands. He was so busy examining the object he didn't notice me enter.

"That's exactly what I was looking for," I told him.

He jumped and I took it from his hands, then landed a hard punch to his face, knocking him unconscious.

"Thanks!" I turned to run back toward the entrance, the item in hand.

It seemed like an hour had passed when I broke back into the lobby, but I still didn't expect Robin to be done with what I had asked. So imagine my surprise to see the courtyard filled with regrouping Wyrforra and not a single human. I rushed to the back of the building, and there she was—with about a hundred of our soldiers. All that were left.

"They'll be following us soon." She took a deep breath.

"I know. Take them all a few miles that way, into the woods.

There's a safe space there. I'll get everyone from the first-aid tent and meet you there."

"All right." She turned to gather up our troops, but I didn't have time to help. I made my way to where Dr. Hanson has set up cots. She was flitting from person to person, and I rushed over to her.

"We have to leave. How many of these people can come with us?"

"All the ones still alive can walk. Safe place in the woods?" she asked, always one step ahead of me.

"You got it."

"Help Cap walk. I've got to carry as many supplies as I can."

Cap hobbled over to me and I threw an arm around him, taking on as much of his weight as I could. He was sweating, and his grunts of pain directed me to carry him as quickly as I could out of the tent, but I stopped by an occupied cot. A sheet covered the person, but a familiar tuft of sandy hair was showing. I couldn't tear myself away this time.

"Fox?" I wasn't sure if I was calling out to him or just asking if that was who was under the sheet. I struggled toward it, dragging Cap with me, and reached for the sheet.

"No, son. Stop! Daire, don't do that, we need to leave," urged Cap, trying to pull me away.

My hand shook as I grabbed the sheet but stopped before I pulled it off the body. *It's not him,* I told myself. *It couldn't be.*

"It's not him, Daire! It's not Fox. Now we have to leave!" Cap shouted, trying to get through to me.

I let go of the sheet. I willed myself to believe Cap's words until I could almost convince myself that the figure under the sheet looked nothing like Fox. It took everything I had to turn back toward the woods. Dr. Hanson was bringing along everyone who could come, and I was half-carrying Cap. We trudged along with all the speed we could muster, knowing that they'd be on our tail in a matter of minutes.

Tears stung my eyes as we made it to the tree line. Cap was lying to me, and we both knew it. But if I stopped to think, I would break down and we would all die. So I kept moving. Somehow I made myself keep moving.

"We're far enough away now, son," Cap said, gentle but strong.

We lurched to a stop. I looked back over the treetops to see the Fort rising against the sky. The moon shone down on the beautiful building that we had had to abandon. Dr. Hanson and our wounded soldiers had gone on well ahead of us, and the others were deep in the woods by now. Cap and I were the only ones relatively near the Fort, besides hundreds of enemies.

"It's my home," I said without really meaning to.

"I know, Daire. Mine too. But we have to do this."

The strange remote-like device was still in my hand. Cap and I could only stare at the building as I forced myself to flip a tiny switch on the machine. For a long second, nothing happened.

And then, the hundreds of pounds of C4, the stuff we had found so long ago, placed throughout the Fort exploded. The cracking of concrete echoed through the sky and fire blossomed in window after window. Then, with a deafening crumbling sound and the screams of hundreds of Cats, the Fort began to collapse.

Cap pulled me away, nearly falling in the process. I caught him, turning my back on the building. We started moving again toward the safe point, away from the weight of this enormous sacrifice. We didn't turn back to watch clouds of smoke blot out the stars.

99 MAD CAT

THE SOUND of laughter rang out in the night.

It took me a second to realize that I was the one laughing, cackling at the sky and iron and stone and dirt. They were all just so *funny!* First, the walls had held me, trapping me for years. Or was it hours? But then, just then, the walls had opened up! It seemed like the sun had taken hold of them as the walls coughed fire and heat. They shook with fear as the sun tore them apart, reducing those walls I had grown quite fond of into little pieces of rock and then smaller pieces of nothing. The bars on the window mourned their loss, twirling inward and bending in grief, before finally shaking from their bonds and leaving.

The walls—those sneaky, *sneaky* walls—they had tried to take me with them. They had thrown things at me, hitting me with bricks and choking me with heat and smoke. They turned the power of that sun against me, hoping to bury me in their own remains. But I, the Mad Cat, was too clever, too clever for them! While the window bars were still tumbling, one of them was shaken free, leaving a hole just big enough for me. I crawled using my hands and feet and the eyes on my arms and scrambled out from under the walls. They tried to smother me in their dying convulsions but I was too fast for them! *Ha-ha, too fast!*

I clambered into the night as smoke covered the silver god in the sky—waning now into a crescent—and for a moment, I didn't know what to do. What was a poor, lonely old cat to do? But then I realized —I am so clever to realize this—that I could do anything! I was free to do whatever I wanted! I could chase all the butterflies in the world!

That, I think, was when I began to laugh. But then I stopped in fear as the building itself began to chuckle, doubling over in laughter. I felt it would fall on me so I ran, ran far into the woods, ran until my paws started to bleed. And as I ran, my laughter echoed off the trees and spiraled up into the sky, free to go wherever it liked.

Free. *Ha ha ha! Free!*

100   ROBIN

I PACED around the clearing where the whole of our soldiers gathered. I counted them. Then I paced. Then I counted them again. And again. And again.

It seemed like hours before Cap and Daire finally stumbled through the trees. I breathed a sigh of relief when I saw them, battered and hurt but alive. Really, definitely alive. Thank God. I rushed over to them, taking Cap's free arm around my shoulders.

"We saw the explosion," I said, as the doctor came over to check on Cap. "We lost the Fort, but it must've taken out the entire Cat army."

Daire didn't respond. He helped Cap, handing him over to Dr. Hanson to look over. Daire's downcast eyes seemed to confirm my suspicions, but I had to know for sure.

"Fox isn't here," I said, just above a whisper.

"I know."

Daire's knees trembled, and then he folded to the ground. I knelt beside him, dropping to the Earth just like my heart did.

"My...my best..." Daire was holding back sobs. Pain and exhaustion and grief weighed upon him—upon us. Tears were welling up behind my eyes but I forced them away, forced my hands to stop shaking, forced myself not to think about this right now. There was just no time. We had to help our soldiers. We had to keep moving. There was no time for grief.

That's what I told myself, but there are some things that just couldn't be pushed away. Kneeling there on the cold ground, I wrapped my arms around Daire. He rested his head on my shoulder. There, for a moment, we shared our strength. We faced pain but we faced it together. And we both knew we would have to save the funeral for another day.

As much as we wanted to stop and cry our hearts out, we had to get somewhere safer first. He looked up to me, his forest eyes meeting mine, and we shared an understanding. We had lost someone incredibly dear to us. But we would have to grieve later.

But we would have each other, and in that, we would somehow find the will to keep moving.

"What now?" I asked, hoping he would have some plan.

"Cap and I discussed that. Next, we meet up with the rest of the... the Resistance. We follow their trail north and when we find them, we locate a place to set up camp. After that...I guess we find a new base. And then—I don't know. Just keep living, I guess."

"Not just living. Fighting."

"Yeah. Fighting." Starlight reflected like hope in his eyes. "Until this damned war is over."

"Hey, guys!" came a youthful voice.

"Port." Daire smiled, relieved to see a familiar face. But the smile faded quickly as he turned to me, sharing an unspoken thought. We would have to tell him about Fox.

"The smoke is starting to clear, so we can navigate with the stars again," Port said. "Are you ready to go?"

"I think..." I looked back toward where the Fort used to be. But then I looked forward, toward the northern horizon. "I think we are."

101 TYLOS

MY HANDS SHOOK SOFTLY on the bike handles as I walked back through the snow. The bike was heavy as I pulled it alongside me, but I barely felt the weight. I barely felt anything. Darkness set as I followed the bike's track, stumbling through the fresh powder. I didn't think about what I would do when I got back. I tried really hard not to think about anything.

Finally, the doctor's cabin came into view. It was well dark by the time I leaned the bike against the side and dragged myself to the door. All the lights were out, but as I knocked on the door a single lantern flared to life in the window. After some hesitation, the door cracked open and a gaunt face appeared. Doc stared at me for a moment, taking in my red-rimmed eyes and hands turning purple in the cold. He sighed before slowly pushing the door open.

"I hope you haven't led that army here," he said, leaning against the doorway.

I shook my head. "I saw some of the Wyrforra fleeing to the east. Looks like they were retreating. They didn't see me."

"I suppose it's over then." The old man breathed with relief. "And you, Tylos? Why come back here?"

"I'm—not really sure. I don't know what to do next." I couldn't help but stare at my feet, closing my shaking hands into fists. Everything was so unclear. There was no roadmap for me, just footprints buried under snow. Doc shuffled, as though he was uncomfortable with talking on the porch but was reluctant to invite me inside. He glanced over his shoulder, then back to me.

"Why not rejoin the army?" he asked softly. My teeth gnashed together of their own accord and I had to force my jaws open to speak.

"I can't. They started this war and killed thousands. They killed Arianna. I can never go back."

The doc sighed again and ran a hand through his sparse hair. He examined me with dark, scrutinizing eyes. I was too tired to care as I hunched against the wind on his doorstep, broken and lost. I didn't expect him to take pity on me.

"Look, Tylos. You seem like a nice kid. But a soldier. A killer. I can set you up somewhere, but I have to be able to trust you."

I almost managed a chuckle. "Look at me, Doc. I fell in love in a warzone. I'm too naive to be a threat. I don't want to hurt anyone. Not anymore."

"I believe you. Tell me, how do you feel about going into medicine?"

I could only look at the man in confusion.

"There's this small settlement a few miles from here," he said. "Not a Resistance base, just a little community of survivors. I'd be willing to take you on as an apprentice if you agreed to live there and help those people. I'd give you supplies, a place to stay, and food. But most important, a purpose. What do you say?"

"I...well, there isn't much choice for me, is there. I don't know much about healing, but I'd be more than willing to learn. Thank you, Doctor."

He grumbled to himself, almost smiling. I almost smiled in return.

"Do we leave in the morning?" I asked.

He paused, looking over his shoulder again.

"...No. Let me load up my old snowmobile with supplies and get some gas for your bike. We'll leave now."

102 CAP

TWO DAYS HAD PASSED since the battle. The Resistance had moved miles into the woods. We didn't know where we were going, or how much farther we would have to travel, or if we would ever find another home. We just walked, and talked, and somehow held on to whatever hope escaped the burning Fort.

My legs hurt more and more with every step, and I was glad when we stopped to rest. Port barely left my side for our whole journey, which I was grateful for, but at the same time, we all needed our own space to grieve. I was no exception. So when Doc Hanson asked to talk to me in private, I happily accepted and hobbled off into the trees a ways until I was certain we were alone. The doctor turned to me and pulled a vial from the pocket of her torn and burned lab coat. She handed it to me without a word and I took it, examining the thick red liquid inside.

"Is this blood?"

"Yes. It's the blood test I took from Robin a few days ago."

"Did you get any useful information from it?" I asked, honestly not expecting much.

"A little... I think I know what the Cats are."

I nearly dropped the vial in surprise. "How?"

"Science! Well, actually, from the blood and some things that Tylos told us and a little educated guessing. But it's just a theory, so take it with a grain of salt. Also, you may want to sit."

I obliged, parking my ass on a tree stump.

"Imagine a few million years ago," began the doctor.

"Can't you just tell me, without a history lesson?"

"No. Shut up. Imagine a long time ago a group of nomadic early humans—people who would one day evolve into *Homo sapiens sapiens*. But this group was threatened by something, so they made their way someplace else: specifically, the Arctic Circle. Now, this group of people would either die...or adapt. They would have to eventually evolve like us only different. They would have to have protection against the harsh cold and severe winds."

"Protection like thick skin... And wounds that close quickly so they wouldn't lose body heat!"

"And eyes that protect them against sun blindness, but also help them in the months without a sun."

"So, what you're saying is, they're us?"

"Not exactly. I don't know for sure and it would take years of research to figure it out entirely, but I think...they're us, but from a slightly different evolutionary track. So they're sort of human, only..."

"Oh my God." I ran a hand over my head, as the implications ran wild in my thoughts. "Oh my God."

"The Cats...the Wyrforra..." breathed Dr. Hanson. "They're the next step in human evolution."

103 TYLOS

I DRANK a hot cup of tea at my kitchen table, looking out the window and into the trees. Steam curled up from the cup, swirling through the air in a way that would have been beautiful if I could focus on it. But I had far too much on my mind. I had been in this little town for a week, but it felt like an eternity. Anaximander, they called it. Odd name for a tiny settlement, but I didn't really care. I was having a hard time caring about anything. But I couldn't complain. I had more than I had ever possessed in my entire life.

Doc had given me my own house. It wasn't big, and two of the three bedrooms were made into hospital rooms for patients, but it was warm and nice. The walls were lined with bookshelves and the kitchen and bathroom had all the amenities I could ask for. It was—I don't know. A house. An empty house holding a lonely, miserable Cat.

The sun was rising, which came as a bit of a surprise. I had forgotten to sleep again, it seemed. There was a little girl down the road with a fever, and Doc and I had spent the whole night making sure she would be okay. This was my life now. I was learning on the job and the doctor said I was good at it. So that was good. I guess. I liked helping people. It was fulfilling to save lives. And my happiness —well, I suppose that didn't matter. I would live, and the people in this town would live, and that was all that was important.

Movement through the window caught my attention. I slowly set the cup on the table, wondering if it was my imagination but keeping a sharp eye on the trees. And *there it was again!* There was someone in the tree line, watching my house.

I wondered for a moment if it was some kind of human assassin. Thus far, nobody had even mentioned that I was a Wyrforra. They seemed too desperate for my help to care. But maybe one of them was out for my blood. And I decided to find out.

Casually, I stood, and moved away from the window. I didn't go for any weapons. I didn't even consider it. I just put my coat on and went out my front door. I didn't head straight for the trees. Instead, I went down the overgrown road like I was out on a very early, very cold morning stroll. I walked as far as my curiosity would let me before turning and heading into the woods, circling back to where my house was. I crept through the brush, thankful for a fresh layer of snow to soften my footsteps.

Eventually, I stumbled across a fresh trail, which I couldn't help but follow. Small, clumsy footsteps led to an old green tent propped up on a hill of snow. The area wasn't heavily traveled, so I guessed it was just one person, but someone who had been there for a while. My suspicion grew as I followed the trail the other way and quickly came into view of my house. The tent was less than a half-mile from my back door, and the footprints led right to my window. And then they went...nowhere. They wandered back to the tree line and vanished. At that point, I began to wonder if I should have brought a weapon.

The hairs on the back of my neck stood up. Someone was definitely watching me at that moment. I acted as though I were confused and made a bit of a show about wandering around, while I followed the footprints. It didn't take me long. I was a soldier once, after all.

"Come down now. I want to talk," I called, but was met with only silence. "I know you're there."

I turned and stared up into a large fir tree, where a figure was crouched in the branches. I couldn't see their face, but their body stiffened as I looked right at them. They were dressed in black, with a thick hood obscuring their face.

"Come down before I take you down," I threatened with all the intimidation I could muster.

The figure hesitated, but finally dropped down into the snow. They kept their hood down, casting a heavy shadow over their features. The only thing I could tell about them was that they were lean and rather short. Human? I couldn't tell.

"How long have you been watching me?" I asked. "And why? What do you want?"

They didn't answer. Their hands clenched into fists at their sides.

"If you're here to kill me, please just do it. I won't fight. It's not worth it. Besides...I promised I'd never fight again. So go right ahead."

I wish I could say I was lying, but in that moment, I didn't want to live. Not without her. And not with the guilt of getting her killed. But the figure didn't move, just stood there staring at me with eyes I couldn't see.

"Get it over with!" I raised my voice, hoping it would shock them into doing something. "I deserve it! I met the most amazing human on the planet and she's dead because of me. I robbed the world of someone so caring and loving that she could even feel something for a monster like me. So I really, really hope you're here to kill me. Because I...I don't want to miss her anymore."

A lump caught in the back of my throat as the truth in my words threatened to reduce me to tears. I found that my hands were shaking, but so were the stranger's. Slowly, they lifted those hands to their hood and pulled it back, revealing hair that fell like tidal waves around storm-cloud gray eyes.

"Ar...?" I could barely breathe, and her name came from my throat like a dying whisper.

"Tylos, I'm sorry." There were tears in her voice and bruises under her eyes, but it was her. "I thought you'd be safe if I—"

She stopped when she saw that I was running at her full speed. Her eyes got wide as I rushed at her, and in a reaction that even I didn't understand, wrapped my arms around her. I tackled us both to the ground, careful to put my body between her and the snow so she wouldn't get hurt. I buried my face in her jacket as we lay there, snow soaking into our clothes. She didn't move for a long moment, and I didn't know if she was surprised or scared or hurt.

But then, she seemed to melt into me, returning my hug with the full force of a storm. Tears squeezed from her eyes as she gripped me tighter, as though she was afraid I would try to leave.

"I missed you too, you stupid Cat," she cried in a soft, beautiful voice.

I wanted to respond but I found that I couldn't speak. For the first time ever, I was too happy for words. I don't know how long we lay together in the snow, but I know that every second with her was a lifetime, but still far too short.

I am not a perfect creature. That's for certain. But maybe, if even she would come back for me, there was some hope for me after all.

I HAD NEVER BEFORE SEEN the High King so...*unsettled*. His eyes were wide with anger and a deep, poorly hidden fear. His was enunciating his words just a little too sharp, as though he was flustered. I'm quite certain he was even shaking a little. It was just *beautiful*.

"Are you sure?" he asked the soldier for the fourth time in a row. "None of them?"

"Yes, sir." The man was shaking too, but that was understandable. He was badly injured and bringing bad news to the King. He had every reason to be afraid.

"But you and a few others were fine," said the King.

"Yes, sir. My squad was far enough outside the wall that we had time to get clear. But everyone else was caught in the explosion."

The King stood suddenly from his chair, causing the soldier to flinch. I glanced around the round room, eyeing the guards and watching Erenvyr do the same. I half-hoped he would be reduced to pacing, but he just sat down again and gripped the armrests.

"Not even General Hellman?" he asked. Again.

"N-no, sir," stuttered the poor soldier. "He was crushed."

Erenvyr ran a hand through his hair, messing it up without realizing it. From my place beside his desk, I had to force myself not to smile.

"Almyrr must have survived," he said, looking for reassurance.

"No one has seen him, sir. We searched, but...we didn't find anything."

"I..." The King trailed off. He was thinking, but for the first time I could remember, there was weakness scrawled across his face. There was fear.

"Leave. Now!" he commanded, and the soldier did so with a start, rushing from the room.

The High King stood again and moved to a window. His eyes, reflected off the glass, showed a delicious uncertainty that I imagined the King was unfamiliar with.

"We lost a battle," he muttered.

"Yes, but it was just one battle out of hundreds. We'll win the war, sir," I said in a calming voice.

"Yes... Yes, of course. You're absolutely right." He sounded as though he believed me. He sounded as though he would have believed anything. I was glad his attention was elsewhere, for I could not hide a tiny smile.

"Odyra," he said with a facade of composure.

"Yes, Your Majesty?"

"I have lost two of my most trusted companions today. I want you to stay with me more from now on, filling Almyrr's job as my personal bodyguard. I need to keep those I can trust as close as possible."

"Of course, sir. I'm honored."

"Yes. Good. Thank you." I could almost hear him begin to fall apart, piece by piece.

I bowed my head in response, as a symbol of subordination, but also to hide my smile. Things couldn't have gone better if I had planned them myself. I hadn't expected that fool Almyrr to die, but now that he had there was a position in the King's court that needed to be filled. And now that I was in position, moving up would be a simple matter.

But for now, I had to wait until the time was right. Luckily, I had all the patience in the world. I would wait, and watch, and when the perfect opening finally presented itself...

I would take *everything*.

ACKNOWLEDGMENTS

This novel would never have existed without the help of Jayna Young, the very first reader, who inspired me to keep working until it was published. My dad, Bret Miller, tirelessly read through draft after draft, and helped in every step until it was finally ready. He honestly deserves a medal for the insane amount of work he put into making this book a reality. My grandpa, Tom Piantanida– also a writer– inspired me with writing wisdom and helped me get the book to its final stages. My mom, Tara Piantanida-Kelly, who researched and worked and read and did everything she could to help– this never would have been possible without her. It'd take another book to name all the people who made this happen, but here's a short list of people who deserve far more credit than they're getting here: Michael MacDonald, Mary Miller, Robert Kelly, Peyton Heesch, Mark and Jack Miller, Lynne and Al Miller, Jack Hicks, Angie Disanto, Vandy, Eric, Kelly, and Nick Shrader, every English teacher I've ever had (except my undergrad Shakespeare professor)– especially Jim Whorton who suggested I try Twitter and Mr. Taylor who encouraged me to write no matter what the subject was, every author who inspired me, every friend who stuck by me, and every cat who curled up on me.

Of course, it goes without saying that this never would have happened without the phenomenal folks at Vintage Hill Press and Trifecta Publishing House. Diana Ballew, Doug Burmeister, and Lori Lyn: thank you all, sincerely, for taking a chance on a young, scared new author. I thank my lucky stars every day that we found each other.

ABOUT THE AUTHOR

McKenna has always had a passion for the written word and is absolutely thrilled to turn her writing dreams into a reality! She worked as a freelance writer for four years and has written as a hobby her whole life. *Wyrforra* is her first novel.

After graduating with her BA in English from SUNY Geneseo in 2016, McKenna is currently studying for her MA at the State University of New York at Brockport. She works on campus and spends her free time writing, reading, tweeting, drinking wine, and playing video games. She lives in New York with her family and her orange tabby, Ravioli.

For more information:

CPSIA information can be obtained
at www.ICGtesting.com
Printed in the USA
BVOW09s0935140817
492002BV00002B/114/P